A CUP OF ZODIAC

A CUP OF SERIES
BOOK ONE

ALEXIS GORGUN

DEDICATION

For anyone who has celiac, IBS, food intolerances, and food allergies... this one is for you.

To my lovitas: without you, life would be meaningless.

CHAPTER 1

*S*ixty is such a slutty number.

At least to me it is. Divisible by twelve different numbers, it gets action from all sides. I used to be a sixty—slutty, carefree, the life of the party.

Now I'm a five. A stable, boring, unsquishable five. It doesn't fit my Leo sun sign.

The woman behind the counter is a total pro at handling the nonstop coffee orders. She's totally a seven. A stud in her nose, an intricate flower tattoo sleeve on her right arm, and overall badass appearance solidify my guess. Sevens are fun and pointy until they're flipped on their side, becoming a weapon.

She must be a Scorpio.

This coffee shop is like stepping into another world. One full of wood. The barista is behind a sweeping wooden counter, curved in all the right places. Mahogany chairs and worktables take up the space, but the ceiling is where it's at. It's made up of wooden rectangles clustered close enough for them to touch, but all of them ending at different lengths. If I were high, I would totally think the ceiling was moving like a wave. That'd fuck with me so hard, I might just have to come back and try it out.

Not wanting to wait in the never-ending line, I claim a seat next to the window decorated with painted ornaments and snowflakes, matching the holiday cheer on the rest of the main street. The black, elegant couch is the perfect ratio of stiffness and squishiness. When the line dies down, I'll order something.

I've been in Portland for twenty-four hours, but I can't spend all my time in my depressing shoebox-sized apartment. I need to learn about the city, my new home.

Amore isn't just any coffee shop. According to the local newspaper, it's been the trendiest coffee shop for the last three years. The drinks are apparently unique and draw a huge crowd since they're not found anywhere else.

But I'm not here for the coffee.

Not when I hate the stuff.

No, I'm here to eavesdrop on conversations and pick up the vibe of the city and its patrons. Coffee shops just so happen to be the perfect place for this. At least, that's what my Aunt Addie relied on when she lived in Portland years ago.

I pull out my phone and pretend I'm busy, when a trio of college-aged women sit at the table next to me. Their excited babble grabs my attention and I tilt my head in their direction.

"Brittney, did you see your horoscope for the day?"

"Not yet. What does it say?"

"That someone has a secret and you're about to be blind-sided."

They all gasp and lean closer to each other. "No way."

"You know Zodiac Way of Life app is always right. We've proven it time and time again ourselves," says the cute blonde, sipping her tea with her bright smile. I'd bet the two hundred dollars in my bank account she's a Gemini.

They continue their chatter, this time about who they're hooking up with. I tune them out and continue scrolling on my phone.

"...Zodiac Way of Life."

I jerk my head up and look around. That's the second time someone has mentioned this thing.

The words come from a nearby table with two forty-something-year-old women in athletic gear. I lean back to hear more.

"You didn't."

"I gave in, but Joy was right. It's so accurate, it's scary. I can't believe it just launched a week ago. It's a smash hit already."

Okay, so this app seems important to the people here. I immediately download it.

The app is sleek and easy to use, all in blues, whites, and grays, which is soothing rather than boring. I input my birthday, time, and location of birth. A pop-up appears demanding payment. Twenty dollars a month.

Shit.

Twenty dollars a month? Are they trying to rip everyone off?

I need every penny in my bank account to make rent for January since I had to prepay December. Twenty dollars is too much.

I back out of the app and read the reviews. Everyone has the same thing to say—it's so accurate that it has changed people's lives.

Well, if anyone needs their life changed it's me. I rub my temples and sink further into the couch.

My phone rings.

I glance at it for a moment before the name flashing on the screen registers. Lilly, my younger sister. She's refused to answer a single one of my one hundred and twenty-two calls since The Event That Shall Not be Named a week ago.

I scramble to press the green button. "Hi."

"I'm moving the wedding to February 11th." She spits the words out as if each one is a poisonous dart aimed for my heart. She pauses for a full minute, as if waiting for the poison to sink in. "Will you be there?"

She's abrupt and I can't blame her for it. She's moving the date because of me, because of my actions. On the plus side, her fiancé won't forget the date. He barely remembers her birthday, which isn't promising given that they've been together for ten years. That's not something she'd want to hear, not right now.

So instead, I say, "Of course." I squeeze my eyes close and ask the question that's been plaguing me since she cut all communication. "But do you still want me there?"

She doesn't respond, and I grip the phone tighter. Before I made a mess of everything, we were as close as close can be. But now, our relationship hangs by a precarious thread that I fear will snap any second now.

All because she can't forgive me.

And I don't blame her one bit.

Not when I can't forgive myself.

"You can come," she says. "But I'm asking someone else to be my maid of honor."

I suck in a sharp breath at her words. We made a pact when we were kids that we'd be each other's maid of honor. We've had our weddings planned out for over twenty years. It's gutting that she's taking that honor away from me. That she's demoting me. An ache spreads in my chest toward my abdomen. This moment right here hurts more than everything else from the past week.

It's the last snip of the thread holding our relationship together. One she's yanked so far from me, there's nothing to grab onto anymore.

And what's worse is that I'm disposable to her. I pinch the bridge of my nose and inhale, keeping the tears at bay.

I tell her in a monotone voice, "If that's what you think is best."

"It is."

"If you need anything in the next few months, I'm here for you."

She snorts. "You've done enough. I'll send you an email in a couple of weeks. You can RSVP... or not."

"I'll be there," I say with conviction.

I wouldn't miss it for the world.

She hangs up on me after that. I stare at the black screen and swallow hard. I'm not sure how to even try to repair everything with her and our parents. After getting kicked out of my parent's Thanksgiving dinner, it's clear no one wants me around.

Apparently losing everyone's money in a terrible investment is grounds to disown me. But if I'm invited to her wedding, then I might still have a chance at redemption. To show them I'm different, changed. That I'm trustworthy and reliable, even if they think I'm the opposite.

I sit taller on the couch.

Yes, that's it. I can totally change in two and a half months. Become a better person and win them back. To return to how we were—a family.

But just as fast as the confident energy comes, it gets sucked right out of me and I deflate back into the couch.

Who am I kidding?

My decisions led to this entire disaster with my family. The only way I'd be able to revamp myself would be if someone else helped. Where I can rely on them to decide everything for me. Like a personal assistant, life coach, and nanny all rolled into one.

My phone vibrates with a reminder from ZWOL that I still haven't paid.

I pause.

What if... what if I rely on ZWOL to make my decisions for me? Get a head start on what's going to happen in my day and maximize my cosmic energy. Twenty dollars would be cheaper than hiring a real person to help me.

Addie was a firm believer in horoscopes and zodiac signs. What if... she's guiding me? Isn't that what we all hope for once someone dies?

The pain of her absence permeates my being, causing an undeniable ache. If Addie is really guiding me, I have to do it.

With a quick prayer to the stars and to wherever

Addie may be, I click on the subscribe button with a promise to myself to follow it to a T.

After subscribing, it explains that it's different from all the other apps because it uses a combination of my sun, rising, and moon signs to deliver an accurate horoscope every day. In the evening, it'll send a reminder for me to judge the accuracy of the day's prediction.

My first horoscope loads, and I almost pass out after reading it.

CHAPTER 2

"*T*ired of life's little setbacks, Leo darling? Need a pick-me-up? A coffee might do the trick, but honey, pay attention. There's more to be found in the magical elixir than a mere caffeine jolt. Open your eyes and peer past the steamy surface. Who knows, there might be a job within there. There's a world of possibilities swirling, just waiting for you to take a bold, caffeinated leap. Love always, ZWOL."

Is this app fucking psychic?

How could ZWOL possibly know I'm in desperate need of a job? Either this app is a genius or a data thief. But does it really matter if it's promising me a job?

I look around Amore. Does it mean to apply here?

There's a sign on the window next to my head. It faces the street, but it's clear it's a help wanted sign.

Goosebumps rise on my arms. Okayyyy, this is eerie.

I open my purse. The resumes I stuffed inside before

leaving my apartment stare back at me, as if saying "see, I told you to bring us."

The thought of applying for a job makes me break out in a cold sweat. I haven't had to interview for a job in over eight years. I'm so out of practice and my teal Hugo Boss dress doesn't really match the vibe of this place. At least the app didn't propose I apply for an engineering job. If I'm going to turn my life around, I need to leave behind everything from my past, including my old job.

Maybe I can start by ordering a drink to get a feel for the place and build up the confidence to apply.

Yeah, that's a good idea.

I place my scarf on the table and enter the line. Amore is spelled in red bricks on the entire right side of the wall in case anyone forgets. How they got the bricks to look elegant with cursive writing is beyond me. But it's sleek and edgy at the same time. Every part of this place plays on contrasts and it really adds to the experience of being here.

Time passes by far too fast and before I know it, there are only a few more people in line until I'm up to order. Then I'll be asked the question I dread most in the world —what do I want?

If only it were so easy to answer.

I used to know, but now I'm lost. Swimming in an ocean begging for a life preserver, as wave after wave hits me. And I'm drowning.

Moving here to Portland, or more like fleeing here, is my last-ditch effort to find something to grasp onto before I go under for good.

The urge to turn around and walk out of this place

vibrates through me. ZWOL and I might be headed for a love-hate relationship if it keeps forcing me out of my comfort zone.

Like the healthy, well-adjusted adult that I am, I avoid the menu and the looming decision by guessing the zodiac sign of another person.

The man sipping what appears to be a cappuccino near the roaster is definitely an eight. Stable, hardworking, seemingly a businessman based on his sharp suit, and reliable. I bet he's a Capricorn.

"Next," the barista calls to the man in front of me.

I pull my attention away from number eight. It's time. I've got to decide.

Maybe I should order a cappuccino like number eight. It would be an easy out, and I'm all for easy outs right now.

But all thoughts grind to a halt and leak out of my ears when I take in the gorgeous specimen of a man behind the counter. He wasn't there when I first walked in. He's sporting a five o'clock shadow-style beard. His brown hair is shaved on the sides starting an inch above his ear and all the way down to the nape of his neck. The top is longer and styled so effortlessly, it lifts in the front and flops to the left like he's stepping off the set of a fashion magazine.

He must've sold his soul to get hair like that.

His green flannel shirt, with the sleeves rolled up twice, exposes countless tattoos on his forearms. He's like a wet dream of a lumberjack. I bet he can cut a log in half with one swing. I saw a guy do that on TikTok once and it was hot as hell.

Fuck me running. He's the hottest man I've ever seen in my life.

Do all men look like this here? It's only my first day in Portland, but damn. It might've been the worst decision ever to escape here if this is considered standard. My vagina's closed up shop for the rest of my life, and I don't need some sexy lumberjacks challenging that decision.

But most interesting of all is no number or zodiac sign pops into my head when I take him in. My Aunt Addie and I used to play this game in her bakery. She'd focus on zodiac signs, and I would make up a number and a reason they'd be that number based on small details I'd notice about the person. Addie would always laugh in response, and my assessments would become more and more ridiculous just to make her smile.

And yet, I've got nothing on him. This has *never* happened.

"Next," he calls and focuses in on me.

And I stare back at him, unable to speak.

He frowns. "What would you like?"

Shit.

Sweat trickles down my back. The answer should be easy. I'm in a coffee shop, after all. One I chose to enter and join the line. The line I've been waiting in for four minutes. Two hundred and forty seconds have passed, but my mind is still blank.

A cappuccino. That was my out, but I didn't think it through. Not just because I despise coffee, but that's a lot of milk. I'm not a fan of the aftertaste. I scan the milk alternatives on the menu. There are four, and that's three too many. What if one causes diarrhea? Or what if the coffee beans used here somehow have gluten in them and I have a reaction? Or what if it's too simple of a drink to order when I want to work here, and they judge me for it? Should I order something more complicated, or would that label me as a snob?

Ever since The Event That Shall Not Be Named, it's become painfully obvious the decisions I make always lead to disaster. All the micro decisions that add up in the day are my enemy. I used to be the person friends would seek out advice from. Now, my brain refuses to cooperate and can't even get its act together enough to order a coffee.

"Umm." That's all I got. That's my answer. I can't even form the words I practiced mentally after seeing number eight's cappuccino.

The woman behind me huffs. "Just choose something so we can all move on with our lives."

I glance over my shoulder and the woman has an 'I Heart Portland' shirt on. Her New York accent paired with the shirt gives off tourist vibes. She's totally a Karen. Moody, dramatic, and a Cancer.

I gulp again and turn back to the Lumberjack of hotness. "What would you recommend?"

He arches an eyebrow and takes me in from head to toe. "Our fruit punch cold brew."

"Ew."

Oh fuck, please stars tell me I did not just say that out loud. Judging by Lumberjack's face, I did. But I don't want a cold drink, not when it's cold enough to freeze my tits off outside. I've got to turn this around. I'm fucking everything up one word at a time.

I clear my throat and give him a winning smile. "Wait, sorry that came out wrong. What I meant to say is sure. I'll take one of those."

He glares at me and punches my order into the machine with far more aggression than necessary.

"Name?" he demands.

"Zoey."

He gestures to the payment machine. My hands shake as I tap my card. I stand off to the side and pat at the sweat dotting my hairline. I've made the executive decision to never order anything ever again in my life.

The Karen asks for her to-go mug to be filled with black coffee while the tattooed barista—the seven—makes my drink.

Ms. Seven calls out my name, and I grab the coffee and head back to my table.

I sip the drink Lumberjack dude recommended, and a burst of grapefruit and kiwi explode on my tongue, followed by mint and bitter coffee. It's the most interesting drink I've ever had.

Coffee and I have a hate-hate relationship. The taste is just flat out disgusting. But I need to change my tune and stop being such a Judgy Julia.

I need any vice I can get my hands on—as long as it's legal and won't kill me.

Which doesn't leave me with much to work with.

Coffee could be an option. I could learn to like it.

I take another sip and suppress a shudder.

Or not.

I glance at Lumberjack, and he's already scowling in my direction, like I personally offended him.

Well, if I wanted to leave a lasting impression on the staff here, I accomplished that. Unfortunately, it was a negative one.

After delaying for as long as I can, the line finally tapers off. Heaving myself out of the chair, I throw back my shoulders and fluff my shoulder length, caramel waves. I'm seriously starting to regret my decision to wear my business dress, heels, and my black suit jacket today.

But these clothes are the only thing I have left from my old life. A throwback to the time when I felt powerful and on top of the world. And I need to feel powerful today when it's my first full day in a new city.

Lumberjack notices my approach right away. His gaze never strays from mine during my walk up to the counter.

I smile, hoping it'll soften him. "I saw your sign about the open position."

He looks me up and down. Again. "It's filled."

"No, it's not," Ms. Seven says.

"It is." He crosses his arms and glares at me. "And if it weren't, why would I hire you? You clearly don't know anything about coffee. Or even like it."

Anger flushes my cheeks, but I keep my voice steady. Professional. "Can I speak to the hiring manager?"

He smirks. "I am the hiring manager."

Well shit, of course he is. "I do know about coffee." It's a lie, but fake it until you make it, right? "I was nervous about applying earlier and blanked on my order. Can you please give me a chance? It's clear you're crazy busy and could use the help."

"No." He shrugs, as if it's not a big deal.

I clench my fists at his dismissal. At his refusal to even consider me as a candidate.

With nothing to lose, I whip out my resume and hand it to him. "In case you change your mind."

He stares at the paper in my hand for a good ten seconds before finally taking it. I spin on my heels and take measured steps to leave the shop, refusing to storm out and make a scene. No, I'm the epitome of professional. There's no doubt he'll call once he reads my resume.

The bell announcing my exit sounds more ominous than anything. Once outside, I look back through the window and find Lumberjack tearing my resume in two and tossing it into the trash.

I gasp.

He did not just do that. He did not just destroy my chance at getting a job I so desperately need.

The old me would've stormed back through those doors and confronted him. Would've given him a piece of my mind to make his rejection easier to bear. But I'm not that woman anymore.

My shoulders sag as I stare at the ground, swallowing hard and trying to get a handle on my despair. I trudge back to my apartment two blocks away.

I CAN'T HELP the nausea I experience every time I enter the studio apartment that is now my home. It's dark and cramped. All that's inside is a dark gray, saggy couch and that's it. The couch is my entire life as it also functions as my table, chair, and bed. The fact that the bathroom is so small I can use the toilet and shower at the same time is the icing on the cake.

It's all I could afford, at least until I get a steady income flowing.

The kitchen is super basic, and the oven doesn't even work. A pang goes through my chest at the size. It's nothing like the massive kitchen I used to have back in Atlanta, where I'd bake to my heart's content using Addie's recipe book. The book is nothing more than a three-pronged folder with handwritten recipes inside, but it's the most important thing I own.

There'll be no baking in this oven, and barely any cooking. But I need to remember this is only temporary. Just until I can get on my feet and figure out life.

The gray garment bag holding my maid of honor dress is nestled in the far-left corner of my clothes rack. We searched for three months for that dress. Baby pink, A line, with a lace bodice. And now I won't get to wear it.

The rest of the clothes on the rack are a mockery of my old life. Full of tailored designer outfits I've built up over the years.

It's only been one week, but it feels like decades. One week since I informed my engineering job about moving cities, which made me disposable. Even if they have an office in Portland, they weren't willing to find me a job in it. It was as if all the hard work I did and all the money I generated for the company didn't matter between one sentence and the next. I became a burden, one they wanted to get rid of and replace as soon as possible.

I collapse onto the couch. Fucking ZWOL lied to me.

That job was supposed to be mine, and I was naïve enough to believe I'd get it.

I thought for once something was working in my favor, but I was wrong.

I need to make a list of job vacancies in the area and apply, but I'm tired. Tired of life, tired of things being hard. I'm so out of touch with the working world; I really thought it'd be easy to get a job. That all I had to do was show my resume and, just like that, I'd be hired. I applied for an entry-level job as a barista, something even a high school student could do, and yet I couldn't manage to get it.

All because of Lumberjack Asshole.

CHAPTER 3

"*L*eo, don't you dare let a little drizzle dampen your fiery spirit. When life throws you a storm, grab an umbrella made of confidence and dance in the downpour. Remember, darling, setbacks are just an invitation to showcase your resilience. Wear something red today to help flick those droplets of doubts away and roar your way to success. Love always, ZWOL."

I SLEPT LIKE SHIT. And my horoscope sounds like today is going to be a doozy.

But I can't wait around for ZWOL to mention a job again, not when I need one ASAP. I compile a list of available vacancies in the area. They range from service industry to corporate assistant positions, and it takes far longer than I care to admit deciding which place to visit first. There's nothing like inputting all the locations into a random name chooser online to pick the starting place for me.

Technology for the win.

The name that popped up was the furthest away. I plan to walk to it, even if it'll take an hour. It'll be worth the gas savings, and let's be honest, I've got nothing but time.

Umbrella in hand, I choose a red Armani dress to follow ZWOL's advice, along with thick leggings TikTok made me buy and waterproof black boots. With copies of my resume printed out in my purse, I'm ready.

I've got this.

It's the type of day where rain hangs heavy in the clouds, threatening everyone in the city. I guess that can't come as too much of a surprise. It's not like the Northwest is known for its amazing weather.

My black peacoat doesn't keep the chill in the air at bay, but at least I look good. And it hasn't started raining yet so the waves that took twenty minutes to put in my hair are still holding up. That might have something to do with the massive amounts of hair spray I used, but it'll be fine.

Everything's fine.

Just because the Lumberjack Asshole tore my resume up and refused to hire me doesn't mean everyone else will.

One hour and twenty minutes and multiple wrong turns later, I make it to the first company on my list with the bottom of my jacket and my tights soaking wet. Umbrellas do nothing to hinder sideways rain. No wonder no one is using one but me. I'll need to invest in a proper raincoat to fit in with the locals whenever I get some money.

I wring out the bottom of my jacket and hope the law office looking for an assistant will overlook my partially wet outfit. I didn't call ahead of time, wanting to surprise them and show initiative. I have an inherent distrust in online applications. There are too many filters and the possibility of losing out on a good person is a real issue, especially for someone looking for a career change. Like me. But once they meet me in person, they'll for sure hire me.

I enter the building behind a woman and take an elevator decorated in tinsel and playing Christmas music to the third floor. The second I step through the door the receptionist gives me a guarded look.

I smile. "Hi, I know this is really unusual, but I have a favor to ask you."

"Okay?"

"I'm here for to apply for the assistant position." I hold out a resume for her. "Can I talk to someone in charge of hiring?"

She lifts her hands in a stop motion and doesn't take the paper within reach. "Oh no, you need to apply online."

"I know, but I would still appreciate the opportunity to talk to someone."

"That's not possible."

"Please, I need a job and I can prove my skills—"

"Listen, lady." She crosses her arms across her chest. "I get what you're saying, but you need to apply online."

"But—"

She places a hand on the receiver of her desk phone. "I'm going to need to call security."

"Whoa." I hold my hands up in a placating gesture. "There's no need for something so drastic. I'm just trying to go the extra mile to apply for a job. To show how much I want it and how capable I am."

"You're not going the extra mile; you're being creepy. I'm going to ask you one last time to leave."

I heave a sigh. There's no use. She's doing her gate-keeping job and I'm shit out of luck. "Fine."

I return to the elevators and smash the down button ten times, hoping it'll come faster the more times I press it. Someone really needs to invent that.

Once I'm out of the building, a light mist of rain coats the air. I check the next place on my list. It's a seven-minute walk. It's okay, I've got this. I came on too strong for that one. I can adapt my tactics for the next place. There are twenty places on the list. One rejection isn't the end.

In the next ten places, I make it through the door without any threats to call security. But they either inform me they already filled the position or that they'll pass my resume to the person in charge.

The next on my list is for a receptionist at a dental office. The hiring manager kindly brings me to their office and takes my resume.

I watch her read it, hoping to understand her facial tics, and wring my hands in my lap.

When she's finished, she looks at me. "You graduated with a degree in mechanical engineering from Georgia Tech?"

"Yes?" I'm not sure where she's going with this.

"I'm having a hard time understanding why you'd want to work here. You're clearly overqualified."

I cringe. "A quarter life crisis?" Really, it's a thirty-three point three percent crisis, but that doesn't have the same ring to it. Also why do all these crises assume we're going to live to one hundred? What a sham.

She laughs as if I told a joke. But it's the truth.

"Seriously," I say. "I need a job and I'm looking for anything that I could add value to."

"Hmm, well, I have your number. I'll call if we decide to proceed."

She says it in a tone that tells me to not expect that call. I give her a strained smile and exit. I'm cold, wet, hungry, and ready for the day to be finished. There's only so much rejection I can deal with before it becomes unbearable.

Almost every place I've visited today gave the same response: I don't have experience in the field. Changing my career feels next to impossible when I'm not able to tick the boxes someone placed on a piece of paper. How fast someone learns and their attitude is more important than having experience for a job that is easy to teach. At least, that's what I always thought when I hired new employees.

The closer I get to home, the angrier I become. And of course, of fucking course, it starts pouring rain when I'm ten minutes away. As if this day could get any worse?

I duck my head and try to steady the umbrella against the gusts of wind trying to rip it from my hands. I'm on a one-track mission to get home. To get dry, to eat something, to warm up. It's not worth the gas savings to be this miserable and—

Something hard slams into my side.

I fall back into a freezing puddle and look up, trying to figure out what the fuck just happened. Honey brown eyes glare down at me, but he still extends a hand to help me up. I bypass the hand of Lumberjack Asshole and stand myself. He bends down and collects my now drenched purse and umbrella from the ground. He holds them out for me.

I snatch them from his hands and muster as much dignity as I can while sopping wet. "Watch where you're going."

He snorts. "You ran into me."

"I did no such thing." I can't help but bristle. Most people would ask if I'm okay. Offer their apologies. But, of course, he's not the type of person to do that. I didn't add "asshole" to his name for nothing.

"Keep telling yourself that, princess."

My shoulders hike to my ears at the term. Princess is what my dad calls me. They just so happen to say it in the same way. As if I'm less-than, as if I'm an annoyance that should go away.

He frowns as he takes in my reaction. I shoulder check him as I push past, as if I'm a linebacker in the NFL and he isn't almost a foot taller than my five-feet-five-inch stature.

I make it back to my apartment and strip out of my sopping clothes. My shower barely heats up enough to be considered lukewarm, but it still burns against my frozen skin.

Once my body stops shivering, I eat leftover gluten-free pasta from last night. I might need to start skipping meals soon to stretch the little money I have left if I don't find a job. Gluten-free food costs at least three times more than the wheat-filled standard.

Fucking celiac disease screwing me over yet again.

I collapse onto the couch and reread my horoscope from this morning. Where did I go wrong? Today was like a test I didn't sign up for.

I rub my temples. Moving here was a mistake. Buying the app was a mistake. Everything I do is a mistake. I'm no closer to transforming myself or impressing my family. I'm still stuck being the same Zoey as a week ago.

Zodiac Way of Life doesn't accept refunds. I paid for the month, and I have it for the month. I aggressively toggle off automatic renewal and toss the phone next to me. I've been conned... again.

How many times will it take for me to learn my lesson?

If Aunt Addie were still alive, she'd know what to do, or at least find a way to make me feel better. If we were on speaking terms, I'd call Lilly or mom. They'd make a joke, probably at my expense, and we'd have a laugh about it all.

But they don't want anything to do with me, and there's no one else. No one who would take my call, who would care.

I snuggle into the cushions and close my eyes, begging the stars for a good night's sleep.

I just can't deal with anything more today.

CHAPTER 4

Days in Portland: 4
Money left in bank account: $150
Number of job offers: 0

A hangover due to crying is the worst, and it's become my new normal over the past three days. I wake up every day and try to make my blue-gray eyes appear less red and puffy. But applying eyeliner to puffy eyes is a hopeless cause. So is applying for jobs. My job prospects are looking pretty abysmal at the moment, and every day that passes causes my stress levels to rise.

Every job I've followed up with has informed me they've hired a more experienced candidate. Candidates younger than me are more experienced. How is it possible that someone can be overqualified and yet not qualified enough at the same time?

My experience managing a team of engineers to

develop a fully automated drink preparation kiosk for Spark, the top selling soft drink on the market, means nothing to them. I had a budget of millions of dollars to design, test, and implement the new technology as well as troubleshoot any problems. Now I'm not trusted to answer phone calls and schedule appointments.

Oh, how I've been demoted in every aspect of my life.

This weekend, I'm going to need to come up with a new plan. I could sell my car to buy myself more time to find a job. But the thought of selling it causes me to panic. Addie picked it out with me. Unless I find something soon, I may need to part with it. Portland is trying to push me away, and damn if that doesn't sting.

I've got to say, getting rejected by a city is not something I wanted to add to my list of life experiences.

But here we are.

Addie always talked about Portland as if it were a magical city. It's where she discovered what she wanted to do with her life—baking. I've heard about her Portland stories my entire life, so much so they've almost become part of me. I feel like I already know the city, even though I've never been before.

When I needed an escape after Thanksgiving, the first place that came to mind was Portland. I was hoping to have a similar experience to Addie, as if by being here I'd feel closer to her, and her spirit would guide and support me.

Turns out, I'm delusional as well as a horrible person who tore my family apart.

The only highlight of my days is passing Amore and giving the window my middle finger. At first it was subtle, like using my middle finger to wipe my cheek. Yesterday, annoyed at yet another failed job search, I held up both middle fingers as I passed. To blame all my bad days since moving here on the person responsible for my first bad day is petty, but it's the most rewarding kind of petty.

I don't look into the window of Amore when I do it. I don't care if Lumberjack Asshole sees or not, or what his reaction is. This act is only for me and it's the first straightforward decision I've been able to make in ages because the consequences don't matter. I've already been turned down from the job and I'll never set foot in that place again.

When I almost reach Amore, Ms. Seven is sitting by the window and observing everyone who passes by, as if she is watching a movie. Instead of her usual flannel uniform, she's wearing all black.

Her gaze locks on mine, and she smiles. I duck my head and forgo giving her the finger. It's not like she did anything to me. There's no need to be rude.

I make it three steps past Amore before a voice calls out, "Zoey, wait."

I freeze and turn around to find Ms. Seven walking toward me. "How do you know my name?"

"I made your coffee a couple of days ago." She stops one foot away. "I have a knack for remembering names."

"That's not creepy at all." I take a step back.

She laughs, light and tinkering. "You want to grab a drink?"

"I..." I stammer as I look around expecting an excuse to say no to suddenly appear out of thin air. She probably only wants to hand me a restraining order.

She threads her arm through mine and is leading me down the street before I'm able to turn her down. "I'm not taking no for an answer, and drinks are on me. I'm Ruby, by the way."

"I'd introduce myself, but there's no point." It comes out with more snark than I meant, but she just chuckles in response.

For some reason, I say nothing else and walk with her. Maybe it's because she's the first person to want to talk to me, to have me around, in far too long. Or maybe I'm just sad enough to cling to another person so I don't feel so alone, if only for a moment.

"You drink alcohol?" she asks.

"Daily."

It would be true if I had enough money to fund it. She laughs her fairy laugh and guides me to a bar that's decorated in dark greens, wood, and lights with some sort of wicker basket thing around them. It'd look ridiculous if it wasn't so fucking cool.

Ruby snaps open the menu and places it in front of me. "This is Toddy's, one of my favorite bars."

I scan the glossy menu and tense. There must be at least fifty options, and I'm already overwhelmed after scanning just the top few lines. I'm too exhausted to deal with choosing something and over-thinking how this will come back to bite me in the ass.

"As in a hot toddy?" I ask to buy time.

"Exactly, and they just so happen to specialize in them. I'd recommend the apple one."

"Apple sounds great." I relax back into the chair and

breathe through the relief at not having to choose something myself.

Ruby walks to the bar and chats with the pretty
bartender, all red hair and pale skin. She must be a Pisces,
listening to people moan about their life all day. That also
makes her a three, which reminds me of half an ear.

I straighten the Santa hat candle in the center of the
table while I wait for Ruby to return.

"So…" I begin once she's back. "Why did you accost me
on the street?"

She laughs. "I'm curious."

"About?"

"How you get my boss riled up."

The server sets our drinks down and I take a hearty
sip of mine. "He's an asshole."

She lifts a shoulder. "Not really, but I can understand
why you'd think that."

"Why does it matter if I rile your boss up or not?"

"Because." She takes a dainty sip of her drink. "It takes
a lot to get under his skin."

I snort. "Seems like all it takes is applying for a job."

"The position is open." She gives me a secretive smile.
"Do you still need a job?"

I nod, hesitant to admit the truth. I'm not sure where
she's going with this.

"Perfect." She claps her hands together. "I'll get you the
job at Amore."

I huff. "Your boss tore my resume up after I gave it to
him. I think it's clear he doesn't want to work with me."

"He won't say no to me."

"Because you're his girlfriend?"

She laughs, and laughs, and laughs some more for good measure before wiping a tear away. "No."

"So what? You're evil and want to torture him with someone he hates?"

"That does have a nice ring to it, but no. Anders needs help but he's too stubborn to admit it. That's where you come in."

Lumberjack Asshole's name is Anders. Why the fuck does he have to have a hot name? But what Ruby's saying can't be real. She's going behind Anders's back by offering me a job and the only explanation is this is some sort of sick prank. Dangle a job in front of the desperate woman and then snatch it away. Ha ha, very funny.

"Sorry, but I really don't care about your asshole boss. I'm not interested in playing into whatever joke is going on here."

I grab my jacket.

She raises her hand. "This isn't a joke. You need a job, and he needs help. It'll be mutually beneficial. The pay is twenty an hour plus tips, free lunch, and unlimited drinks. Not only that, but there's potential to expand your responsibilities and move up to a managerial role."

I pause, intrigued. "In what way?"

"I read your resume." At my confused look she says, "Got it from the trash. Your background and skills running a project and a team are exactly what we need to help get a new location up and running."

I settle back in the chair. "Amore is expanding?"

"Not exactly. It'll be a new concept all together, but almost nothing is complete and we're on a time crunch.

That's why I need you, and so does Anders. But he's a man, so he's a little slow on the uptake."

I couldn't agree more with that assessment of Anders. But the most irritating part is the fact that excitement sizzles in my blood. She's hinting at the type of jobs I love most in the world: projects with a time limit. They're like catnip to me. Conditions like these are what I thrive under.

I settle back into the chair and take another pull of my drink, trying to act nonchalant. I can't take another day of rejections like today. It's only been four days of job searching and I'm already over it. How do people do it for months or years on end? Even if I have to work with an asshole of epic proportions, it'd be worth it to pay my bills. To keep a roof over my head and food in my stomach.

I run through all the ways this is a bad idea in my head, but I can't help but come back to the one answer I want to say. The one that's been sitting on the tip of my tongue since she made her proposal.

Yes.

Zodiac Way of Life promised a job at a coffee shop… and it's delivering? I'm going to have to toggle on automatic renew if it keeps this up.

"If you can get him to board," I say, "which I seriously doubt by the way, then I accept."

"Perfect." She grins. "Give me your number and I'll text you this weekend with the details of your first shift. Expect to start on Monday."

Today's Saturday. She might just be my kind of delusional if she thinks she can convince Lumberjack Asshole to hire me so soon, but I do as she asks, not wanting her to reconsider.

After we exchange numbers, I down the rest of my drink and stand. "Thank you for the drink and the job. But I need to get going."

She smiles. "Sure thing. See you Monday."

I speed walk home, trying to temper my excitement. But no matter how much I try to suppress the hope bubbling inside, it's a losing battle.

Maybe this is the start of my luck turning around. Maybe the stars were testing me, to ensure my dedication before following through on a job offer.

Well, they better not test me anymore, because time is ticking away until Lilly's wedding and my apology tour. Not to mention January when my rent is due.

It's time for the stars to stop messing around and to start delivering.

CHAPTER 5

"*H*ey there, bestie. The universe is sending you a clear message—it's time to ditch those screens and get your butt into nature. It's time to recharge those batteries of yours after a difficult past couple of weeks. Whether it's a stroll through a scenic forest or a visit to a Christmas tree farm (because, hey, even lions need festive vibes), immerse yourself in the enchanting beauty around you. Enjoy, Leo. Love always, ZWOL."

NATURE?

When I think of nature, I think of hiking, and I'm allergic to that level of activity.

ZWOL is really challenging my resolve to follow it today. But I'm here to maximize my cosmic energy to become the best version of myself. All to prove to my parents and sister that I deserve a second chance. That I'm not a failure at life.

ZWOL's idea to go to a Christmas tree farm sounds like something I can manage. I haven't been able to enjoy or appreciate the festive season. The stress of moving here has taken up all my headspace.

But that's all about to change.

There are a few farms within a thirty-minute drive, and they aren't that expensive. Cheaper than a fake tree. I'll just have to go without ornaments or lights this year, but that's fine.

I bet mom and Lilly have already decorated our family Christmas tree by now. Normally we do it the morning after Thanksgiving, but after the disaster of this year's dinner that didn't happen.

A pang goes through my heart thinking about them. I miss them more than I ever thought possible. There's nothing like this time of year to remind me how much I lost. Way more than the money. They're my family, my stability.

Shaking off thoughts of them, I grab my skinny black jeans and a hunter green sweater. The color brings out my grayish blue eyes. They're my defining feature thanks to the almond shape with a slight tilt upward at the corner. My black puffer jacket and black winter boots complete my look.

My appearance, my clothes, are all I have left. And I refuse to let go of them. It doesn't matter that I'm dirt poor or that I'm jobless; I refuse to look like it. Not when I used to earn six figures in my previous job.

It's easy to find Hilltop Christmas Tree Farm. I park my silver Mini, the car Addie helped me pick out, and hop out. My perfect mini tree is waiting for me.

The farm is adorable. There's a bonfire surrounded by stalls that sell every Christmas decoration imaginable as well as coffee.

A man in a red flannel shirt and hiking boots approaches me. I glare at the sky and the cosmos when I catch sight of his face.

Really, stars? Do you hate me that much?

It's Lumberjack Asshole, again. Apparently known to his friends as Anders.

His facial expression doesn't change from his typical resting asshole face the closer he gets. "What are you looking for?"

I look between him and the "Christmas trees for sale sign" next to me a couple times and snark, "A Christmas tree?"

He rolls his eyes and in an exasperated voice says, "Yes, but what type?"

"A green one."

"I mean a Douglas, Nobel, or Grand Fir…"

I nod like that all means something important to me, even though it's all nonsense. "A small one. What type is that?"

He snorts. "Follow me."

His strides are so long, I have to jog to keep up. I never thought I was that short, but damn, he's putting that to the test. After a five-minute speed walk in silence, he points over to a selection of small trees. Row after row of them.

"Pick one, chop it down using the hand saw, and either wait for the tractor to bring it around or carry it yourself to your car. You'll pay then."

"Okayyyy."

I blink, and he's already gone. I take inventory of all the tree options and take far too long to narrow it down to my five favorites. They're all good options. I need to narrow it down to one, but how? With a critical eye, I walk around each one, hoping for a reason to jump out at me.

I don't know a single thing about Christmas trees. I'd normally go for smell, but as they all smell good what the fuck can I use instead?

Fullness is the only criteria I can think of. The engineer in me screams at the horror of using only one criterion, but I shut that bitch up with mental duct tape. It's a fucking Christmas tree. It doesn't have to be rocket science.

I somehow manage to narrow down my options to two which are close to each other. Both beautiful and fuller than I'd have expected for a four-foot tree.

A crushing sensation takes root in my chest at the thought of narrowing it down even further and having to choose. To decide.

What if I choose wrong? What if it's going to die tomorrow and I should've chosen the other one? What if the needles all fall off on the way to my car, or the tree I choose has a disease?

Doubt after doubt attacks me and I can barely breathe. This is why I hate making decisions. The last big decision I made caused my life to blow up so spectacularly that I'm still burned by it all.

I've been out here for ages. My toes and hands are numb and it's no longer fun. But I can't do it. I can't decide. The sun's getting lower in the sky, and the closer the sun gets to the tree line, the angrier I become. At myself and my inability to choose.

This should be easy, and yet I'm paralyzed. If I had the money, I'd cut down both just to avoid the decision.

I'm so sick of myself and my issues. I came here for a tree, and I'm fucking leaving with one. Yes, I can do this. I've been making decisions my entire life; I've got the ability.

Maybe?

Even my pep talk leads to doubt. How pathetic.

I blow out a long breath.

Fine, if I can't decide myself, I'll need to leave it up to chance. I close my eyes and spin around a few times with my pointer finger extended. The tree closest to whatever direction I'm pointing at is the one I'm getting. I open my eyes and my back is facing both trees.

Exasperated, I try again and when I open my eyes, my finger points to the tree on the right.

Ugh, finally.

I pick up the saw, but the tree I chose is a thick bitch, and I'm already regretting my choice. But I can't leave a partially cut tree out here. That'd be rude.

My nose stings with the telltale sign that tears aren't far behind. I just wanted to get a tree, and a simple journey has taken up my entire day and just reinforced how useless I am.

I need to get help, but I can't ask Anders. It's not a good look to appear incapable in front of a potential boss. I should be able to chop down a tree myself.

"Hey there," a man, blessedly not Anders, calls out.

He's hot with his short dark hair, chiseled jaw, and tawny-colored eyes. "We're closing soon, and your car is the only one left in the lot. Can I help you with anything?"

I force a smile, hoping I don't look like I'm about to cry. "Yeah, just having some issues chopping the tree down."

"They're tricky bastards. You've got to work them just right and butter them up."

I almost smile. "And how does one go about buttering up a tree?"

"By whispering sweet nothings to it. Obviously." He takes the saw from me and completes the job in two seconds flat.

I snort. "Obviously."

He's totally a ninety-one. Playful, but with a secretive smile. Ones can be written in three different ways. They're adaptable and you never know what secrets the person holds.

He walks back to the parking lot with the tree in his arms. He doesn't make me run to keep up with him like Anders did.

After a few minutes, he says, "I don't think I've ever seen someone choose a tree like you."

I whip my head to the side and meet his gaze, his eyes dancing with mirth. "How did you see me?"

"Security feed."

I groan. Can today get any worse? "Don't tell me Anders saw it, too."

He laughs. "I plead the fifth."

"Fuck," I mumble under my breath. "So what? You drew the short straw to help me?"

His eyes crinkle at the corners when he grins. "I'll wrap this in a net really quick. You want it in the backseat?"

"Sure." I open the back hatch and push down the back seats to fit the tree, all while trying not to focus on his non answer.

I dig into my purse for some cash. "How much is it?"

"It's on the house."

"What? No. I can pay no problem."

He puts his hands in his back pockets. "Didn't say you couldn't. It's a gift. 'Tis the season and all that bullshit."

"Are you sure?"

He arches an eyebrow. "Are you always so bad at accepting gifts?"

I cringe. "Maybe?"

"Merry Christmas."

I murmur a thank you and climb into the car. Finally, something good is happening today.

But ten minutes after leaving the tree farm, my steering wheel begins to vibrate accompanied by a loud flapping noise.

Shit, shit, shit.

I pull off to the shoulder of the road and get out to inspect the car.

My rear tire is flat.

Shit.

I take a deep breath through my nose and promise to buy myself some alcohol to drown my sorrows in when I get home.

It can't be that hard to change a tire, right? I'm a mechanical engineer. This *should* be easy. But fuck, let's be real.

Equations aren't going to do me any good here. Neither is leading a team to perform the job. Or calculating any force on the vehicle. Or drawing how each part functions.

So, on a scale of one to one hundred of the likelihood of me changing the tire myself, it's a clear negative ten. But I have to try. I don't want to spend the night on the side of the road.

Thank the stars for Google. I pull up my browser and watch a tire changing video twice before opening my trunk.

The spare is there, but I don't have any of the tools needed. Of course not.

Tears trickle down my cheeks, and I try to think of a solution. I can't afford a tow truck or a repair service. Dad was right when he recommended getting roadside assistance for the car, but I didn't listen. I never did listen to his advice.

My best option would be to either wait for a stranger to pass by or call the tree farm for help.

I look up and down the country road. The empty roads are ominous, and it's almost dark. Yeah, I'm going to nope out of waiting for a stranger to pass by. I'd have better luck getting murdered than getting help.

I kick at the dirt and call the farm. It rings endlessly and I call again. And again.

Fuck.

I scroll through my contacts. Ruby is the only person I know here. It's weird to call someone I just met and assume they know how to change a tire and are even willing to help. But here we are.

"Hey, you," Ruby answers on the third ring. Music pumps in the background and I can barely hear her. "Good news, I got you the job. You start Monday."

"Wait, what?"

"I got you the job," she shrieks with more excitement than I thought was humanly possible.

"Wow. Thank you."

"See you Monday…"

"Wait," I shout. "I'm actually calling for a favor."

"As if getting you a job wasn't favor enough?"

"Ha. Ha," I say. "But seriously, I'm in a bind here."

"What's wrong?"

"My car has a flat, and I can't fix it. I don't have any tools."

"Did you order a tow truck?" she asks as if it's the most obvious course of action.

I'm already regretting calling her.

"No, I can't… afford it." I say the last words in a whisper, hoping she didn't hear them, and I won't feel as humiliated as I do right now.

Ruby's silent for a few seconds before she says, "Alright, send me your location. I'll see if I have any friends who can help."

"Thanks." I hang up and do as told.

Ruby calls back three minutes later. "I've got a friend on the way. He'll be there in about ten minutes."

"You're a lifesaver. I owe you one."

She laughs and I can't tell if it's at what I said or if she's laughing at someone next to her. Not when it's so loud on her end and I have to strain to hear her.

She says, "We'll see about that. Call if they don't show up."

She hangs up before I can say anything else. I blow out a long breath and drum my fingers on the steering wheel. I'll be okay, help is on the way.

Counting helps pass the time, and it allows me to focus on something other than being alone in the near dark on the side of the road.

Or how close to a breakdown I am.

Or how miserable my life is.

Or any of it.

Numbers are comforting, and they're the perfect distraction.

Three hundred seconds later, headlights appear in my rearview mirror and grow closer until a truck stops behind my car. A figure steps out of the truck and approaches my window. I remain in the car, refusing to get out until I know it's a friend of Ruby's.

Anders knocks on my window, and I blink in shock. This can't be happening. Why does he keep coming into my life and witnessing me at my weakest?

Of course, he is Ruby's friend. And he was at the farm and therefore nearby. Why didn't I put two and two together?

I unlock the door and he steps back for me to get out.

He doesn't say anything, but disapproval radiates off him. My shoulders tense, uncomfortable he's the one to help me.

"Thank you for coming," I say, trying to be nice.

He ignores me and my attempts at kindness and turns back to his truck. Okay then. No talking.

He grabs all the necessary items to change the tire and returns to my car.

"Hold the light for me." He follows up his demand by forcing the flashlight into my hands.

I don't bother responding and instead direct the light to the flat. He doesn't talk, but his movements are practiced, as if he's changed thousands of tires in his life.

Who is this man? And why does my body heat up while watching him? He's so capable, and there's something so sexy about that. My ex, Eric, didn't know his way around anything besides computers.

His hand cranks the wrench and holy shit. Have a pair of hands ever looked hotter than now? With the veins popping out at the exertion paired with the thickness of them. They'd almost be muscular, but that's ridiculous. I'm no doctor, but muscular hands? Fuck, I need a drink because I'm imagining things.

Every movement is so smooth, I can't help but pin Anders as the type of man who excels at everything he does. Inside or outside the bedroom. Eric couldn't find my clit. He probably wouldn't have been able to even with a map tattooed on my skin.

But Anders? Whew, I can tell just by looking at him that he'd be great in bed.

Ugh, and why the fuck has my mind gone to sex while watching Anders? Way to stay professional.

When he finishes, he wipes his hands on a rag he just so happens to have in his back pocket. Who carries a rag in their back pocket?

"You should get that changed ASAP. The spare is only temporary."

I make some sort of humming noise in agreement, not wanting to lie to him outright. Not if we'll maybe be working together.

He frowns. "I'm serious."

"I know." And I do, but food is more important than a car. I really hope I'll get the job, because if not, I'm going to be screwed on so many levels.

Thanks to that helpful reminder at the worst possible moment, the dam of emotions from the day breaks. It's too much. Everything that's happened today, my inability to choose a tree, my life, and my money issues. The list is endless at this point.

A flood of emotions hits my system, and I turn around so I can fall apart without an audience.

I grit my teeth and force out a strained. "Thanks again."

It's rude to dismiss him so abruptly, but I can't have him see me cry. He'd probably make fun of me.

"Wait," he says.

But I ignore him and stride to my driver's side door, desperate to escape to the inside of my car before I break. I reach for my handle, but his hand grips my bicep and stops me from opening the door. His hold is loose, and he tugs gently on my arm, asking me without words to face him.

I blow out a breath and turn around. He doesn't crowd me, but I can barely breathe with him so close. He smells dangerous. Not in the "I'll kill you in one hundred ways" kind of way, but in the "you'll be addicted after one night" kind of way.

Spicy with a hint of caramel.

Intoxicating.

Tingles travel through my chilled limbs at the heat radiating off him. His honey-colored eyes stare down at me as if I'm a puzzle he can't figure out. I stare back, fighting against the building tears, hoping he doesn't notice in the dim light. His gaze roams over my face, taking everything in, and I have a sinking sensation he sees everything I've been trying so hard to hide.

It feels like hours before he takes a step back, but it must have only been seconds.

He runs a hand through his perfect hair. "Six a.m."

"What?"

"Come to Amore tomorrow at six." He doesn't wait for a reply, and instead walks away and gets back into his truck.

I'm left stunned and confused. I have no idea what just happened. He honks his horn and I jump into motion and get back into my car.

I wait for him to pull out on the road, but he waves for me to go first. He follows behind me the entire way back to the city and to my apartment. I find a row of spots one block away. He parks and hops out of his truck and comes over to my car.

Without speaking, he opens my back seat and takes out the Christmas tree.

When I remain staring at him with wide eyes, he asks, "Where to?"

"Why are you helping me?" I don't get it, not when he's been nothing but rude to me.

Some emotion passes over his face, but he shuts it down before I can read it. He clenches his jaw. "I'm helping Ruby, not you, princess. She demanded I see you all the way home, so here I am."

His answer hurts. I'm a burden and an obligation to him. I thought him asking me to come to Amore was a step in the right direction, that he was beginning to let go of his animosity toward me. But no, he did that for Ruby, too. Ruby who laughed when I asked if they were together, but clearly, he has feelings for her if he does everything she asks.

"Well, you've delivered me home. Job complete," I snap back.

I pull the tree out of his arms, and it immediately drops to the ground. Gritting my teeth, I heft it up. Not only is this tree a thick bitch, but she's a heavy one. The needles poke at my freezing hands, but I refuse to struggle in front of him. I want someone to help me because they're a good person, or because they're my friend, not because they're trying to win over another woman's affections.

I storm down the street. At least I won't have to carry this thing for too long at the speed I'm going.

I've got to add work on my upper body strength to the endless list of things I need to improve about myself. I have to stop five times on the stairs before I make it to my apartment.

Dragging the tree inside, I prop it against the wall. It'll need a holder. Ugh, of course it does. I shoot off a text to Ruby, informing her that I'm home and thanking her again for her help.

I head right back outside to buy a bottle of wine and a Christmas tree holder. If I'm going to Amore tomorrow, then at least I'll get paid for the day to compensate these purchases.

When I get home, I set the tree up in front of the couch. It'll be the first thing I view when I wake up and the last thing I see when I go to sleep. It's perfect. As I eat some rice crackers with peanut butter, I realize I need to come up with a game plan for tomorrow with Anders.

He already has such a low opinion of me, I need to impress him. Because whether I like him or not is irrelevant. I need this job, and the money.

Our first interaction was a disaster of epic proportions. But now, I'm going to impress him so much, he'll forget that ever happened. I'm nothing if not good at research and being analytical. That part of my engineering work was my favorite.

I start by reading the reviews for Amore. Everyone loves the coffee, but every now and again there will be a mention of one of the baristas being an asshole—that they are grumpy or mean. It must be Anders. I'm not surprised, if he treated me like that, he must treat others the same way.

I lose myself for hours in videos about the different types of coffee beans (four types), the best temperature for steamed milk (between one hundred forty and one hundred fifty, but there are different thoughts on this), and how the ideal temperature changes depending on the milk type. Forty videos later, and I'm an expert at tamping the grounds. At least, theoretically. I wish I had a machine to practice on. How do you judge if you have applied twenty to thirty pounds of pressure consistently over the entire surface?

My mind whirls with all the ways I need to be consistent to ensure an amazing cup every time I make it. I study the menu online and all the drink offers. Google is helpful in decoding some of the drinks, but others appear to be the owner's own mashup. The drinks are from all over the world, and it makes me wonder about the owner and how they created this menu. I make flash cards and test myself on each of the drinks and memorize them plus their price.

It's three in the morning when I finally stop. I'll just have to push through the day with little sleep, but it'll be worth it.

Anders is going to be so impressed with me, he'll kick himself for not hiring me sooner.

CHAPTER 6

"*L*ooks like someone's got a cosmic green light to start something new, Leo. But hold your horses, cowgirl. Don't go galloping off into the sunset just yet. It's crucial to stay grounded during this exciting time of change. Remember to trust in your abilities and stay the course, even when faced with the occasional tumbleweed or flock of sheep. So, saddle up, partner, and ride off into the sunset of your dreams. Love always, ZWOL."

AT FIVE FIFTY on the dot, I'm waiting outside the coffee shop. It's dark inside, and I dance a little while waiting in the cold. Two minutes later, the lights turn on and Anders appears in his green flannel shirt and dark jeans. His face remains blank when he sees me, but he does unlock the front door for me to enter before relocking it.

I'll take that as a good sign so that I don't have to wait eight minutes in the cold.

"Good morning," I say, trying to start off in the right way.

"Morning."

He hands me a matching flannel shirt and gestures for me to put it on. I remove my sweater and keep my black cami on.

He doesn't avert his gaze. No, he watches with rapt interest, as if I'm going to do a strip tease. My nipples pebble in my bra, but I ignore it. He has no right to look at me like that when he's trying to get with Ruby.

I slide on the shirt and keep it unbuttoned, but I do tie it at the bottom. My dark jeans match his. I didn't realize they had a uniform here. I just assumed he liked flannel so much he owned one in every color they make.

"What now?" I ask.

"I'll teach you the register and show you the cleaning supplies."

"Will I also be making coffee?"

He snorts. "Definitely not."

His answer is full of so much disbelief, like I'm silly for even thinking about touching his precious beans and machine. I store that fact in my back pocket, to use my new knowledge to my advantage when the time calls for it.

I love proving people wrong and did it repeatedly through school and at work. Especially at work, when my colleagues didn't think a woman could outperform them. But I did it on the regular with a smile on my face and sugar on my lips.

"Do you accept cash here?" I ask, changing the subject.

"Yes, but most people pay with a card."

He spends the next few minutes teaching me how to work the register, and it's simple enough. He pretends to be a customer and orders a chai tea latte. I fumble through the order, getting familiar with the buttons. When it's time to pay, he places his card on the reader.

"Wait, why did you do that?" Ruby mentioned free unlimited drinks as part of the employee perks.

He ignores my question and says, "The machine will print two slips of paper. One is the receipt for the customer and the other is the order. Write the customer's name at the top and place it here." He points to a spot on the counter. "So I know what drink to make."

"What's your name?" I ask following the next step in the process. He's serious about the training if he paid for a drink that doesn't need to be made.

"Ben."

I write Ben in my loopy writing and place the ticket on the counter where he showed me. He jumps behind the counter, literally slides across the counter like from the movies. My mouth gapes like it's trying to catch a dick.

Who the hell is this man? Apparently walking the ten extra feet to go around the back was too much.

Snapping myself out of my amazement, I watch everything he does with a laser focus. His movements are so smooth; it's like he was born to be a barista.

A million questions sit on my tongue, but I bite them back. Now's not the time to understand the drink making process.

When he finishes, he hands me the drink with the fake name written on it.

I give him a quizzical look, but he rolls his eyes and commands, "Just drink it."

I eye it skeptically. I saw him make it, and I know he didn't fuck with it. But why did he make me a drink? It doesn't make sense.

He gestures for me to take a sip and I do. It's... meh. He used cow's milk and I'm not a fan. I would've gone with almond or coconut.

He crosses his arms. "And?"

"It's okay." I try to keep my expression neutral, but I must do a shit job at it because his shoulders tighten and he scowls, like I offended him by saying his drink is just okay.

He waves to a closet and says, "In there are the cleaning supplies. I expect this place to be spotless by the time we open at seven."

"Sir, yes, sir."

He ignores me and cleans his precious machines, checks the stock of everything, unloads boxes of pastries and sandwiches, and begins a cycle on the bean roaster in the corner.

While he's cleaning, I sneakily dump the tea down the drain and finish up my opening tasks with seconds to spare. The place is gleaming, and I'm ready for the crowd.

When Anders flips the sign over from closed to open, the line already snakes around the block with no end in sight.

The first couple of customers are straightforward, but when customer number five asks for a cappuccino with half oat milk and half almond milk with a pump of hazelnut syrup, I'm not sure how to input it in the system.

With a line out the door, I'm scared to ask. So, I write the request at the top of the ticket by hand.

When Anders sees me do it, he makes an unhappy noise, loud enough that it can't be missed. But I've got to move on. I'm being agile and working with what I've got.

"Next," I say.

The next person steps up to the counter and says, "I'll take a skinny, iced soy latte with three pumps vanilla syrup, one pump hazelnut, and cinnamon on top."

Holy shit, I've got no idea how to do this. It's off menu, but I think about the additions and calculate a price in my head.

I input the cost into the machine and write the order on the top of the slip again.

This time, when Anders reads it, he crumples the paper in his hand. He shoots me a death glare as I ring up the next customer, and the next.

The moment there's a lull, he motions for me to step away from the counter.

"You keep messing up," he says. "You have one job to do, and a simple one at that. I need you to do better."

I frown. "How am I messing up? There've been no complaints."

"We don't accept any drink changes besides swapping out the milk. We're not one of those shitty chain stores and if anyone tries to add some syrup shit to our drinks and ruin the perfection that is our menu, we kick them out."

"But that's—"

"—how we do business here. It's how we separate ourselves from everyone else. Each drink on the menu took weeks to perfect. We know coffee better than our customers."

"Okay, I understand." I don't, but I let it go. No need to get into an argument. "Thank you for informing me of that."

"I already did inform you, this morning."

"I'm sorry, but I don't remember that." Is this a test? I'm sure I'd remember a rule that makes my life easier. "How many people have you trained before?"

"Only Ruby. We're the only ones who work here."

"Hmm." I give him a look like that says, "it appears like you're the one who's fucked up, not me."

But he ignores it and says, "Do better. I expect you to remember everything I say, or else why the hell are you even working here?"

Anders doesn't believe in a learning curve. Making mistakes isn't part of his list of acceptable behavior. Years of working in the corporate world keep my face free of emotion, even though I feel like taking off my apron and having a pity party in the back.

Instead, I use my customer service voice on him, the one I reserve for difficult clients and bosses. "Thank you for the feedback. I'll be sure to implement this learning from here on out."

He looks at me as if I've grown three heads.

Huh, that's good to know. Being professional shuts him up.

It becomes a blur of buttons, writing names and tickets as I work through the line as fast as I can. After the first hour, I get the hang of it. Once there's a pause in the line, I do a quick wipe down of the tables and gather all the empty mugs and trash. Then the next rush comes in. The same rhythm repeats itself for the first three hours.

Anders either ignores me or glares at me for the entire three hours. There's no in between with him. It's become a lesson in restraint to ignore him and not let his behavior get to me.

Once there's another lull, Anders tasks me with restocking the pastries and cleaning the bathroom. I do everything he asks without complaint.

When lunch time rolls around, Anders hands me a panini from the food window. "Lunch is included. There's a break room in the back."

Lunch is included for employees, and this is the first time he's referred to me as one. I don't react, nor do I ask for details. Details don't matter right now, not when I've still got half a shift left. "Thanks, but it's not necessary."

His sigh is full of exasperation. "Take the damn sandwich."

"I'm good. I'll run home and get something."

"Do you have something against the food and drink here?" He crosses his arms across his chest.

Hoo boy, someone's still a little testy that I didn't like his chai tea latte. It takes all my willpower to not make a quip about it.

Instead, I say, "Yeah, I do." He bristles and opens his mouth to say something, probably to fire me, but I cut him off. "I can't eat that sandwich because I have celiac."

His anger leaves him between one breath and the next. "Oh."

"Yeah, oh. And even if that." I point to the sandwich. "Were on gluten-free bread, cross contamination is a no go. Also, I don't like cow's milk. I prefer almond or coconut, especially since oat milk isn't gluten-free unless made with certified gluten-free oats."

"I see." He has a contemplative look on his face as he places the sandwich on a plate and off to the side.

"Be back in thirty," I say and leave without waiting for a response.

I speed home and scarf down a peanut butter and jelly rice cake before heading back. When I return, Anders has a cup in his hand with my name on it.

"What's this?" I ask.

"There has to be something here you like."

I arch an eyebrow. "Why do you care?"

"Because this is the best coffee shop in Portland, and probably the region. It's impossible for you to find everything on the menu disgusting." He curls his lips when he says the last word, as if he really means he's disgusted with me.

He's totally giving off small dick energy, which is something I never thought I'd say about Anders. He sure takes everything personally when it comes to Amore, especially when he doesn't even own the fucking thing.

What a dick.

I take the cup and take a sip.

It's better than that cold brew shit I had when I first came, due to the chocolaty undertones. But damn, it still has the horribly bitter aftertaste of coffee.

"And?" he asks, impatiently.

"It's fine, but you'd have been better off just handing me a piece of chocolate."

"You've got no palate. This is the perfect balance of

chocolate, coconut, and coffee. How can you not appreciate it?"

I roll my eyes and don't even bother responding. Not when it won't do any good. He mumbles something under his breath before staring at the ceiling, as if praying to the coffee gods to smite me on the spot.

He turns away and snaps, "Get back to work."

I dump the coffee down the sink before focusing on my job. We're continuously slammed. It's no wonder this place desperately needs an extra pair of hands. I don't understand why it's so understaffed, but I hope the new place isn't going to use the same staffing model as here.

I don't have time to sit the entire day, and I don't take another break. Anders has a smug look on his face every time he offers for me to take one, but I refuse. He doesn't take one and eats his lunch between completing orders. It's almost like he's daring me to take a break so he can prove he's better than me. That he can last longer without one.

It doesn't matter that I'm dead tired after my late night, or that my feet ache. I don't give in. When six rolls around, and he finally flips the sign, I breathe out a sigh of relief that it's over.

When all the closing tasks are complete, he approaches me with his phone in hand. "What's your phone number? I'll text you your schedule for next week. For this week, you'll be here every day for training."

"Will you also be training me to make the drinks?"

He gives me his best resting asshole face. "Depends on if you're able to meet my standards."

"And let me guess, they're high?"

"Through the roof."

I deadpan. "Looking forward to that."

He inputs my digits into his phone and calls me so I can save his number. I grab my jacket and leave without a goodbye. Not like he'd care, anyway.

When I enter my cold apartment, I set the heat to fifty-five. I can't afford it to be any higher, and it's freezing in here, but I won't die from the cold.

I skip dinner, too tired to boil water. My splurge on wine and a Christmas tree stand has my bank account balance dropping below one hundred dollars. I've got to conserve where I can and keep any money in case of an emergency.

At least until I get my first paycheck.

ZWOL pings with a reminder to input my results for the day. So far, it's been accurate, and today was full of ups and downs. But I stayed the course and wasn't fired. That's a win in my book.

I barely make it through my night routine before falling onto the couch and snuggling under the blankets.

I set my alarm for five and doze off to the scent of my Christmas tree, which unfortunately reminds me of the farm I got it from... and Anders.

CHAPTER 7

"*T*he universe is rolling out the red carpet for you, Ms. Social Butterfly Leo. The stars are shining so brightly today, you may need a pair of shades just to handle all the attention. Gather your squad, invite new acquaintances, and let your magnetic energy ignite an evening of unforgettable revelry. It's time for you to bask in the glow of newfound friendships and create memories that will forever shine in the constellation of your heart. Love always, ZWOL."

OH SHIT. I'm supposed to spend time with friends, and yet I have none. Well, maybe Ruby, but I don't want to burden her.

I shove my phone to the bottom of my purse and pretend like I didn't read it. If I can't see it, it doesn't exist, right?

Anders opens the door for me at five fifty. He asks me to sit at one of the tables while he makes us both a drink.

He slides me a cappuccino and places the same one in front of himself. "I have a feeling you don't even know what this tastes like. It's made with almond milk."

I bristle. "Of course I know what a cappuccino tastes like."

"Ours is infused with clove, so I highly doubt that. If you want to make drinks here, you need to know how they're supposed to taste."

I don't comment and lift the offending drink toward my lips. He scrutinizes my expression while I take a sip.

After my second sip, he leans back into the chair, expression smug. "You hate it."

"Hate is such a strong word..."

"I knew you hated coffee."

"To the surprise of no one."

He rolls his eyes.

"Why does it matter if this tastes like nothing more than bitter almond and clove milk?" I ask.

He stiffens. "Bitter... almond?" He closes his eyes and takes a deep breath before scowling at me. "If you want to work here, you need to understand that this isn't just a cappuccino."

"Fine, I'll bite. What is it then? Soup?"

He glares at me. "Coffee has the power to transport you to another time, another place. I could be drinking this in Venice at the Piazza San Marco while watching pigeons overrun the tourists. Or I could be in Bari with the sea by my side, the scent of salt and freshness in the air, and the sun kissing my face."

As he talks his face transforms from a glare to one of

longing, as if he's visited the places he mentioned and misses them.

"For a brief moment," he says, "I forget I'm here in Portland, where it's so cold it can snow. So yes, it matters. This is what we give our customers. An experience."

This is the most he's said to me since we've met. I've never heard someone speak so passionately about coffee before. Most people demand it to function. I've never heard someone talk about it related to memories. I can almost picture the scenes in Venice and Bari. A longing for places I've never been fills me.

His gaze doesn't waver from mine, and it's uncomfortable to be under his scrutiny. So, I try to make light of the situation. "That's a lot of expectation to put on a cup of coffee."

He doesn't react to my quip. "Why do you think people have drunk it for hundreds of years?"

"Because of the caffeine and the fact that our brains become addicted to it."

He snorts. "No, because it's an affordable, simple pleasure."

"Tomato, tom-ah-to."

The corner of his lip twitches, as if he has the impulse to smile, but of course he wouldn't smile around me. He's allergic to smiling in general.

But I get it, his passion for something so simple and yet so complex. He views coffee as an escape, like how I view baking. I remember my Aunt Addie the most clearly when I bake her famous brownies. I'm transported back into her kitchen, eight years old and covered in flour. She taught me, without a hint of annoyance, no matter how much mess I made. Every time I make pie dough, I'm thrown back to when we'd talk about what was going on in our lives while we rolled it out.

Every single one of my favorite childhood memories revolve around baking with Addie. I was lucky she lived across the street from us, a place I could go to whenever I wanted. I used it as an escape more times than I can count when my parents would argue.

The grief over losing her is still there, nestled under my rib cage. Even after almost a year, the grief has only just started to become cushioned with new memories.

Anders clears his throat and I snap my gaze back to him. "You don't have to finish it but, memorize the flavor, the feel on your tongue and in your mouth. If you ever become competent enough to make the drinks, you'll need to know this."

I nod, and he begins his morning tasks. I take two more sips before dumping the rest of the drink down the sink. Anders frowns at my actions and doesn't acknowledge my presence for the rest of the preparation time.

Five minutes before opening, Ruby walks into the shop wearing a green flannel shirt. Actually it's a reworked version of the shirt, cut and resewn into an edgy dress with pins and holes in strategic locations across her shoulders and abdomen.

It's badass. Just like her.

She points to Anders. "I need a double espresso. Stat."

He smiles, an honest to goodness smile with a dimple forming in his right cheek. Oh fuck, I didn't think it was possible for him to have any expression but resting asshole face due to his smiling allergy. Boy, was I wrong. And apparently, all it takes to get that kind of reaction out of him is Ruby ordering him around.

A tightness twists my stomach, but I refuse to look deeper into it. It's not like I'm jealous.

Nope.

He's hot, but stars, at what cost? His personality is toxic and there's no need to go there.

Ruby gives me an easy smile, unaware of my inner turmoil. "How's it going?"

"Fine. Thanks again for getting me the job."

Ruby glances at Anders for a second and says, "No problem. Glad to have you here."

I need to fulfill my horoscope for the day, and Ruby's my best shot.

"You want to go out tonight?" I blurt out, even if my bank account weeps at the offer.

"Sure. What did you have in mind?" I'm impressed she doesn't hesitate or have to think twice about it.

"Well, I've only been in Portland less than a week, so I've got no idea."

"I've got the perfect place in mind." Ruby focuses on Anders. "You in?"

Well damn, I did not intend for the invite to include him, but I can't uninvite him. That'd be ridiculous.

He grumbles, "Fine."

He sounds as excited to come as I am for him to join. Ruby laughs and gives him a side hug. "Oh, come on. It'll be fun."

"It'll be fun if we go to Theo's. At least we'll get great drinks there."

Ruby pushes out of the hug and snaps at him. "Why would you do that to me?"

Anders grins. "Because you know I'm right."

Ruby storms for an apron. When she turns back around, Anders already has her drink ready, as well as a spoon piled high with whipped cream. A cherry sits on the top of the cream. Ruby smiles and softens at the sight. Her anger disappears as fast as it came.

They chat quietly until opening, lost in their own world. A world I don't exist in.

I ring up the order for our first customer. He's a businessman, who I'd guess is an Aries based on his sharp suit. Plus the fact he was first in line, and the general aura surrounding him that says, "back off and get out of my way." Total seventy-seven vibes right there.

I go through the motions of ringing him up, but I'm still stuck on their interaction and how Anders knew exactly how to calm Ruby down. That only comes from knowing someone on a deep level.

The rest of the morning passes with Anders ignoring me completely, which isn't much different than yesterday. Ruby makes it fun and chats with me between customers.

When lunch rolls around, I feel faint. Maybe it wasn't a good idea to try to save money by skipping breakfast. Anders offers for me to take my lunch break first, and I don't question it.

As I hang my apron, he passes me a white paper bag. "It's gluten free."

I stare at the bag like it's full of poison. No one, not even my family, has ever bought me takeout food. They always leave me to fend for myself, with the excuse that celiac is too complicated to understand. Eric, my ex, didn't believe it was a real disease and would constantly contaminate butter and cream cheese containers with a gluten-filled knife. My mind can't wrap itself around the concept of Anders buying something for me.

I peek inside the bag and there's a pressed panini, as well as a huge peanut butter cookie with chocolate chips. My stomach growls at the sight. I swallow down my building saliva to form a question. "Did you check—"

"No cross contamination, no gluten in any of the ingredients, and they made the panini on a cleaned press."

Emotion chokes my throat. "Thank you."

He shrugs like it's not that big of a deal. "Lunch is part of your employment. You've got thirty minutes."

The break room is small, with a round table and four chairs surrounding it and no room for anything else. On the walls are a few pictures of the coffee making process from bean to cup. I rip the bag open and devour the chicken, mozzarella, and pesto panini like it's my first real meal in days, possibly weeks. Because it is.

Rice cakes and plain pasta can't compare to the amazingness that is real food.

I break a piece off the soft cookie and get lost in how the peanut butter and chocolate meld together. It's the perfect balance of sweet and savory.

The itch to bake, to try to recreate the recipe for the cookie, courses through me. But it doesn't take long for reality to hit. My oven doesn't work, and if it did, who'd eat the cookies?

Eric thought sugar was the enemy and refused to eat any of the desserts I made. He didn't like when I wore my hair down, so I wore it in a ponytail. He didn't like the color white on me, so I stopped wearing it. It's taken me far too long to realize I changed a lot for a man who didn't change anything for me.

I thought it was compromise, and that's how relationships were supposed to be. But I was the one who kept giving for an entire year, and he took and took and took until there was nothing left to give.

When I return to the front, Ruby brushes a hand across Anders's bicep. He smiles and says something that makes her laugh.

When Ruby notices me, she says, "I'm going to take my break now."

Anders doesn't react when I get situated at the register. He remains silent throughout the rest of the afternoon.

And so do I.

It's not until we've finished cleaning up the shop after closing that he says to me, "You need to go home for anything before we go out?"

"Nope, but I'll just pop in the restroom first."

I quickly lock myself in the restroom and fluff out my wavy hair. I pinch my cheeks to add some color to my pale skin and hope for the best.

When I exit the bathroom, Anders and Ruby are deep in conversation. Their backs are toward me.

"What do you think?" Ruby asks.

"Why did you force me to hire her? She's... unimpressive."

"Your wrong, she's good for Amore and good for the new—"

"Don't start with that," Anders says. "You've only known her for five seconds, you can't make a judgement yet."

"You need help. The new shop is behind schedule."

"No, what I need is to not be dealing with Zoey, who is nothing but messy. Just like Courtney. I never should've hired her."

My throat closes at his statement. It's like a slap in the face to know he's regretting hiring me, and a second slap on the same side to know that Ruby forced his hand.

"I think she might be going through a hard time..." Ruby says softly.

Anders snorts. "Who cares?"

Before Ruby can say anything more, I clear my throat to get their attention. I don't want to hear whether she agrees or not, don't want to have to decide if the one friend I thought I had here is really my friend.

Ruby spins to face me and has the decency to look ashamed on Anders's behalf. Anders places his hands inside his jacket pockets, looking far too casual, like he wouldn't mind saying everything he just said to Ruby to my face.

I ball my fists, digging my nails into my palms. The pain distracts me enough to say the words with more confidence than I feel. "I prefer the word chaotic instead of messy."

Anders shrugs his shoulders, as if he doesn't care one way or another. "Noted. Chaotic it is."

I'd be impressed at his nonchalance if I wasn't the one on the receiving end of it. "Now that we've cleared that up, I just remembered I forgot to say yes when

Netflix asked if I'm still watching. Catch you another time."

I take measured steps out the front door and down the street. Boss or not, life's too short to fake wanting to be around Anders. Damn my horoscope and its ridiculous idea to have a social outing.

"Zoey, wait," Ruby calls out.

I stop and wait for her to come to my side.

"I'm sorry about that. What you heard was out of context."

"Was it?" I ask. "Because it sounded to me like you had to force Anders to hire me."

She winces. "Anders declined every application we received at Amore for months. So yeah, I forced his hand. He needed to get his head out of his ass. Are you okay?"

"Sure. I'll catch you tomorrow."

I continue walking, cursing ZWOL and its stupid idea the entire way home.

CHAPTER 8

"*A*lright, Leo, listen up! It seems the cosmos is whispering in your ear, urging you to dust off that crown and consider accepting apologies. Yes, even mighty lions like you can stumble, but hey, it takes a real lion-hearted soul to forgive and give a potential friend another shot. Embrace forgiveness and watch as the universe serves up a double dose of fun, perhaps in the form of a night out or a romantic escapade. Love always, ZWOL."

ANDERS ISN'T at Amore the next day, but Ruby is.

According to ZWOL, I'm going to need to forgive her and give her a second chance. That, I can do. She didn't actually say anything hurtful herself.

Ruby pulls me aside the moment I enter. "How are you holding up?

"I'm fine. Nothing like the words of an asshole to put an end to the night." Ruby is somehow able to overlook his flaws, or maybe he's just nice to her and she doesn't see that side of him often enough to count it as a red flag.

She nods. "Last night he was definitely an asshole."

"Did you still go out?"

"No, I left right after laying into him. You're my friend, too, and his behavior wasn't acceptable."

"Thanks for the support."

"Of course, we've got to stick together. Do you want to have a redo tonight?"

ZWOL mentioned having fun tonight. "Fine, but just us."

She mimics crossing her heart with her finger and says, "Promise. Is he training you at all?"

"Not to make drinks."

She snorts. "That sounds like him."

"Would you?" I wave a hand at the machines, and she grins.

"Obvi. Let's start with a cappuccino. It's one of the main orders we get."

"Sure."

She walks me through the steps and tries the drink I make before teaching me how to adjust my technique. "Anders wants the person drinking it to feel like they're in Italy when they take their first sip."

"Yeah, he already gave me that spiel. He's super dedicated for someone who just works here."

She gives me a funny look. "He's the owner."

Oh shit. Anders owns this place?

"I see." All the air leaves my lungs on a wheeze. Oh my stars, please do not tell me I've been a complete bitch to the owner. Why didn't my horoscope clue me in on this?

I'm totally going to get fired.

Fuck, fuck, fuckity, fuck.

I need to get wasted tonight; it might just be one of my last nights in the city if I can't find a new job fast.

"Are you okay?" asks Ruby.

"Oh yeah, just freaking out that the boss is about to fire me."

She laughs. "He won't fire you, not without talking to me first."

"Oh? And why's that?" How does she have so much sway over Anders?

"Because he's so far behind schedule, the opening of the new place might be delayed. He won't accept my help, or anyone else's, and that's where you come in. I'm going to force him to work with you."

I fidget with my apron, needing to do something with my hands besides flap them about in my panic. "There are so many things wrong with this plan…"

"Oh, I know but I'm desperate. And so is he. He's my best friend and I refuse to stand by and watch him fail because he's too stubborn."

She's a good friend and clearly cares for him and his businesses. I can't fault her and her actions. At least she's on my side, so maybe she can buy me some time before Anders fires me for real.

"How about you make the next cappuccino ordered?" she asks.

I cling to the subject change. "Sure."

When the day ends, we both run home to change and meet back at Amore. I'm sporting a white blouse with a deep V and sparkly silver sleeves. Black skinny jeans and

71

my black motorcycle boots complete the look. Darker eye makeup, more blush, and I'm good to go.

Ruby does a wolf whistle when she sees me. "Love the outfit. What kind of vibe you're looking for tonight?"

"The kind where we drink until we're blackout drunk and dance until our feet fall off." Hardcore partying sounds like the perfect antidote to all of my life's problems.

She laughs. "You forgot to add the most important part of that list: to fuck until we pass out."

"My current luck with men involves more of a solo Netflix and zero chill kind of night. But you do you."

"We'll talk about that little tidbit once I get a few drinks in you." She throws her arm around my shoulder and guides us down the street.

A friendship, or at least a possibility of one, sparks between us. I've been without a real friend for so long, I forgot what it felt like.

Ruby brings us to a bar best known for its tapas, at least according to her. The feel and appearance of the bar is like a cellar. Concrete covers the space with bottles filling every wall from ground to ceiling. The only other colors in the room come from the chairs. Every single one is a different shade, encompassing the rainbow and everything in between. The bar also has splatters of paint on it, representing the color of every chair.

It's funky and cool, and a great place to have a girls' night.

I settle into a lime green chair, and Ruby picks a neon pink one. Most of the tapas have gluten, something Ruby is apologetic about, but I don't have the funds to pay for dinner and drinks. Besides, anytime I eat out is a risk of getting glutened, especially in a new city. It's not worth it.

Instead, I make an executive adult decision to drink cocktails as my dinner, with a side of smoked almonds. I'd rather use my limited funds on alcohol than food. At least I'll get a buzz out of my choices tonight.

Ruby doesn't comment on my decision and raises two fingers to one of the bartenders. Within minutes, he brings over two margaritas. That's some service right there.

Ruby dances in her seat to the Spanish music pumping through the speakers. "When it gets later in the night, they'll move the tables to create a dance floor."

"Don't tell me you're one of those people who likes to dance."

She snorts. "And you're not? What happened to the "let's dance until our feet fall off" part of our night?"

"It was more of a euphemism. I'm going to need more alcohol before I even think about it." I'm that girl who was born with no rhythm. The type someone would make a meme out of if they caught my moves on video.

"Well, good thing I excel at getting free drinks."

"Oh?"

She smirks. "It's a special talent of mine."

"Teach me, oh wise one." Help make this night easier on my bank account.

She laughs. "It's easy. I know the bartender, and we have an agreement. Free coffee for free cocktails."

I look between her and the guy behind the bar she points out. The same one who gave her two margaritas when she held up her fingers. He's lean with shaggy blond hair. There's a constant smile on his lips while he stirs a drink with flare. Two customers break out into an argument in front of him, and with a few words, both customers visibly relax. He's totally a Libra and the number one hundred and twenty-one. Balanced on both sides, and if you add the end digits together, they equal the middle number.

I ask, "And does this arrangement consist of free dick, too?"

"Obviously."

I chuckle. "But what about Anders? Have you ever..."

"Anders is like a brother. I would never." She shudders.

It's an interesting reaction, and I can't help but push for more information. "I was definitely picking up on something between you two the other day. Maybe he likes you as more than a friend?"

"Aren't you mighty interested in who Anders likes." She sips her drink.

"Not at all, just curious about your dynamic since we all work together."

She grins. "I've known him and his family since I was five. They've all been there for me when I was at my lowest, and Anders is my best friend."

"Uh-huh."

Her grin widens. "I know Anders isn't interested in me because he keeps trying to push me on his brother, Theo."

Ruby got upset when Anders mentioned going to Theo's when we were going to grab drinks all together. Before he called me messy.

"Wait. Theo is Anders's brother?"

"Yeah, and my mortal enemy."

"What did he do to you?"

She looks me dead in the eye and says, "Exist."

I snicker and she says, "Enough about me. Tell me more about you. Why Portland? When was your last relationship? You know, all the fun stuff."

"You mean let's rehash all the horrible things that've happened to me recently?" I chug more of my drink.

She winces. "That bad?"

"Let's start easy. Why Portland? My aunt used to live here. She loved it so much, I thought I could love it too. As for my ex? We broke up three weeks ago and he's part of the reason I moved here. Let's just say I hope he always gets overcooked food at restaurants, catches all the red lights while driving, and constantly shits his pants."

"Brutal, and I love it." She raises her glass. "Cheers to that."

We polish off the rest of our drinks.

"What about you?" I ask.

"Easy, I grew up here and my last relationship was..." She pauses and counts on her fingers. "Eight years ago."

She mouths the word eight to herself again and her entire attitude changes from her usual badass self to something smaller, sadder.

"Eight years is a long time..." I prompt.

She doesn't look at me and instead picks at the colorful, paperboard drink coaster. "Yeah... my ex did a number on me and afterwards I realized I don't believe in love. Or relationships." She flicks her gaze to mine. "Just casual sex."

There's a lot to unpack in those sentences, but she's clearly uncomfortable and I don't want to push for more.

She shakes herself, as if shaking off memories best forgotten, and asks, "Have you slept with anyone since your ex?"

"No, it hasn't been that long since we broke up."

"Pff, it doesn't matter. Jump back in the saddle."

"Did it help, with you?"

"Definitely, that's why I know you won't regret it."

"I don't know… let me check my horoscope." It did allude to getting lucky today.

"Did you just say horoscope?"

I put my index finger up to silence any comment she may have and pull up my ZWOL app to double check it.

Now that she's pointed it out, it doesn't sit right that Eric was the last person I slept with. Removing every last crumb of him from my life, purging myself of him, would be one of the biggest steps I could take in transforming myself. Lilly would totally be on board with this idea if she were here.

Ruby turns my phone so she can read it and beams at me. "See, even your horoscope says it's the best idea ever. And sidenote, I love how dedicated you are to this. It's cute."

"Oh, fuck off."

She cackles. "Let's find someone here for you to hook up with."

"Or not." I give her a pointed look. "I don't need an audience when I fail at picking someone up."

"This isn't something you can fail at. You're hot and fun. That's enough to attract any single guy here for sex. Let me get some more drinks while you think about it."

She skips to the bar and flirts with her bartender.

Knowing my luck, I'd probably end up with an STI or have the worst sex in the world. On the other hand, it'd be nice to have an orgasm from a person instead of my vibrator.

I'm not fully convinced, but my horoscope clearly says I'm due for a tumble in the sheets. I promised myself I'd follow it and would stop second guessing everything.

Okay, I can do this. I can pick a guy up, right? It's just sex, it's not like I'm asking him to marry me.

Ruby appears with more drinks, and we drink them as if they're water. I'm tipsy enough to dance, and Ruby, the little mind reader that she is, pulls me toward the small dance floor.

The designated area is full of people by the time we make it there. Ruby faces me and begins to move her body to the beat. "You can always have a quickie in the bathroom if you find someone. Wham, bam, thank you ma'am, style."

I scrunch my nose. "Bathrooms are so dirty."

Ruby gets knocked closer to me. "You don't get undressed fully. Do it up against the wall and pull down any clothes in the way. Or move them to the side. Simple."

"I should've worn a dress."

She grins. "You'll manage."

I laugh. Ruby points behind me and wiggles her eyebrows up and down. I turn my head as a man grinds into my ass. Brown hair, kind of cute, and looks like he has enough muscles to hold me up against a wall.

That's good enough for me.

It'll be like ripping a Band-Aid off. I just need to get it over with. I don't miss Eric. After seeing his true colors, it's been easy to get over him as a boyfriend. But I'm not over the hurt he caused or how much he ruined my life. Hooking up with someone would be a great fuck you to the year I wasted on him.

Yeah, I've got this.

I give my possible hookup a wide smile and he places his hands on my hips and pulls me into his body. I lean back into him and enjoy his hands on me. When I close my eyes, I imagine a certain Lumberjack Asshole touching me.

I snap my eyes open.

No. No. No. That's not going to work.

Anders doesn't get to star in my fantasies. Even if he and Ruby aren't a thing, even if he's the most attractive man I've ever seen, it's not going to happen.

I turn in the guy's arms and face him. I lean into his ear, grab his junk, and say, "Bathroom?"

Subtle? Definitely not.

Effective? Surprisingly, yes.

His gaze heats and I barely have time to wave to Ruby, who gives me two thumbs up, before we're in the dark hallway that leads to the bathroom.

With both doors locked, he decides to pass the time by trailing his hands down my ass and squeezing. He kisses the side of my neck, but it does nothing for me.

My traitorous brain decides to bring up Lumberjack Asshole... again. Ugh, fine. It's a quickie and I need to be ready. I can work with this fantasy.

It's fine, totally fine.

The second I close my eyes, it's Anders's hands on my ass, his lips on my neck, his body pressing into mine. And damn, I'm ashamed to admit how wet I get in under two seconds flat thinking of my nemesis.

The door to the right opens. A man ducks his head and speed walks past us and back into the bar. We enter the now vacated bathroom, and oh my…

It smells.

Not like the normal kind of public bathroom smell of urine and disinfectant and something musty underneath.

No. It smells like someone just had a massive case of diarrhea. The kind where you need snacks in the middle because you're on the toilet for so long. Where you weigh five pounds lighter because of the mass exodus.

My hookup doesn't seem to care as he pushes me against the door and locks it. He leans in for a kiss, but I'm about to gag, so I guide his mouth back down to my neck.

Oh my stars, am I being cock blocked by someone else's bowel movement? My defining moment to reclaim myself after Eric is being ruined by shit, literally.

I stare at the ceiling and curse all the zodiac signs and stars I can name.

What kind of bathrooms are Ruby used to having sex in? If this is what she puts up with, and she finds it sufficient, I might need to revoke her friend card.

My hookup grabs my ass and crushes me against the wall. I wrap my legs around his waist, and he grinds into me. He captures my lips and licks my teeth.

Licks. My. Teeth.

Like a motherfucking toothbrush.

I can't hide the shudder that goes through my body,

couldn't have even if I'd tried. Though I don't try that hard.

Ew. Just ew.

I push against his chest. "I can't... the smell."

He nuzzles my ear. "Who cares? You won't think of anything except me when I'm inside you."

He moves back to my poor neck and sucks, as if he'll find buried treasure under my skin. Getting neck hoovered isn't on my list of things to do today.

Ugh, worst decision ever.

I unlock my legs from his waist and push him back. "Yeah, it's gonna be a no from me."

The smell is all I can think about. How can it be worse now than when we first entered? I should be desensitized to it by now. Right? I'm starting to worry it's imbedded in my skin, my hair. That thought alone makes me gag.

How the fuck does it not bother him?

I gag again and he jumps back so far away from me, he hits the sink.

Hand over my mouth, I turn the lock and whip open the door.

Blissful, fresh air fills my nose. I gulp it down as if I've been holding my breath for the last ten minutes and am reacquainting myself with the act of breathing.

The guy brushes past me in a huff of annoyance. "You're not worth it."

He storms off, and a giggle escapes my lips. I slap a hand over my mouth. It's not funny, but if I don't laugh, I just might cry. Cry at the unfairness of trying to have casual sex and it blowing up in my face.

My decisions always lead to disaster. When will I learn?

I sag against the wall and laugh until I actually do start crying. I hope anyone passing by thinks I'm one of those people who cry while they laugh. Because I'm so close to a breakdown, it's not even funny.

"Are you okay?" Ruby asks. "I saw the guy come out of here, but you weren't behind him."

I turn to her and laugh harder, my stomach cramping in response. "I'm fine."

"Was it good?"

"I couldn't go through with it. The guy who used the toilet before us had a massive dump." I wave a hand toward the door. "Smell for yourself."

She pushes open the door a few inches before slamming it shut with her hand covering her nose. "Holy shit."

"Literally."

Ruby joins my laugh attack. Well, technically I'm crying and she's laughing, but same difference.

She takes a few deep breaths to compose herself before saying, "Come, let's get out of this shit hole."

I chuckle. "Maybe I should leave a shitty review of this place."

"Or maybe we can cause some shit and complain?"

I tap my chin. "Let's not be shit stirrers. You don't want to lose your bartender hookup."

She busts out in another fit of laughter as she guides us back to the dance floor. "Hiring you was the best decision I've ever made."

I grin. "Obviously."

CHAPTER 9

"*T*he universe is tossing you a little challenge to flex those problem-solving muscles of yours, Leo. But don't sweat it, because you're about to show that obstacle who's boss with your quick thinking and resourcefulness. Just remember, don't be afraid to shake things up and take a few risks. Go forth and slay that challenge like the boss you are. Love always, ZWOL."

THANKS A LOT, horoscope. Quick thinking while still drunk? ZWOL needs a talking to.

It takes far too long to realize I'm on a bed and not my couch. I sit up and stare at the room I'm in. There's a picture on the nightstand of a group of random guys and a bottle of cologne.

Wait, I didn't go home with someone last night, did I?

I'm alone in the room, and fully dressed. My bag and phone are conveniently lying next to the picture, and I tip toe out of the room, hoping for more information. A man snores on the couch, so loud the walls vibrate with it.

Where am I? And who is *he*?

Is this the obstacle I have to overcome? Make a daring escape from a stranger's home and hope I don't die?

What did I get myself into last night? It gets hazy after Ruby insisted on tequila shots followed by kamikazes, and then more tequila.

I creep closer to the front door, trying not to breathe in case I wake the stranger on the couch. Just as my hand touches the handle, a door opens across the living room.

A sleep rumbled Ruby emerges, rubbing her eyes. "Hey, where are you going?"

"Well, I was about to sneak out of an unknown apartment before I got murdered."

She grins. "Just get ready here. You can use my shower and makeup and we can head into work together."

"Who's that?" I point to the man on the couch.

Ruby walks to said man and shakes his shoulder. "Ian, you can go back to your room now."

Ian grumbles at Ruby for waking him before trudging to the room I just came from.

I cover my eyes with my hand. "Please tell me I didn't just steal your roommates' bed."

"You didn't steal his bed." Her deadpan statement tells me everything.

I peek through my fingers to find Ruby smirking at me. "What? How?"

"Doesn't matter." She laughs. "The shower is through my room, and I'll make us some coffee."

"I don't drink coffee."

"You do today."

I scoff, but she interrupts. "Anders will lose his shit if we both show up still... drunk or hungover?" She looks at me to complete the sentence.

"Drunk."

"Same here." She grins. "Point being, you have the task of looking normal."

"Why do I have to be the sober looking one?"

"Because you're new."

"Thanks a lot," I say sarcastically.

"Hey, I don't make the rules."

"You're right. Good old killjoy Anders does."

She cackles. "I love that nickname. Don't worry, I'll make sure to give credit to the person who invented it when I use it today."

I give her the middle finger as I go to her room to shower and get ready for the day. I get dressed in my smoke-soaked outfit from last night. At least my pants are black and hide a sticky spot on my right thigh. Spilled alcohol perhaps? Wouldn't surprise me. I douse myself and my pants in a spray deodorant I find on the counter. There are spare flannels in the break room so at least that won't smell of smoke.

Anders arrives ten minutes after us and gives us a once over, like he can sense we're both still drunk.

Ruby ignores his look and says, "Good morning. You better have brought lunch today because I missed breakfast."

Anders frowns. "How many times do I have to tell you—"

"—how important breakfast is." Ruby pitches her voice to sound just like Anders.

I laugh at her impersonation, and Anders glares at me. I mime zipping my lips and it just makes him glare more. Yup, it's official. I'm still drunk.

Ruby snickers and places a hand on his arm. "But in all seriousness, lunch? Yes? Or better yet, breakfast *and* lunch."

He sighs. "Fine."

"Fine to both or only lunch?" I ask.

Ruby giggles and Anders glares at me some more before gesturing to the table where he usually forces me to drink coffee.

"Let's go over another drink and what it's supposed to taste like," he says.

Oh no, I can't. My stomach rebels just at the thought of drinking anything right now. This is supposed to be part of my training, to try the drinks even though I'll never be trusted to make. But damn, I'd rather eat a spoonful of cinnamon.

Thanks to Ruby, I now know he's the boss. I'm on borrowed time here. It won't work out long term with the animosity between us. I need the paycheck, so I try to think of a professional response.

Ruby, bless her, saves me. "Let's wait until we eat first, yes?"

Anders's gaze roams over my body, as if he can find the cause of my ailment. "Are you okay?"

I wave him off. "Just peachy."

His eyes narrow and he turns his glare to Ruby. "What's wrong with her? She's... peppy."

"Anders, meet Drunk Zoey. Drunk Zoey meet Killjoy Anders."

"Drunk?" he sputters.

I groan. "Why did you have to out me like that?"

Ruby ignores me and pats Anders on the shoulder. "Don't worry, we can walk in a straight line."

"You too?" He rubs the bridge of his nose.

Ruby bats her eyelashes. "No way, I would *never*."

Anders and I snort at the same time. He startles, and our gazes meet for a split second of comradery. But then he spins away from me, as if burned. I roll my eyes at his back.

Huh, maybe I should come to work drunk more often. It's like I'm wearing a shield because I'm not at all bothered by his behavior.

Have I just unlocked a new adulting level?

Maaayyybeee?

But then my rational side kicks in and yells at me for being unprofessional and showing up still drunk, and my good mood disintegrates.

Ugh, killjoy brain in cahoots with killjoy Anders.

"Any mistakes, and I'll send you home," he threatens us both.

"Sir, yes, sir," I say with a salute and all.

His gaze heats when I say sir, and just like that, I'm thrown back into my fantasy from last night of Anders touching me. Well, before it all went to shit. Literally.

Ruby throws her arm around my shoulders. "You're my favorite person. Ever."

"Hey," Anders says, put out.

"You, too. You're tied," she amends.

"Get to work," he demands.

Ruby turns on some music and we dance and laugh through our opening jobs. Anders doesn't scold us again, but he watches. Not Ruby, but me. Probably to avoid the liability if I hurt myself, but he doesn't look worried or angry. He looks... hungry.

Huh, maybe he skipped breakfast, too.

When the shop opens, Anders sends Ruby to buy some breakfast and lunch for us all.

Five minutes later, a man with blue eyes and blond slicked back hair comes to the counter. A well-fitted forest-green sweater and dark jeans cover his lean frame. He's attractive in a sophisticated way, but it's his eyes and the laugh lines at the corners that elevate him from handsome to hot. At least in my book. He gives off Capricorn vibes.

"Hi," he says.

"Why hello there." I smile, so glad I'm still drunk. It makes flirting with hot men easier. "What can I get for you?"

"One medium black pepper coffee and a truffle grilled cheese. For here."

"What's your name?"

"Nick."

I hit the buttons on the machine, but nothing happens. The screen's black, as well as the card reader.

Oh shit.

I turn to Anders. "Umm, Anders. There's an issue with the machine."

Anders comes over to press some buttons while I step to the side and focus back on Nick.

"Sorry about this. It'll just be another minute. Thank you for your patience."

"No problem," Nick says. "I haven't seen you here before. Are you new?"

"Yeah, I just started a couple of days ago."

He smiles and leans a little closer to the counter. "Would you like to—"

"Zoey, come here for a moment." Anders tugs on my arm and leads me a few steps away from the counter.

"What's going on?" I glare at him, annoyed that he interrupted whatever Nick was going to say.

"We've got a major problem. I can't get the machine working." He squeezes the back of his neck while he looks at the line out the door. "We're going to need to close down until someone can repair it."

Anders looks gutted by that admission. I should be happy I don't have to work, that I'll probably get to go home early. I might be able to sleep enough to bypass my pending hangover. But I'm not. Addie was in a constant state of stress about her bakery, and how a bad day or two could influence the entire month.

Sometimes she'd barely have enough money left over to pay herself a salary after paying her two employees. I never envied Addie for owning a bakery, and it's not that big of a stretch to assume Anders is under a similar pressure.

It's like Addie is on my shoulder, demanding I help him. To support someone in need. And ZWOL did mention I'll need my problem-solving abilities today.

I blow out a long breath. Okay, I can do this. I need a solution, and fast.

This type of situation is what I lived for when I was working, where it's all hands-on deck. I make a split-second decision, not worried about the implications. Anything is better than losing all the customers.

I ask Anders, "Do you have Venmo on your phone?"

Anders flicks his gaze at me for a moment before staring at the antsy customers. "Of course."

"Let's use that and your QR code for the customers to pay."

He frowns. "But—"

"We don't have time to second guess this. People are about to walk out of here. You're the owner. Get the money directly."

He stares at the disgruntled customers, who are already complaining about the hold up, before nodding. "Okay, here." He passes me his phone and the QR code.

I raise my voice to be heard over the chatter in the room. "Sorry about the delay, everyone. We've got a problem with the register and card reader. We'll take payment via Venmo or cash if you have it."

I step back to the counter and to Nick. "That'll be thirteen seventy-five."

It's easy to do the math, even if I'm tipsy. I memorized the prices the night before I started. I write the order down on a notepad next to the register and pass it to Anders while showing Nick the QR code to pay with.

Anders stares at me like I've grown three heads again. What did I do this time?

"That's impressive," Nick says, "to calculate the price in your head."

Mom and Lilly were never impressed. When I used to

calculate the total before the cashier finished ringing up their shopping. They acted like it was more of an annoyance. They thought it was weird, and that it wasn't a cute quirk. So I stopped saying it aloud, and kept it to myself around. Except Addie. She loved when I did it in her bakery. The only place I felt like I could be me.

I say to Nick, "It's easy when you don't have sales tax."

He laughs and steps to the side so I can take the next customer's order. Anders stares at me for a beat longer before grabbing the paper I wrote the order on.

The next twenty minutes becomes a blur of customers, math, and payments. My idea works flawlessly. It's comforting to know I've still got my problem-solving abilities. I thought I lost that along with everything else when my life blew up.

When Ruby returns with food, she quickly stashes everything in the backroom before joining us behind the counter.

"What's going on?" she asks Anders as she takes in the dead machine and me holding Anders's phone out to the customer.

He fills her in on the events of the past twenty minutes.

Ruby grabs the paper for the next drink order and begins to make it. "So, you're a human calculator now?"

I grin. "Apparently."

"How?"

"I've always had a knack for numbers," I say.

Anders says, "Either way it's impressive."

I glance at him out of the corner of my eye. He gave me a… compliment? I'm so shocked the next customer has to repeat their order twice before I'm able to process it. I'm too drunk to unpack that, so I pretend like it didn't happen.

When there's a moment of quiet, Anders makes a call to the repair company and Nick approaches the counter.

"How was everything?" I ask while restocking the food offerings.

"Good, but it'd be even better if I could take you out to dinner tonight."

My hands still. "Like a date?"

"Like a date," he confirms.

"She'd love to go with you," Ruby says, coming to my side.

I glare at Ruby. "She can speak for herself."

Ruby laughs and returns to the coffee machines.

Nick's smiles at our antics and I say, "I'd love to go out."

I write down my number on one of the slips of paper next to the register and pass it to him.

"I'll message you the details," he says.

"Stop trying to score a date with my staff and leave," Anders says, coming to my side and crossing his arms.

Nick glares at Anders before saying, "See you later."

Once he's gone, I turn on Anders. "What was that about?"

"Nothing."

"Uh-huh." I roll my eyes. "Any idea when they'll come and repair the machine?"

"Lunch time."

My phone beeps with an incoming message.

> Unknown: It's Nick. What time do you
> get off?

I'M giddy Nick wrote to me immediately and didn't delay it.

> Me: Seven. Meet me at Amore then?

> Nick: Sure, see you then

THE HAIR on my neck rises and I spin around, only to find Anders right behind me and clearly looking over my shoulder.

"What are you doing?" I snap.

"I should be asking you the same thing." Anders bristles. "You have a date? With a customer?"

"So?"

"That's not allowed."

I laugh. "Says who?"

"Says me."

"Let me guess, it's written in your employee handbook."

"If it'll deter you. I'll make one."

"You do that." I turn my back on him and continue to restock the sandwiches.

"You don't even know the guy." Anders hovers over me.

I glare at him and remain silent.

"He's too boring for you."

I snort. "As if you know anything about what I want or like in a man."

"Well then, enlighten me." Anders leans a hip against the counter. "What does Zoey like in a man?"

A customer walks through the door, and I breathe a sigh of relief. There's no way I'd ever tell Anders the answer. I'm sure he'd just find a way to use my words against me. But more troubling than that is I don't know the answer myself. Someone the complete opposite of Eric sounds like a good start, but other than that, I've got nothing.

As the day passes, and I get more sober, I begin to regret accepting a date with Nick. I swore off all men when I moved here, so what the hell am I doing going out on a date with one? A hookup here or there to clear the cobwebs is fine, but a date? Ruby's right, maybe just hooking up is the answer.

I need to stay focused on improving my life so that my family accepts me back into the fold. I should cancel. No, I need to cancel. But my horoscope did say to take risks today. Maybe it meant that I should take a chance on Nick?

I check the time on my phone. There's five minutes before he shows up. No way out of it now. I go through the motions of changing into the outfit I packed during my lunch break. Black dress pants, gray-silver sweater, and heels. Simple and elegant.

When I step out of the bathroom, Anders is there with

his arms crossed. Ruby whistles when she sees me. "You're smoking."

Anders takes his time perusing my outfit and I tense, preparing myself for his vitriol. "Where is he taking you?"

I'm caught off guard by the demand in his question. It almost sounds like he cares, but that doesn't make sense.

"Not sure."

"Don't you think that's irresponsible? To go somewhere with a stranger."

I rub some gloss on my lips and smack them together. "It'll be fine, Dad. Is my curfew still set for ten?"

Anders scowls at my words, and I laugh.

"I'm just trying to make sure you're okay," he says.

I roll my eyes. "Yeah, sure."

"I'm serious."

"And here I thought you'd be happy if I never stepped foot inside here again."

Anders jerks back as if I struck him. "That's not—"

"It's fine. I'll message Ruby the location." I grab my purse. "See you guys tomorrow."

I'm out the door before he can say something to annoy me and ruin my date. Nick is already outside by the door. "You look amazing."

"Thanks, you too." He's in the same outfit from earlier.

When we arrive at the Italian restaurant, I shoot off a quick text to Ruby. The maître d' whisks us off to a table by the windows. It's all white linen, red roses on the table, and candles lighting the inside. It's romantic and fancy.

Too fancy.

I can't afford this place if he decides to split the bill.

Oh stars, what do I do? If I tell him I can't afford it, he

may think I'm pressuring him to pay for me and that's embarrassing on so many levels. But I don't think I can swing a salad that costs thirty dollars. And that's the cheapest thing on the menu.

A fine trail of sweat slides down my lower back, and I wring the crisp napkin in my lap.

"May I start you off with some drinks?" the server asks.

"Do you like red wine?" Nick asks me.

"Yes, but—"

He speaks over me to the server, "We'll have a bottle of Emidio Pepe. 2008."

I chew on the inside of my cheek as the server disappears.

"You okay?" he asks.

"That sounds like an expensive bottle of wine," I hedge.

He lifts a shoulder. "I've developed a taste of the finer things in life the older I get."

"I work in a coffee shop…"

I really hope he's picking up what I'm throwing down, so I don't have to explain it to him. To verbalize the embarrassment of not being able to afford a salad, let alone an expensive sounding wine.

His eyes soften with understanding. "Tonight's on me."

"Thank you." I smooth out my crumpled napkin in my lap before asking, "So, you're a regular at Amore?"

"I live nearby."

I should've researched first date questions before coming, but I didn't have time between the time he asked me and the actual date. Is asking what his highlight of the month is too personal or job interviewy? Or should I find out his zodiac sign first and see if it even matches my sign? Do I stay boring and ask what he does for work? I really should've put more thought into this.

It's been so long since I went on a first date. With Eric, it was easy. I knew him from my time at Georgia Tech and we reconnected right after Addie died. At that time, grief consumed me. Showering was at the bottom of my concerns, let alone dating someone. I didn't care what kind of impression I made on him, and I barely remember our first few dates. Eric was patient and understanding through it all. When I eventually dug myself out of my grief, we'd already been together for months. It wasn't awkward by that time, and I didn't have to worry about going through this.

The server interrupts my internal freak out by pouring a small bit of wine in the glass for Nick to try. He sniffs and swirls it like an expert before giving his approval.

I raise my glass to his and he clinks it against mine.

"To new beginnings," he says.

I smile and drink. Notes of cherry, smoke, leather, and raspberry burst on my tongue. It's an interesting mixture and something I'd never order for myself.

Silence hovers over us, and he straightens the cutlery.

I can't take it anymore. It's making me anxious and awkward, which is never a good combination. "What do you do for work?"

"I'm a manager at an automotive company in the area."

"Do you have an engineering background?" I ask.

"I do. Mechanical. Most people don't ask that question."

"I'm also an engineer." I lift a shoulder.

His eyes widen. "Really? What type?"

His disbelief is annoying. I bet he's one of those managers who assign women in management positions to meet a quota.

"Also mechanical. Went to Georgia Tech."

"What in the world are you doing working at a coffee shop?"

"Trying something new." I leave it at that and change the subject. "You from the area?"

"Yeah, born and raised."

Nick is stable, smart, and has money, at least based on his job title and outfit. My parents would still hate him, though. They'd hate any man I'd chosen, especially after Eric.

Nick used to be my type, before I lost everything. But as I'm sitting here sipping expensive wine, I'm bored. I don't have any desire to know more about him. There are no flutters in my stomach.

The dinner passes by slowly. I keep up with the conversation, trying to force myself to be interested, but I'd rather be reading the user manual for Amore's espresso machine than be here.

Fuck.

When we leave, he stops on the sidewalk.

"I had an amazing time," he says.

"Me too."

He leans toward me, going in for a kiss. His cologne clogs my nose, it's so strong. I can practically taste it, and it's almost metallic. Holding my breath, our lips press against each other. He holds them there for a good thirty seconds before pulling away with a smile.

My heart beats steadily, refusing to react to the kiss or his nearness. Ugh.

"Come, I'll walk you home," he offers.

"That's okay, I've got it from here." There's no way I want him to see my building or try to see my empty apartment.

"You sure?"

"Yeah. Good night."

"Night."

I turn and walk back to my place. It wasn't a bad date. We have a lot in common, from our engineering background to our taste in music, but there's no chemistry between us.

I'm not sure if I should give him another chance. Maybe I should wait until my horoscope gives me an indication either way.

Wait, that's the best idea.

I'll let ZWOL rule my love life.

What could go wrong?

CHAPTER 10

"*L*eo, you're getting the green light to spill some tea today, but there's no need to be a Chatty Kathy with just anyone. Trust your gut and carefully choose who you share your juicy tidbit with. When done right, this could be your chance for some serious liberation. Spill away. Love always, ZWOL."

"How was your date?" Anders asks when I enter Amore.

"Fine."

"Fine doesn't sound good." He can't keep the smugness from his voice as we sit at the table that's become my training table before we open.

I arch my eyebrow. "Do you want to hear all the dirty details, then?"

The lie comes out before I can stop it. I don't want him to know the date wasn't the best. He'd dig into all my issues with men, and probably hit all my triggers too while he's at it.

He stiffens. "You *fucked* him?"

"Careful, it sounds like you might be about to imply I'm a whore."

He slides an espresso cup my way. "Seems like you saved me from saying it."

I roll my eyes so hard it hurts.

Typical. A man judging a woman and her sexual history. "Been a long time, hmm? Your blue balls getting to you and making you lash out? Or is this"—I wave a hand to encompass him—"just you on your man period? Low libido is normal during that time of the month, you know."

He chuckles. "Man period, huh? I like it."

I take a sip of the drink he placed in front of me to cover my surprise. He took the joke like a pro and didn't become defensive. And that's hotter than hot.

No. Nope. Not going to happen. I can't go there.

I swallow the hot liquid and immediately regret it. It's spicy and bitter and so not my thing.

"This is our jalapeno espresso." His grin is arrogant, as if he knows how much I hate the drink. He enjoys torturing me with coffee a bit too much.

"Do you hate your customers?" I choke on my words, mouth on fire.

"You clearly have no taste when it comes to coffee."

"Well, maybe I'll develop a taste when I start learning the machines."

"You'll learn when I feel like it." The corner of his lip twitches in what could almost be a partial smile.

"Of course. We must all bow down to the one and only Anders... wait, what's your last name?"

"Watson."

"Anders Watson," I whisper. "Good name."

He can't keep the amusement off his face. "My mom thinks so."

"I bet she does."

"Hey, I—" Ruby stops whatever she's about to say when she spots us. "What's going on here?"

"Training," Anders says. "Obviously."

"Looks more like two friends chatting away."

We both glare at her in response.

"Okay then." She holds up her hands. "I'll just be right over here doing my thing." She points to the counter and ducks behind it.

"I should get to work." I stand.

"Yes, of course."

The rest of the morning passes with Anders pretending I don't exist, and me returning the favor.

When Anders is on his lunch break, a man breezes through the door. He looks too much like Anders for it to be a coincidence. His darker hair is styled in that messy, just-fucked look, but they have the same jaw.

Damn, he's hot.

Ruby stiffens next to me, and I shoot her a look, but she just shakes her head.

"Hey, you must be Zoey," he says.

"Uh huh, and you are?"

"Theo, Anders's older brother." He extends his hand for me to shake, but when I grasp it, he kisses my knuckles. He does it so smoothly, as if he's practiced it a thousand times.

"Do that move on all the ladies, huh?" I laugh and pull my hand out of his.

He winks. "It's never failed."

"Until now."

"I wasn't even trying."

I laugh again, delighted he isn't a raging asshole like his brother. "Don't believe anything Anders told you about me. He thinks I regularly indulge in heinous activities like refusing to drink tea with milk."

Theo grins. "Well, I had to meet the woman who finally made my unflappable brother... flappable."

"Theo," Ruby warns.

He sears her with a look that would melt my panties if it were pointed my way. Ruby throws him the middle finger in return and calls over her shoulder, "I'll be in the break room if you need me."

Theo doesn't take his gaze off Ruby's retreating figure. Even when she's gone, he still stares at the hallway she went down.

"What's the deal between you two?" I ask.

"Nothing."

I snort. "Uh-huh. Why are you really here?"

He leans against the counter. "I wanted to invite you to my bar."

"I've heard about this bar."

"Of course you have. It's the best one in town." He slides me a business card with a skull and the words 'Grave Digger' embossed above it.

"And why do you want me to come?"

"To piss off my brother, of course."

"That is a valid reason, though I'm not sure why he would care."

Theo chuckles. "Trust me, he'll care."

"Well, if I do come, I'm bringing Ruby." I'm not sure why it feels necessary to warn him of this, but I do.

"Of course." He stuffs his hands in his peacoat pockets. "She won't be easy to convince, so let me give you something you can use to help sway her. Drinks are on the house if you both come."

With that, he leaves just as fast as he came. I slide his card into my back pocket and wait for Ruby to return.

Once she does, she takes one look at my face and says, "No."

"You don't even know what I was going to say."

She unloads the dishwasher and wrinkles her nose like she's smelling something bad. "I'm not going to Grave Digger."

"Even for free drinks?"

"Theo offered free drinks?" She freezes with a mug in hand. "He must really want you there."

"Funny, he only offered that to convince you to come."

She frowns.

I push my advantage, too curious about Theo and why he wants to rile Anders up to pass on this. "Come on, worst case we can get drunk and leave. It'll be fun. Also, you owe me."

"And how do I owe you?"

"Zoey." I pitch my voice to sound like her. "It'll be easy to find a hookup. Just do it in the bathroom."

"Ugh, fine." She coughs out a laugh. "You're lucky I like you."

"And when we're there, you can tell me all about your history with Theo."

She glares at me. "Don't push your luck."

I laugh and get back to work. Tonight can't come soon enough.

* * *

WHEN THEO SAID he owned the hottest bar in town, I thought he was exaggerating, but the line out the door proves me wrong on so many levels. Ruby marches up to the bouncer, and he lets us in immediately.

Theo's waiting for us as soon as we enter. "Welcome, ladies. Thank you for coming."

Ruby snorts, but I'm struck silent when I get a view of the place. It's a Halloween-themed bar, which is so cool, especially with Christmas only a few weeks away. It feels like I'm being naughty, going to an anti-Christmas themed place.

It's all dim, red lighting with smoke billowing from skulls on every table, and cobwebs strategically placed throughout. It's a total vibe. But the best part is the tables. They're shaped like tombstones and they're perfection.

"Whoa," I say.

Theo shoots me a grin and leads us to a table in the middle of the room. "Here you go. The staff knows you're my VIP guests, so everything you want is on the house."

"I plan to take advantage of that," Ruby states calmly.

Theo licks his lips. "Wouldn't expect anything else." He glances at me quickly. "Enjoy your night."

Theo makes his way through the room, giving attention to everyone and making them laugh. He has them hanging on his words and looking at him as if he's their reason for living, which is total Gemini behavior. He's the type of person that makes you feel instantly comfortable and secure. It's refreshing to be on the receiving end, even if he'll turn around and do it to the next person he encounters.

No wonder he's in the service industry. He's charming. Too charming for his own good, but great for business.

I lay my phone face up on the table and ask Ruby, "What would you recommend?"

She leans closer to the table. "Everything. Let's order every single one of their signature cocktails."

I scan the menu and the ten signature cocktails on it. "You're evil."

She cackles. "Yes, but Theo deserves it."

"Did you ever..."

Her gaze finds Theo chatting with a group of men on the other side of the room. "Once. And it was the biggest mistake of my life."

Ruby flags down a server and orders all ten of the signature cocktails for each of us. The server doesn't even blink at our order, and instead asks if we would like them all at the same time or spaced out.

"Same time," we say in unison and then laugh.

The server smiles along with us and disappears to put our order in.

Ruby and I laugh about the customers from today until the drinks arrive. They barely fit on the table, and we're getting confused stares from nearby patrons, but we don't care. The server even labeled each coaster, so we know which drink is which.

Ruby lifts one that's in a skull shaped glass and smoking on the top. "Let's start with this bad boy here."

I raise my glass and clink it against hers. Smoke, bitters, and orange explode on my tongue and, holy shit, it's amazing. Never thought I'd like something so smoky, but I'm converted.

We each drink half the glass in one go and giggle like schoolgirls afterwards. A notification pops up on my screen from Zodiac Way of Life. One that reminds me to mark if the horoscope came true or not.

Ruby notices and nods her head to my screen. "You still a slave to your horoscope?"

"Yeah, I'm using it to improve myself. Do you believe in horoscopes?"

"Sure, when it suits."

I snort. "It's been on point, for the most part."

"What did it say about today?"

"That I should be prepared to reveal a secret."

Ruby taps her chest. "Okay, lay one on me."

"I haven't had sex in over four months."

"Four?" She chokes on her drink. "But wasn't your breakup three weeks ago?"

"Yeah…" I run my finger over the condensation of the glass.

It was a place in my relationship with Eric that was always lacking. I accepted it because I was in love, or at least I thought I was, but damn, I wasted a year on him.

Maybe I'm just not good at sex.

"Even more reason to find a hookup." Ruby nods to a man sitting at the bar.

Buzzed black hair and thick eyebrows add some dimension to his otherwise round face. His muscles are one wrong move away from breaking through his long-sleeved black Henley. He's hot enough, but not my normal type. I don't need all those muscles. They're too intimidating. My body is too soft for someone like him. He's giving off twenty-two vibes. Strong, confident, steady. I bet he's an Aries as he clearly loves the gym.

"Not this again," I say. "Remember last time? Shit storm?"

"In all seriousness I know him. He'll do good by you and treat you right."

"But all those muscles…"

"Are a gift. He could carry you everywhere and wouldn't get tired. Imagine the stamina in bed."

I down the rest of my drink and pick up another before pounding half of it. She does have a point. A random hookup will cut one of my last ties with Eric, even though the last attempt was a failure. I'm tipsy enough to go through it, even if ZWOL didn't mention anything about getting lucky tonight.

"How do I?" I wave my hand toward him as if that explains everything.

Ruby cackles and takes a moment to compose herself before saying, "You don't have to do anything. If he looks this way, catch his gaze and give him a sly smile before looking away. He'll come over with that invitation."

"That's it?"

"Yup."

I stare at her for a few beats, trying to decipher if she's joking, but she's not.

It can't be that easy.

"Watch and learn." She scans the room and doles out a few smiles here and there. One of the men smiles back and strolls over to our table to talk to her.

I tune out their conversation and make eye contact with the man at the bar, the one Ruby thinks would be Mr. Stamina in the bedroom. I repeat what Ruby did and take a sip of my drink and wait.

"Hello, there."

"Hi," I say. Holy shit, it really worked.

He takes in my appearance from head to toe and then scans the table. "I would offer to buy you a drink, but it appears like you're set for the night."

I laugh. "I couldn't decide and wanted to taste every single one."

He hums and pulls out the stool next to mine. "May I?"

"Sure. Do you want one?" I nod to the drinks lining the table.

He lifts his half full glass to me. "I'm good with my whiskey."

"Who goes to a cocktail bar and orders a whiskey?"

He laughs. "Good question, but the real one is who runs a cocktail bar and hates cocktails."

I tilt my head to the side. "I thought Theo runs this place?"

He smiles. "He owns it, but I'm the manager."

Ahh, that's how Ruby knows him. I make a tsking sound. "Drinking on the job then?"

"It's my night off, but they asked me to come in since

there were some VIPs here." He gives me a meaningful stare.

I throw back my head and laugh. "I'm far from a VIP. More like I'm doing a favor for Theo."

The man leans closer. "And what kind of favor is that?"

I lift my shoulder and his gaze dips to follow the movement. "We both wanted to annoy someone."

He takes a sip of his whiskey, gaze locked on mine. "Interesting."

"Hugo," a voice I know all too well says from behind me.

I stiffen as Anders crowds my back, so close he's touching me.

Hugo looks between the two of us before laughing. "Hey man. What are you doing here?"

"Theo called and needed my help with something."

"I'm sure he did." Hugo glances my way. "Do you two know each other?"

I sit taller and move away from Anders' body. "He's my boss."

Hugo tilts his head. "Theo's in the office."

Anders remains behind me and doesn't say anything verbally, but whatever face he's making has Hugo smiling widely.

Once he leaves, Hugo chuckles. "That was fun."

Hugo looks like someone who just accomplished something they've been wanting to do for ages. I deflate. He must be in on it, on ruffling Anders's feathers. He didn't approach me because he's interested. He was following his boss's orders.

All I wanted was to break my dry spell and now I've

ended up tangled in a joke between friends. It's official. The universe is against me having sex. What do I need to do to get some action around here? Burn some sage and remove whatever bad juju is following me around?

I take a sip of a new drink to calm my rising panic. I can barely taste the chocolate mixture. My mouth is nothing but ash at the reality of my situation. "Theo's more thorough than I gave him credit for. Did he ask you to come over?"

Hugo's smile drops. "Not explicitly, but he did want me here to see Anders get his panties in a twist."

"I see." But I don't. It feels like I'm the punchline of a joke Theo engineered. Having him confirm it makes it all the more brutal. A slimy feeling of being used coats my stomach.

Hugo covers his hand over mine. "Anders is a good friend, but I'm not going to lie. I wish he wasn't right now."

I give him a strained smile and down the rest of my drink. I need to get out of here before the tears come. Tears for trying over and over again and still failing. I can't even get a random hookup right. It was supposed to be easy, but no matter what I do, I fail at it. Eric can't be the last person I had sex with. I can't let him have that power over me.

It's all too much. I grab my purse from the table and stand. It was a mistake coming here. "I need to get going."

Ruby pulls herself away from her guy. "Already?"

"Yeah. Catch you at work."

She waves and I ignore Hugo as I make a beeline for the door. The more I walk, the drunker I become. As if the alcohol was lying in wait for me to move before it strikes. I thought the drinks weren't that strong, but, oh my, was I wrong.

I'm far more drunk than I realized.

Shit.

I make it onto the street, and the cold air does little to cool down my overheated body. I felt like things were finally falling into place and I was about to take a healthy step forward in becoming a different person, but it was an illusion.

Of course, Hugo didn't want me.

He just wanted to play a joke on his friend.

A joke I still don't get. Why would Anders care who I talk to? It's not like he even likes me. He should've been more interested in Ruby picking up some guy.

I try to contain the tears threatening to fall, and pick up my pace, but I'm so drunk I'm swerving from side to side. I'm not even sure if I'm heading in the right direction.

"Zoey," Anders calls from behind me.

"What?" I groan and whip around to face him, but there was too much whip in my movement. I stumble to the side, huffing when I catch myself.

Anders places a steady hand under my elbow and looks me over. "Why are you crying?"

"I'm not crying. I just have an eyelash in my eye." I stick my finger in my eye, following through with the lie, fishing for a nonexistent eyelash. "Shouldn't you be meeting with Theo right now?"

"Theo's not important. I'll call him tomorrow." His

gaze roams my face, and he frowns at whatever he sees. "Did something happen? Did Hugo hurt you?"

"No." I sigh, exhausted. "I just want to sleep."

He doesn't look like he believes me, but I don't care.

"Let me walk you."

"That's not necessary." I jerk my arm out of his grip.

"It is, especially if you've been drinking." He places his arm around my back, supporting some of my weight.

I don't have the energy to argue with him. We walk side by side with our usual silence enclosing us. A silence that radiates disapproval from Anders's side every time I stumble, bump into him, or sway on my feet.

I'm acting like the messy Zoey he thinks I am.

The messy Zoey that I am.

When we make it to the front of my building, I say, "I've got it from here."

"I'll walk you up."

"What? No."

A line forms between his eyebrows. "Why not?"

I snort. "Well, you hate me, and I don't want you in my space."

"I don't hate you." He grabs my keys from my hand and unlocks the building door for me.

"Keep telling yourself that."

After the first flight of stairs, I lean so heavily on the banister, I debate if I should just sleep here. Damn if that doesn't sound like the best idea I've had in ages. I close my eyes and press my cheek to the worn wood. Anders sighs and scoops me up and into his arms. I'm too tired to protest his actions when the relief at not having to move my body is so strong.

He's not even out of breath after carrying me up three flights of stairs. How does this man stay in such good shape?

When he unlocks my door and begins to push open the door, I yell, "Stop."

He freezes. "What is it?"

"I don't want you to come in."

He frowns. "Why?"

I mumble, "It's embarrassing."

"You're close to blacking out. I don't want you to get hurt."

"I'm fine."

He snorts. "If I set you down and you don't sway, then I'll believe you."

I muster up my outrage. "Fine, I'll show you."

He sets me down and my world tilts to the side as I fall. He catches me with his arms around my waist. My traitorous hands fall to his chest and cop a feel of his strong pecs. Maybe he's an Aries too, because hot damn, he's full of muscles under his shirt.

The strangest thing of all is he doesn't push me away. Instead, he pulls me closer and into some semblance of a hug. It feels too good to be touched. By anyone, even him. Even if he's having to deal with messy Zoey yet again.

I jerk away from him at that thought.

"I thought it was chaotic Zoey," he says.

Oh shit. I said that last part out loud. I glare at him, and he smirks while waiting for me to push open my door.

"I know I just failed that little test of yours, but I'll be fine."

He can't have more fuel to make fun of me. My barren apartment would give him material for years.

Anders raises his hands up in a placating gesture. "Okay."

"Thanks for getting me home." I lean against the door-jamb, trying to act cool.

But I miss the door and fall through it instead, landing hard on my ass.

"Fuck," I groan.

Anders swoops me into his arms but remains in the hallway. "We've got a problem."

"How so?" I lick my lips and stare at his mouth.

His gaze is serious. "You don't want me to come in, but I'm worried you may hurt yourself again. Can I please come in and help you?"

I stare at him for a few heartbeats before I nod.

"I need to hear you say it out loud."

"Fine, you can come in. But please don't comment on anything you see here tomorrow. Or ever."

When he starts to walk, I throw my hand over my eyes to hide my embarrassment. To avoid seeing his reaction to my dingy apartment. The cracks in the ceiling, the saggy couch, the bareness of it all.

He sets me down on the couch and pulls my hand from my face. "I promise I won't say anything. Let me get you some water."

I stare at my sad Christmas tree and listen to him opening and closing cabinets. All empty except for a few essentials.

Time seems to drag on, and as it does, I become more and more tense. It's just a matter of time before he breaks his promise and comments. I'm emotionally stripped bare in front of him and he's seeing all the things I've tried to keep hidden these past weeks. All the things I wish I could hide from myself.

My apartment is a constant reminder of how far I've fallen.

My eyes burn and I suck in a sharp breath to try to keep the tears from falling. But it doesn't help, and it's a losing battle, anyway. What's one more thing to add to his never-ending list of things he can make fun of me for?

The faucet turns on and off. His footsteps draw nearer, and before I know it, he's beside me again.

I blink through my tears and stare at his stupidly handsome face.

"Why are you crying?" His voice is soft, as if he's afraid I'm about to become a sobbing mess. Lucky for him, I'm doing my best to wait until he leaves to have my break-down. I have some standards left, even if I am drunk.

I try to get my voice working over the knot in my throat. "No reason. It's cathartic. You should try it sometime."

His lips pinch together and hands me a glass of water. He nods to the couch. "Does it open?"

I shake my head.

He finds my blankets on the side of the couch and covers me. Tucks me in as if I'm a child. "Where's your heat?"

I nod to the opposite wall. "Please don't put it higher than fifty-five."

"Why not? You're going to get sick." He frowns.

"Don't make me say it out loud."

"I don't understand."

"What's there to not understand? I'm fucking poor, alright?"

"But how—"

"Please..." I close my eyes. "Do you know how embarrassing it is for you, out of all the people in the world, to see me at my lowest?"

"I didn't know..." A range of emotions cross his face, but I'm far too drunk to try to decipher them. He also doesn't finish the sentence, and instead, leans down and kisses my forehead before leaving. "Good night, Zoey."

My world continues to spin and tilt even with my eyes closed. Before I can dissect what it meant, that kiss on my forehead, sleep pulls me under.

CHAPTER 11

"*B*uckle up, Leo, because you're about to go on a wild ride of progress and setbacks. Don't forget to celebrate your successes and bask in the glow of your achievements. Who knows? There just might be a date in your cards. But remember, don't sweat those setbacks because they're just speed bumps on the road to success. Embody the honey badger attitude—stay determined, don't give up, and most importantly, don't give a fuck. Love always, ZWOL."

IT'S a universal truth that hangovers suck balls. But working while hungover? It's making me question all my life decisions. Every hiss of the steamer or clack of metal against metal causes my shoulders to bunch and the pounding behind my eyes to intensify. The headache doesn't budge, no matter how much pain medicine I take.

Anders has been quiet all morning, but he keeps

shooting me looks like he's afraid I'm about to fall apart on him. It's annoying, but at least he's keeping quiet. I'm surprised he hasn't made a snide remark about my hungover state, but I'll take the small miracles when they occur.

It's difficult to plaster on a smile and get through the customers. I'm counting down until lunch. Even if my stomach rebels against the idea of food, I need a break.

"Can I take an early lunch?" It's the second thing I've said to him today. The first being good morning.

He gives me a once over. "You okay?"

"Just dandy."

"Lunch is in the fridge."

When I go to the break room, I find a white bag with my name on it in the fridge.

I peek inside, and the largest burrito bowl I've ever seen sits inside. It's at least three times bigger than a standard size, more than enough for me to take home and eat for dinner as well.

Huh, today is looking up. Also in the bag are containers of salsa, guac, and sour cream. I use a plate from the break room and dump a portion of the bowl inside to heat up. I can ration the rest for later.

Holy shit, it's so good.

I search for the name of the restaurant on the container and bag, but there's none. Ugh, I'll need to ask Anders for the name. This is "I could eat it every day and never tire of it" kind of good. But the thought of talking to him makes my skin crawl, so that's not going to happen.

I scarf down my food. When I'm finished, I lay my

head on the table. A power nap is exactly what I need right now. I set a timer and close my eyes.

The timer rings far too soon and I push up and out to the front of the shop. At least the food and rest have decreased my hangover to more manageable levels.

Anders waits until there's a lull in customers before taking his break. "If a customer comes, come get me from the break room."

"I'll be fine." Anders almost never takes a break for himself while I'm here, but always ensures I have one. The fact he won't train me properly, so he can take a proper lunch, stings. A headache builds at my temples when I try to untangle his actions and discover the meaning, but it's pointless.

He doesn't acknowledge my statement and walks down the corridor.

My phone buzzes with a call in my front pocket of my apron. Ruby.

The second I answer the call, Ruby already starts talking. "Do you have time to talk? I figured there'd be a lull in the customers now."

"Yeah, Anders just took his lunch. What's up?"

"Are you okay?" she asks. "You left suddenly last night."

"All fine, just wasn't feeling the best. I must've drunk too much too soon." The lie comes easily. There's no need to out myself and tell her the truth about her friend using me to get a rise out of Anders.

"I heard Anders got you home safely. I told you he doesn't hate you."

"Well, he's back to freezing me out and I'm one hundred percent down for that."

"Well, speaking of Anders, it's his birthday in a few days. We're going to do a surprise party at Grave Digger."

Huh, that'd make him a Sagittarius. But with his critical personality and general assholeness, I would've put money on him being a Virgo.

"Don't tell me you're planning it with Theo."

"The things I tolerate for Anders." She sighs, as if the weight of the world is on her shoulders.

"Uh-huh."

"You've got to come and save me from a night of dealing with Theo."

"Ugh, fine," I say. "Send me the details, but I'm not able to swing a present so I'm going to slap my name on whatever present you get him."

"Deal."

We hang up and I open my text thread with Nick. Maybe I should invite him to the party. My horoscope said to go on a date, and I was waiting for something from ZWOL before contacting him. If Nick comes, I can make an appearance and bail early. He'll also create a buffer between Anders and me. And the party will create a buffer between Nick and me.

It's a win-win.

I send Nick a quick message asking if he'll join me, and he immediately replies yes.

When Anders returns from his break he asks, "Can you stay after tonight?"

I rock back on my heels. "Why?"

"To train you to make the drinks."

I stare at him while he rubs the back of his neck. His

discomfort can only speak to one thing—what he saw last night.

Oh my stars.

It's like a pity fuck, but instead of an O and getting naked, I'm getting trained.

It's a pity training.

And fuck me, but I have to take this opportunity and run with it. Because I want to learn.

I mentally will a customer to walk in. To interrupt this awkward as fuck proposal.

But no one comes to save me.

"Fine," I say and turn back to the register.

Finally, a customer comes, and I don't have to interact with Anders until closing.

Once the sign is flipped to closed and our duties are complete, Anders holds out a white envelope.

"What's that?" I stare at it, but don't take it.

"Your wages for the entire time you've worked here." He shakes it in his hand, as if urging me to take it. "From now on, I can start paying you daily if that… helps."

Blood rushes to my cheeks. It's the closest he's come to talking about what he saw, and it's embarrassing as fuck.

"You don't need to treat me differently now that you know I'm poor." I swipe the envelope from his hand and stuff it in my back pocket.

"I… that's not what…"

"Can we get on with the training portion of the evening?"

He nods slowly, as if appeasing a wild animal.

"We'll start with a Ristretto. It's a drink that differentiates a good coffee shop from an excellent one."

He walks through the steps, and I copy them.

Or at least I try to.

But I can't get it right.

In any of the nineteen attempts I try.

Anders takes a sip of the twentieth Ristretto I've made and makes a face like he's drinking garbage. "It's too watery, and you didn't tamp the grounds hard enough. How many times do I need to go over this?"

His tone is what does me in. The tone that implies I'm stupid for not being able to get it right. That I can't get his pride and joy drink, the flagship of the shop, correct.

It's the same tone my parents took with me during The Event That Shall Not Be Named aka Thanksgiving. The day I told my family the truth of what happened with Eric and how he stole from us.

My father's normally tan skin turned ruddy. His face contorted with rage, but he straightened his vest calmly. I thought he was going to tell me everything would be okay with that calm move. The way he used to when I got a bad grade. Instead, he called me useless and a waste of space.

His words were like a sledgehammer, breaking everything they touched, starting with my heart. My mother jumped right in and hurled her own insults my way.

It was at that moment I broke. That the emotional sutures I was holding myself together with after finding out about Eric's deceit tore open. I was left alone to emotionally bleed all over the living room carpet.

I didn't argue, didn't defend myself. Not when I had nothing to say. Not when I deserved their scorn.

I throw the grounds into the garbage more forcefully than necessary, snapping myself back into the present moment. "I get it, okay? I'm a failure. You don't need to constantly point it out."

I spin around so my back is to him. I didn't mean to be so honest, and I immediately regret cluing him in on how much his words hurt me.

Trying to contain my building emotions, I bite the inside of my cheek. It's like I'm replaying The Event That Shall Not Be Named all over again. Being told I'm not good enough, a failure, a worthless and stupid person. Now, I'm left a shaky mess on the verge of a breakdown.

It's all too much.

I'm too hot. My apron chokes me. I tug it off, but it doesn't help. Everything is too stifling.

I need to leave, to get out of here.

"Hey." He softens his voice, as if it'll make everything better and erase everything he implied.

I grab my purse and make a beeline for the door, keeping my head ducked. "I'm done for the day. See you tomorrow."

"Wait, Zoey," he calls after me.

I pause at the door, and he catches up to me.

Standing in front of me, he tilts my chin up. "What's going on?"

"I'm not sure why you even hired me when you can't stand me." A stupid tear takes this moment to fall down my cheek.

"I made you cry?" His eyes widen, and a horrified expression overcomes him.

He opens his mouth to say something else, but I don't want to hear it. I can't, not when it might just break me even more.

I jerk my chin out of his grip. "Not tonight, okay? I'll see you tomorrow."

I say it through gritted teeth, trying to be professional when I feel anything but, and wait for him to give me a small nod before escaping to the street.

Only when I'm safe inside my apartment do I let the tears flow. I leave my purse and shoes by the door and curl up into a ball on my couch. The apartment is so cold, shivers rack my body. Just another thing to add to the long list of things wrong with my life.

And the worst part? I left my epic burrito bowl at Amore in my rush to escape Anders.

I grab the blanket next to the couch and curl into it. A crinkle comes from my back pocket. I remove the envelope filled with my earnings and look inside. Two thousand dollars. I recount it five times, but the number stays the same. He overpaid me.

Am I so pitiful that he's now taken me on as a charity case?

Anders blows so hot and cold; I never know where I stand with him. One second, he's nice, and the next he has an uncanny ability to hurt me.

There's a knock on my door.

I lift my head and stare at the door as if there's a burglar on the other side about to break down my door. A polite burglar, of course, by giving me the courtesy of advanced notice.

I heave myself off the couch and run my hands over my tear-stained face. When I whip the door open, no one is there, but there is a white plastic bag on the floor.

I toe it open with my bare foot, and inside is the

container from lunch. Anders must have brought it over. He's the only one who knows where I live.

Is he a fucking food and money fairy now?

I snatch the bag off the ground and bring it inside, grabbing my phone.

Me: Thanks for the food, but you overpaid. I'll bring the extra to work tomorrow.

Anders: No I didn't.

Me: I'm not a charity case.

Anders: Never said you were. You must be misinformed about your hourly rate.

I ROLL my eyes at his antics. There's no way I'm worth even the twenty dollars an hour Ruby proposed, let alone more.

Me: Fine, enlighten me, oh wise one. What's my pay per hour?

Anders: You're good with numbers, you can do the math. Keep the money, I won't accept you returning it.

Me: Has anyone ever told you that you're the most infuriating person they've ever met?

. . .

THREE DOTS INDICATE he's typing. They stop moving, then restart. Finally, his message comes through.

> Anders: Regularly. It's my defining feature, after all.

I SNORT. Did he just make a joke? I didn't think he had it in him.

> Me: Glad you're self-aware.

> Anders: I'm sorry about today

I NEVER EXPECTED him to apologize. To say I'm shocked is an understatement.

Maybe, just maybe, he isn't as bad as I've been thinking. Maybe he's human and makes mistakes. Or I'm just fucked up and have a row full of triggers a thousand miles long and he keeps setting them off.

Unknowingly.

> Me: Let's just pretend it never happened and never speak of it again.

Anders: You have a habit of pretending,
don't you?

Me: That's my defining feature.

Anders: Fair enough. See you tomorrow.

I ALMOST WANT to continue chatting with him. It feels safer somehow, to do it over text rather than face-to-face. I can't hear his tone over text so I can pretend he's saying it nicely. Not like how he acted while making the Ristretto.

Anger resurfaces at the memory of his tone. Ugh, I need a distraction. Everything from The Event That Shall Not Be Named is too close to the surface.

I head to my kitchen. Even if my oven's not working, I can at least knead some dough. I take out all the ingredients I need, brought from my old kitchen. Where my oven worked.

While the yeast, water, and sugar bubble, I feel more in control all ready. Baking has always been my stress relief. It's never about eating the food, though I always do a taste test. It's methodical with exact measurements and processes. It's scientific and speaks to the part of my brain that loves order and numbers.

Addie was the worst cook, but the best baker. She needed exactness to feel comfortable, just like me. She's the only one in the family who also found comfort with numbers.

Stars, I miss her.

I wish I could call her and tell her about everything that's happened, catch her up on life. She'd know what to do about Anders. She'd know what to do about everything.

It's almost been a year, and yet sometimes it feels like I haven't healed at all. Like I'm back to square one. As if I've only just got that phone call, where mom frantically told me she was on the way to the hospital. Addie had collapsed in front of her bakery.

But she was dead on arrival.

Heart attack.

No warning signs.

Gone from my life between one heartbeat and the next.

It was the first time I'd experienced a sudden loss. My grandparents were sick for months before they passed, so we had plenty of time to say goodbye.

And that's the hardest part—not being able to say goodbye. To tell her one last time how much I love her. How much she meant to me. How she was more of a mom to me than my own mom.

I'm lost without her.

Lilly was sad, but not devastated. Mom was, though. She didn't leave the house for two months, and Lilly was there to help her. Like Lilly always is. Like how I was there for Addie.

Now, Addie is gone, and the only family I have left—mom, dad, and Lilly—don't want me.

Loneliness and sadness scald me, like spilling boiling water onto my skin. I knead the dough, and it doesn't help. Nothing does.

When my tears fall onto the dough, I abandon it and snatch my phone off the couch. I open the group chat between Lilly, mom, and me. The chat thread I had with Addie remains untouched. I can't open that one, not yet.

Not ever.

I scroll through the history, the photos. It hasn't been active since Thanksgiving. I can't help but reminisce about what we used to have.

It's the worst kind of pain to be alone.

All because I trusted Eric.

I lean back onto the couch and tip my head to the ceiling. The cracks haven't changed, but there's comfort in counting them. In going back to the numbers I love so much. Numbers never lie, but I didn't double check them when presented with a set. I missed the obvious error and lost everything.

Failure, sour and sticky, coats my throat, but I swallow it down. I can't go there, not today. Instead, I count the multiple cracks in the ceiling until I fall asleep, dreaming of numbers.

CHAPTER 12

"*H*ey there, magnificent Leo! Guess what? It's time to put that royal paw to good use and extend a helping hand to someone in need. Yep, you read that right—beneath your fierce exterior, there's a heart of gold waiting to lend support. So, channel your inner life coach and offer some royal guidance. Whether it's a shoulder to cry on or some sassy words of wisdom, your lion-hearted compassion can make all the difference. Love always, ZWOL."

WHEN I ARRIVE AT AMORE, Ruby opens the door and says, "Hope you came with your A-game today. I'm responsible for teaching you the drinks."

"What happened to Anders doing it?" Maybe I scared him off yesterday with my meltdown.

She leads me to the machines. "No idea, but we're going to spend the entire hour before we open working through the drinks. I'll taste each one after you make it and give corrections. If we can finish the top ten drinks before we open, Anders promised to buy us dessert for lunch. And I'm going to need that dessert, so you better perform."

"Deal."

Anders enters the shop, as if we conjured him by just using his name. He ties his apron on and heads to the cleaning supplies. He must be taking over my opening tasks if I'm working on the drinks with Ruby.

I never knew wiping a table down could be done with so much attitude, but he's excelling at it. I can't help but enjoy how annoyed he is, even if I don't know what's caused it.

Ruby explains each drink, the background behind it, and why it's on the menu. It's fascinating and speaks to the part of my brain that loves to learn. That loves to understand how things work. Learning about the menu and drinks makes me curious about Anders. I wonder what experiences he had that led him here.

Ruby must be my coffee making whisperer because after she tries my first ever jalapeno espresso, she smiles.

"Very good," she says. "Just nine more to go."

I laugh and we continue. When we get to the Ristretto, I can't help but glance at Anders. He's already staring at me. I gulp and focus back on the task at hand.

I can do this.

I follow through the steps Ruby just showed me and wring my hands when she tries it. I scrutinize her face, searching for any indication of what she thinks of it.

Finally, she gives me a nod. "Good."

I let out a relieved breath. Anders comes over, picks up the cup and takes a sip.

"It's perfect," he says, staring directly at me.

My heart melts like metal. His words are so confident, they tear down my barriers. This is something I've worked hard for, something I learned from the ground up. Not like in my engineering roles, where it came naturally, and the praise never hit since it was easy. I had a talent and knew how to twist it to meet the company culture, but I didn't work for it.

There's a difference in being appreciated for something that comes naturally, almost with no effort, and something that comes from hard work, sweat, and tears. I never felt that different until right now. Until this moment.

Ruby bounces on her feet. "Fair warning, I'm going to order so much dessert we'll be in a coma afterward."

Anders grumbles and leaves us alone for the rest of the hour. By the time we open, I'm ready. Anders mans the counter while Ruby oversees my drink making abilities in action.

She offers encouragement and kind corrections until I get the hang of it. By the second hour, I'm ready for anything. I'm filled with the kind of energy that comes after overcoming a challenge. The relief is overwhelming. I can learn. I'm capable. There's a sense of accomplishment pulsing through me, one saying I not only can handle the challenging menu but excel at it.

"Thanks for being the best teacher ever," I say to Ruby.

"Anytime. I'm just relieved we can all take proper breaks now."

"Why don't you take a break now if you're so desperate for one?" Anders snaps at her. "There's a reason only a few of us work here. Keeping a line is important for business. It makes our customers work for it, to feel like they earned their order."

"Okayyyy." I give Ruby a wide-eyed look.

She just rolls her eyes, and we get back to it.

Anders must be on his man period, but I've never seen him snap at Ruby. Anyone else, sure. But not her.

When Anders takes his break, I ask Ruby, "What's up with him?"

She frowns at the back corridor where he disappeared to. "I don't know. He won't talk about it, and I'm worried."

I should leave it, there's no reason to approach him when he's in a mood. But fucking ZWOL predicted my day yet again with far too much accuracy. Which means I'm going to have to go to him. To be his life coach or some shit.

I ask Ruby, "Can I have a few minutes?"

"Sure."

I take off down the hallway and knock on the break room door before entering.

It's empty.

I push open the back door and find Anders sitting on the stairs. He has his elbows on his knees and both hands in his hair.

His shoulders tense when the door slams shut behind me. I make sure to keep a foot of distance between us while I settle down next to him.

"You okay?" I ask.

He flicks his gaze to me. "Yeah."

"You've been pissy all morning."

"So what?" he snaps back, proving my statement.

"I thought you could use someone to talk to."

When he stays silent, I shrug. "Guess I was wrong."

I tried, just like ZWOL asked of me, but now I'm done. I stand up to leave.

"You're right. I'm not okay, I'm stressed." He blows out a long breath, as if exhausted.

I sit back down on the step and wait him out, giving him time and space to share... if he wants.

"I'm opening a new coffee shop in a couple months, but every idea I have for it isn't good enough."

"What was your original idea?"

"I didn't have one." He glances at me. "I bought a building because of the potential I felt it had."

"Must be some building."

"It is." His lips twitch.

"I'm sure you'll find a way."

"There's no need to placate me with empty words."

"Okay, fine. You want the truth? You need help, but you aren't willing to ask for it."

He bristles. "And who can help me?"

"Oh, I don't know—your successful brother, Ruby, or even me."

"You'd help me?" He arches an eyebrow.

"Don't look so astonished. This may surprise you, but I'm really good at a few things and I think I'd be the perfect person to help."

"But why would you want to help me? I've been..."

"An asshole," I say. "Definitely, but you're also the asshole who pays me... so why not?"

He remains silent and stares me down. "What makes you think you're going to be able to help?"

My face drops, and he says, "I didn't mean it in a bad way. I'm curious." When I give him a wary look, he continues, "I'm serious. Please tell me because you're right. I need help with this."

I hold up my pointer finger. "I'm an amazing project manager and have the ability to foresee twenty steps ahead." I hold up a second finger. "Problem solving and finding workarounds are my areas expertise." I hold up another finger. "Design and baking are my hobbies, so I'd be good at flavor combinations for the menu and concept as well as decorating the inside of this so-called magical building." I hold up the rest of my fingers. "And I'm just an awesome person."

"Did you seriously just hold up seven fingers for being an awesome person?"

I give him a deadpan look and he laughs, a real laugh. Not the grunts or huffs he normally gives me, but one that makes him look relaxed, fun, and happy. Happy looks good on him. Too good.

"What do you think?" I ask.

"Can we do a trial for two weeks first?"

"Fair enough, but I expect to be compensated accordingly for the two weeks I work on this."

He grins. "I wouldn't expect anything less."

"When can you show me the building?"

"Right after work?" he asks.

"Sure."

* * *

ANDERS DOESN'T MENTION GOING to the new shop to Ruby. He even lets her leave early, as if hiding it from her. For some reason, I also don't mention it to her.

Anders doesn't say anything as we walk to the building, but he stares at me more than the sidewalk in front of us. It's unnerving.

When we arrive, it's to a corner storefront for a white, two-story building in a hip part of town. The store has cardboard blocking the windows, and he opens the front door with a key stored in his jacket.

It's a construction zone inside with plywood lying about in piles, tarps covering the floors, and paint cans in the corner. It's a large space, with so much potential. He was right about the building.

He doesn't stop at the bottom floor, and instead leads me up to the second floor, which is divided in two. Half of it is a room. The other half is a terrace with fairy lights around the railing. He brings me outside, and there's a canopy for rainy days.

I take in the view of the neighborhood around us. Since it's situated on the corner of the street, it's open and airy. The orange and yellow lights from a taco restaurant across the street shine bright in the sky. The neon green lights from a bar on the other side of the street make me want to stay here.

"It's gorgeous." And it is. There's something special about this building and neighborhood. My mind is already turning over ideas for the space. "I understand why you bought it."

"I love this neighborhood." He turns to me.

"This place has a great feel to it."

"It's why I fell in love with it from the first viewing."

"How do you want here to be different from Amore?"

"Well, I can't have this place cannibalize Amore's customers, so I need to target a different demographic."

"That's fair. Who would you say are Amore's current customers?"

"People who love exotic coffee drinks."

"Yeah," I say, "but I think you have more than those customers. You get a lot of businesspeople who use Amore to work at, people who happen to live close by, and people who like to travel and the drinks remind them of that."

"Hmm, I see what you're saying."

"To start, you can create a target customer for this place like moms, or college kids, or something completely different."

"I want here to be a place for friends to come to when they want to catch up or hang out. Where they want to spend time and make it part of their day."

"So, cozy and comfortable, with awesome food to keep them here longer, but offering something different from all the shops out there."

He thinks a moment before nodding. "Exactly that."

"That's a great start. We have a demographic, and now we need to think about what friends are interested in. What's important to them or what would draw them to your new place?"

"You really are good at this."

"Don't sound so surprised." I smack him on the arm.

He laughs. "It's just... you keep surprising me at every turn. I'm constantly on my toes around you."

"As you should be." I grin. "When do you want to open?"

"First week of March. I don't have a menu, design ideas, or even the colors fixed. Basically, I'm fucked."

"Good thing you have me." I like to solve problems. My old job was something I excelled at, and I was confident doing it. Opening a new shop won't be as technical as my job at Spark, but it'll be fun. Best of all, I'll finally be able to show how capable I am.

I snap some pictures of the interior and can already envision what it'd look like. It's like everything that's happened since moving here has led me to this moment. ZWOL guided me today, and it's worked out in my favor.

A new energy fills me, and I'm excited. For the first time in too long.

"Can I walk you home?" he asks once we're back on the street.

"If you want."

He tucks my arm in his, and we walk in comfortable silence. He slows his pace to match mine and soon our steps are in sync. There's something special about being so in-tune with someone you match their movements. I don't think Eric ever tried to match my pace. He expected me to match his strides, and it was never natural.

I push thoughts of Eric out of my mind as we arrive at my building. Anders makes no move to go home, and I give him a quizzical look.

"Can I come up for a coffee?" he asks.

"I don't have any coffee."

"How about a tea?"

"I don't have tea, either."

He grins. "Then I'll take a glass of water."

"Ugh, fine. Come on."

"Don't sound too excited."

I roll my eyes and he follows me up the stairs without another word. My apartment looks the same as it did this morning, still depressing and still an embarrassment. Even though he's already seen it, it doesn't change the facts.

He takes his shoes off by the front door and grabs us each a glass of water, as if he lives here and knows exactly where everything is.

"Where did you learn to do that?" I nod my head in the direction of his shoes.

"In Japan." He hands me my glass and leans against the kitchen counter.

"How many countries have you lived in?"

"Ten."

"Whoa. That's a lot." I place my phone on the counter next to me and mimic his lean. There's a text from Nick, but I ignore it.

"We moved around a lot for my father's job, but Portland's always been home. My mom's from here and made sure to keep our roots."

"Favorite place you lived in?"

"Italy and Japan," he says.

"I've never even left the country. I planned on it with my aunt, but we never made it happen." Because we put off our trip to one day and one day turned into never after she died.

"Where did you plan to go?"

"Finland. It's supposed to be the gluten-free capital of

the world. Addie, my aunt, researched it and made a whole itinerary for us…" I don't know why we never pulled the trigger and made the trip a reality. We planned to, but we didn't do it. Never took it further than an idea. Grief and regret pulse through me, but I bite my cheek to suppress it. The pain refocuses me.

"Finland is amazing. You'd love it there."

My phone buzzes with a reminder from Zodiac Way of Life. Thank the stars, because if we continue the conversation, I'll probably end up in tears. And he doesn't need to see that. Again.

"What's that?" he asks.

I make a face. "You'll make fun of me if I tell you."

"I promise I won't."

I narrow my eyes at him. "'Cross your heart and hope to die' type promise?"

He waves a hand. "Yes, to all of that."

"I got a horoscope app and made a goal to follow it every day."

"Why in the world would you do that?"

"To get over my thirty-three point three percent life crisis."

He raises an eyebrow.

"It's legit so far."

His shoulders shake as if he's trying not to laugh, but he's totally laughing.

"What happened to your promise? You're laughing," I accuse with my hands on my hips.

He takes three deep breaths to compose himself. "We should've made a pinky promise. Everyone knows that's the biggest promise you can make."

"Good to know for the next time I need it."

"I'm sorry, it's not every day I meet someone obsessed with horoscopes," he says.

"Then you aren't paying attention because everyone here follows horoscopes. Haven't you ever been asked your sign?"

"Yes, but I don't answer."

I snort. "Of course, you don't."

"There's no scientific proof that it's real..." He lets that statement hang, as if expecting me to agree.

"There's also no scientific proof regarding religion and yet billions of people follow that."

He stares at me, as if trying to find out how to fit this bit of information about me to what he already knows. "You're serious about this."

"It's important to me. I need to turn my life around before my sister's wedding." Oh shit, I didn't mean to say that, so I try to cover by saying, "Which I need to take off for."

"Why do you need to turn your life around?"

Of course, he asks a question about the part I clearly didn't mean to say.

"No reason." I brush off his question. "You don't have to understand it or believe in it, but you should know following my horoscope is important to me."

"Okayyy. So, what days do you need to take off?"

"February tenth and eleventh."

He pulls up the calendar on his phone and raises his eyebrows. "Her wedding is in the middle of the week?"

I swallow the sudden spike of emotion through me. It was cheaper to get married on a Wednesday, and my actions forced her to choose that day. Because of my screw up.

"Yeah, she wanted a specific date." The lie comes out smoothly, and I wish it were true. It'd make the guilt riding me disappear. But no, she wanted a summer wedding on a Saturday. To make sure all her friends could attend. But now she's left with a Wednesday, and a much tamer version of her dream due to the budget restrictions she's now under.

"Don't tell me she's into numbers and astrology, too."

I snort. "I wish."

He waits for me to elaborate, but when I don't, he says, "You're a confusing woman."

"Aren't all women?"

"Apparently. What about Christmas and New Year's? Do you need time off?"

"Nope. I can work both days."

He frowns at my response but doesn't push for more. I need all the extra hours I can get, and it's not like I'm welcome at home for the holidays.

I yawn. "I think I'm going to call it a night…"

He grabs an envelope from his back pocket and places it on the counter. My money from working today. He remembered.

"Goodnight," he says.

"Goodnight."

I lock up, change into my pajamas and fall onto my couch. Anders was… nice? And it's throwing me off balance.

It was easier to not like him.

CHAPTER 13

"*L*et's go Leo! Let's go! The stars are cheering you on today while your imagination sparks and brings your ideas to life. If there were ever a time to color outside the lines, it's now. The universe will soon be giving you a standing ovation. Love always, ZWOL."

TODAY'S MY DAY OFF, my first one since starting, but I'm still going to work. Just not at Amore. Instead, I want to work on the new shop. I'm too pumped after seeing the building and the challenge it provides to not work on it.

I research the coffee shops nearby and decide to go to two. One isn't rated well, and the other is.

The first shop I go to is the one not rated well. It's got cyan walls. They're so bright it almost hurts to look at them. They painted the chairs and tables in a gold color, but it clashes with the walls. Both my table and chair wobble.

It's not inviting at all.

I take a sip of my tea and even that doesn't taste good. It has a chemical aftertaste, like the detergent used on the cup still clings to it.

There are two customers in the thirty minutes I stay there. It's clear what this place isn't doing well. I jot down my notes on my phone and head to the next shop.

The second I enter, it's clear it is more popular. It's a beige space with groups of people sitting and chatting throughout.

I order a hot chocolate and wait a few minutes before a table frees up. The baristas behind the counter work like robots. They don't interact, focused on their task, and churn out orders as if in an assembly line.

This place will be Anders's biggest competition. The demographic is similar to the one he wants. I make more notes on my phone and read my horoscope again. At least the stars are on my side with this project.

I pause.

A concept idea for the new shop barrels into me.

My leg bounces under the table with my excitement, but it's going to be a hard sell. I need the full concept laid out in an easy-to-understand way to convince Anders. Good thing I have the day off and making pitch presentations is my jam.

* * *

TODAY IS the one time I wish time would drag at a snail's pace, or the clock to stop working and never reach six p.m. Yesterday, I spent all day and night getting everything together for my pitch to Anders.

But doubt plagues me. What if he hates the idea? What if he decides right here and now he doesn't want my help? And worst of all, what if it's not good enough?

It's too much pressure. I'm feeling a fun mixture of wanting to pass out and throw up at the same time

But if he wants to open in a couple months, we need a decision.

Time marches forward, and before I'm prepared, it's six.

"You alright?" Anders asks while cleaning up.

Of course he notices. He never not notices anything when it comes to me.

"I have something to show you." My mouth is so dry I'm barely able to form the words. Nerves assault me, but I push forward. "It's a proposal for the new shop, but I don't know if you'll like it."

His head jerks back. "Already?"

"Do you have time now?" Shit, I should've asked this morning and set up a time.

"Of course." He gestures for me to sit down. "But first, here." He gives me another envelope for the day's wages.

"Thanks." I bring my laptop to the table and open the presentation. "It's just a rough draft, but I went to a couple of coffee shops yesterday and had an idea for your new place." I look him dead in the eye and ask seriously, "Please, please, please keep an open mind."

"I promise."

"Pinky promise?"

He arches an eyebrow. "It must be serious. Okay, pinky promise."

I hold my pinky out to him to cement the deal. He laughs but wraps his finger around mine.

I blow out a breath and begin the slideshow. "Friendship is the atmosphere you want in the new shop, and I asked myself what are friends interested in? What makes them pick one shop over the other? These are my theories."

I click the slide, and the theories pop up. "A comfortable and cozy place to chat, trying something new or trendy, but most of all, the atmosphere of the shop needs to be friendly and draw them in through the door while the drinks and food keep them there."

"Makes sense."

"I think you can accomplish all of it by going with." I pause and take another breath before the make-or-break moment of the idea. "A zodiac theme for the shop."

He scoffs, but when I glare at him, he motions for me to continue.

"Hear me out. That's for the trendy-slash-trying something new part. We could have recommendations for the drinks based on the person's sign and pair it with food, like a wine pairing, but with coffee instead. No coffee shop does this and it'll set us apart. It's a key part of the concept and it will bring the zodiac theme full circle.

"For the atmosphere, a good color scheme and comfortable furniture is a given. But if the baristas are friends and joking and chatting together as well as with the customers, it'll add to the experience. It'll make people feel welcome, or like they have a friend, and draw them through the door. The entire concept will make running the social media account easy."

He stares at my last slide and then looks back at me. "I still can't believe you made a presentation for me."

"Well, yeah, I have some backup slides on design ideas, market figures, and why I believe this is the right concept."

He covers my hand to still it and flips back and forth between the slides multiple times, studying the presentation.

Finally, after what feels like days, he says, "I like it. It has a clear direction and unique sales proposition."

"Yeah?"

The smile he gives causes my heart to hitch. "Yeah."

"So, you want to do it?"

"Only if you help me. There's no need for a trial run anymore. Congratulations, you can add being a coffee shop developer to your resume."

I snort. "I think we'll need to come up with a better name than that."

He smiles. "Seriously, thank you. You've put so much time into this presentation."

"It wasn't a big deal."

"It is. Are you free now to work on some menu ideas? I'm going to need your help on what the different zodiac signs would like."

"Sure."

"What zodiac sign are you?" he asks.

"A Leo."

"And what am I?"

I laugh. "You might want to get used to answering that question now. You're a Sagittarius."

"Describe Leo's to me in three words."

I think on it for a moment before saying, "Bold, sweet, and a flair for dramatics."

He grins. "Sounds about right." He grabs a black, worn notebook from behind the counter and returns with it. He flips through page after page of artwork.

"Wait." I reach for the book. "May I?"

He nods and passes it over. I flip slowly between each one. "Did you draw these?" There are such lifelike portraits of people, they look real. There are also animals and abstract pictures. All amazing.

He rubs the back of his neck. "I like to sketch."

"This is more than sketching or a hobby. These are really good. Have you ever sold any?"

He laughs. "Definitely not. But I did design all my tattoos, and Ruby's."

I trace my finger over the one always displayed on his forearm when he rolls up his sleeves. A watch face, with the mechanical inner workings showing in the middle and roman numerals for each number on the outside. It's intricate and takes up the majority of his forearm on his left arm, but there's one thing missing. "Why is there no time set?"

"I'll keep it blank until I meet my forever woman, then I'll fill it in with the exact time I meet her."

I flip through the book. "Don't tell me you have a list of random times written in here for all the women you've met."

His gaze sparks. "Jealous?"

"Not at all." Nope, that'd be ridiculous.

He laughs and takes the notebook from me before flipping toward the back and to an empty page. He writes down each word I said about Leos. Oh shit, I forgot what we're doing.

I watch as he jots down flavor ideas next to each word. It's impressive how fast he is at generating ideas.

After about ten minutes, he says, "What about an affogato? We could do a couple of different flavors of ice cream or even do nondairy options. We could top it all with shaved chocolate or whipped cream."

"I think that sounds like something even I'd drink, especially with the nondairy ice cream."

"Well, we've got to ensure you can eat and drink here."

"But then everything would have to be gluten-free."

He lifts a shoulder and says, "Why not?"

I gape at him. "Seriously?" I didn't expect him to run with that. Making the entire shop gluten free is an accommodation I never expected but is more meaningful than he probably realizes.

"You're not the only person with celiac."

"But I thought you hated me?"

He clears his throat. "I owe you an apology. I judged you when you walked into Amore that first day. You didn't order for ages, said "ew" when I proposed a drink, and you were wearing a designer dress. It didn't add up, and I thought it was a joke my brother set up. That thought was reinforced when I saw your resume and engineering credentials."

"But that only explains that first day. What about all the days after? When you discovered it wasn't a joke?"

He rubs the back of his neck. "I have a problem trusting people. With my business."

"So, what? You tried to test me?"

He winces. "Yeah, and I'm sorry. The words don't excuse it, and I was an asshole. But I didn't think you'd make it past the first day, let alone the second."

"And yet, here I am." He tried to drive me away to protect himself. I don't agree with his actions, but I can finally understand them. I need to be careful with him. If he doesn't trust easily, this entire new shop could go up in flames before it even starts.

"Here you are," he repeats.

A charged silence overcomes us, and if I don't break it soon, I'll do something stupid. So, I grab his notebook and turn it to a new page. At the top of the page, I write Sagittarius and the words curious, open minded, and enjoys change.

He slides the notebook back in front of himself. Our fingers brush when I pass him the pen. It's getting harder and harder to ignore the spark between us, but I have to.

I need to think of a food to go with an affogato. Addie loved to add a special to her menu each month, and we'd have a blast trying out new flavor combinations.

She'd pair the drink with waffles or pancakes, but I want to make the dish a touch more savory. I tap my fingers on the table, thinking. What's something like a pancake but not a pancake?

My fingers stop their rhythm.

Of course.

Crêpes.

They just so happen to have been Addie's favorite

breakfast food. It's perfect, and I already have a gluten-free version thanks to her. I can fill it with maple bacon and some sort of sauce. It could be a sweet sauce like maple cream or savory like a jalapeno jam. I grab a paper and pen from the register and jot down the ideas to share with Anders.

When I'm done, I look up to find Anders leaning back in his chair and his gaze on me. "What?"

"Nothing. I like watching you work."

I duck my head to hide my smile and show him my paper. "I have some ideas for the Leo food pairing, but we'd need to try everything together to ensure it tastes good."

"Good idea. For Sagittarius, I was thinking of a pistachio latte."

"Blood orange pairs so well with pistachio. Maybe we could do a blood orange pastry of some sort? Wait, what are the cooking restrictions?"

"Let's get the flavors nailed down first. We can worry about how to adapt it to the shop after. I don't want to hinder our creativity."

"Fair enough. When do you want to do a trial run with these?"

"Tomorrow I'm busy, but what about the next night? You can come to my place, and we can cook there. Send me a list of ingredients and I'll make sure they're there."

"Sure."

Of course he's busy tomorrow. It's his birthday party. The same one I'll be bringing another man to as my date.

CHAPTER 14

"*B*ow Chicka Wow Wow, Leo. The stars are feeling spicy today. Embrace your inner wild child, take risks, and let that adrenaline rush kick your life up a notch. Go ahead and have some fun, pounce on that prey like there's no tomorrow. Love always, ZWOL."

I LEAN CLOSER to the mirror and line my eyes in black. I'm going with heavier makeup tonight and aiming for a sultry look for Anders's birthday party. It'll pair well with my dark gray pencil dress with cap sleeves. It's from my corporate life, but it looks awesome on me.

ZWOL promises me a hookup with Nick tonight, and damn if I'm not going to channel that energy.

Ruby is on the other side of the mirror, adding the final touches to her makeup. She demanded we get ready together at her place after work.

"So, I did a thing," I blurt out.

"Do tell."

"I invited Nick to come tonight."

Her eyes widen. "Why would you do that? You were supposed to be my wing woman, my buffer between Theo and me."

"Well, I need a buffer between Anders and me and Nick will help with that."

I need someone to distract me and to remind me that lusting after my boss is not a good idea. Acting on the physical attraction between us will only end up with me jobless once it fizzles out.

"And why didn't you tell me about this earlier?" Ruby glares at me.

"It never came up."

"Fine," Ruby grumbles. "Where are we meeting him?"

"In front of Grave Digger in twenty."

"Ugh. Worst surprise ever."

"Sorry," I say.

"You're lucky I like you."

"I'll make it up to you."

She perks up. "In chocolate?"

"In chocolate," I confirm.

We head over to Grave Digger and Nick's already waiting outside. The bar is closed tonight, just for Anders. Nick's in a pair of gray dress pants and a navy turtleneck. I guess we both have more of a corporate lean to our attire. That's another thing we have in common.

"You look good," he says, leaning in to kiss my cheek.

"So do you. Thanks for coming tonight. This is Ruby," I say.

Ruby gives him a curt nod before saying, "We need to get inside. Anders will arrive soon."

Ruby turns on her heels and heads inside to where at least fifty people wait. All of Anders's friends and family. I don't even know five people here, let alone fifty.

Nick grabs drinks for us from a server carrying a tray. I down it in one go, not even tasting it. I need the liquid courage tonight.

"Whoa, you might want to slow down there," Nick says.

"Or not. I'm ready to have fun."

"But getting drunk in front of your boss is unprofessional."

I make a humming noise in response and grab another drink from a tray. Boo, he's being a buzz kill already.

"Get in your hiding places," Ruby shouts to the crowd. "He's coming in one minute."

Everyone ducks low and the lights go out. Ruby and Theo stand by the front door and less than a minute later, Anders pushes through.

The lights turn on and everyone yells, "Surprise."

Anders smiles so big it's breathtaking. He's wearing black slacks and a white button down that's rolled up to showcase his amazing forearms and tattoos.

Hoo boy, what have I gotten myself into by coming here? I've not seen him in anything besides flannel, and—holy hell—he wears normal clothes like he's a rugged model.

Theo shoves a drink in Anders's hand as a mass of people descend on him and wish him happy birthday. Ruby heads over to the DJ booth and starts the music.

"Do you want to head over?" Nick asks.

Not really, but I can't not say hi. So, I down the rest of my drink, grab Nick's hand, and drag us both to Anders.

Anders's gaze travels from my shoes all the way up to my smokey eyes. It's slow, as if he's savoring the taste of a fine whiskey. But then his gaze darkens as he takes in Nick next to me.

"Why are you here?" Anders snaps at Nick.

He stands taller. "I'm Zoey's date."

Anders is about to open his mouth probably to say something rude.

"Happy birthday," I say, leaning in and kissing him on the cheek.

His scent wraps around me. Spice with a hint of caramel. I lean into his cheek and inhale deeply, craving more.

I blame it on the alcohol.

Anders freezes under my touch for a split second until he wraps his arms around me in a hug.

"You look stunning," he whispers in my ear.

My heart flutters at his words. Stunning. He thinks I'm stunning. And Nick thinks I look only good. Plain, old, boring good.

I blush and push him away. He lets me go, almost reluctantly, when a woman and man almost twice my age approach. They don't close us out of the circle they form around Anders, but instead include us in their group. I'm about to make some excuse to leave, but the woman smiles at me and asks for my name.

"Mom, dad, this is Zoey. And her date," Anders fills in for them.

His parents look like they run marathons for funzies. They're the oldest people here, and yet they're in better shape than all of us put together. It's intimidating as much as it is impressive. Anders has his father's bone structure, but his hair and eyes are all from his mom.

His dad smiles and gives me a small wave, but his mom immediately pulls me into a hug. "It's so lovely to meet you."

I freeze in her embrace, shocked she's a hugger. Did not expect that. She must be a Cancer, but in the loving, caring, and hugging way.

"Same." I pat her on the back awkwardly before she releases me.

"Have you been enjoying the food?" she asks.

"Food?"

Anders gives his mom a wide-eyed look of embarrassment, like she just revealed a secret.

She either doesn't notice or doesn't care because she plows on. "Anders has been asking for recipes without flour. We've been adjusting and practicing since finding out about your disease."

She looks so puzzled, but I'm the one who's confused. I slide a glance to Anders, but he's no help. He's as stiff as the stick that's normally up his ass.

"He's been asking for recipes?" Every word comes out slowly, like I'm still trying to piece together this information and my brain is too sluggish to connect the dots.

"Yeah, we've had many conversations on how to change my famous burrito bowls or my peanut butter cookies into non-gluten recipes." She gives Anders a reprimanding look only a mom can give. "Don't tell me you haven't given any of the food to her."

"She's had it..." he says, rubbing the back of his neck.

With that statement, it all clicks. He's made all the lunches himself. Every time I thought he bought them from a restaurant, it's been him.

His mom beams. "Did you like it? What was your favorite?"

"I..." I draw a blank on all the lunches I've had, still in shock. "It's all been amazing."

"Wait until later this week, we've been tweaking my lasagna rec—"

"Mom," Anders says and draws a hand across his throat.

She laughs and pats him on the shoulder. "There's nothing to be embarrassed about."

Anders looks like he's about to pick his mom up and deposit her somewhere else. His dad, bless his heart, reads it easily and throws an arm around his wife's shoulders. He must be an Aquarius.

"Darling," his dad says. "Theo's waving us over. It was lovely to meet you, Zoey."

His mom sputters, but his dad guides her away.

I'm still processing what it all means as his parents make their leave. Nick wraps an arm around my waist. I jump, forgetting he was even next to me.

I forgot about my date. All because of Anders.

Anders has the kind of personality that draws you in and keeps your attention on him. From the beginning it's been that way, but now that he's not as hostile toward me, I'm in danger of being sucked into his orbit completely.

Fuck, this isn't good.

"That's nice of you. To make Zoey lunch." Nick says nice sarcastically, as if my employer accommodating my disease is... distasteful?

Anders gives Nick a once-over and sneers, like he finds him lacking. Nick puffs out his chest in response but doesn't say anything.

"I..." What do I say after all that? How do I deescalate the brewing tension?

Before I can decide, Nick grabs my hand and pulls me away from Anders, back to the bar. I turn my head to look back at Anders. His gaze locks on mine. I frown at his tense stance, fists at his side. Theo breaks the connection between us by tapping Anders on the shoulder and saying something in his ear.

Nick orders a shot and throws it back as if it's water. Huh, so it's okay for him to drink, but not me?

"Is there something going on between you two?" Nick asks.

"No way. We hate each other."

"It didn't feel like hate to me."

"I..." It didn't feel like hate to me either, but I can't say that. "We work together. That's it. Let's forget about Anders and enjoy the night."

Nick grumbles, and I hand him a cocktail before taking one for myself. This one is red and tastes like raspberry heaven.

I lick my lips after knocking back half the glass in one go. Nick tracks the movement, but I ignore the heat in his gaze. I can't kiss him here. Not with Anders and his family around.

I move my hips to the heavy beat of the music. "Want to dance?"

Nick shakes his head. "The music is crap and dancing isn't my thing."

"Oh. What do you want to do, then?"

"Stay for ten minutes longer and then leave?"

"I have to show my face. He's my boss, and it's good for my career to stay longer than ten minutes."

"What career?" He laughs. "It's a coffee shop. There's no room for growth."

Just like that, all interest I had in Nick dies.

Funny how working at a coffee shop wasn't a problem when we first met, but now he's judging me for it. Like he's disappointed I'm not living up to some imaginary potential he's placed on me after finding out I have a degree in engineering. It's exactly like how my parents would respond if they knew I worked at Amore.

"I'm going to the bathroom. Be right back," I say.

I leave him at the bar and make a beeline to the toilets. Is it so hard to find someone who accepts me as who I am right now instead of who they want me to be?

I'm three steps from the women's when Anders comes out of the men's door.

"How's your date going?" He stops next to me, close but not close enough.

"Perfectly fine. Thanks for asking."

"Fine means he's bad in bed."

"Not everything is about sex," I say.

"Said like someone who hasn't had an orgasm from Nick."

That comment hits a little too close to home.

"Oh stop being such a dry vagina," I say. Annoying, and the opposite of fun.

"A dry." He huffs out a laugh. "I've never heard that."

"That somehow doesn't surprise me."

"But really." He turns serious. "Do you like him?"

I sigh. "He's turned into a Judgy Julia, so no."

"What's he judging you about?"

"Oh no, you don't get to ask that and gain fuel for your 'I hate Zoey campaign.'"

"But I already bought T-shirts and everything."

I snort and he flashes me a grin.

"Seriously," he says. "What did he do?"

"Nothing I can't handle. If you'll excuse me." I step to the side to get around him, but he stops me with his hand on my arm.

I spin around. "What—"

He crashes his lips to mine, and I'm frozen in place for a millisecond until my hands find their way into his oh so touchable hair.

He pushes me further against the wall, all his hard edges flush with my soft ones. I kiss him like I'm a desperate actress starving for an Oscar, and this is the performance of a lifetime.

And oh my stars, can he *kiss*.

He kisses like he invented the word. It takes far longer than I care to admit to remember that I'm kissing my boss. In a place where anyone can see. While technically on a date with someone else.

I tear away from his lips and stare at him in shock for a heartbeat before ducking under his arm and rushing into the restroom. I lean against the closed door, breathing far too heavily.

Ruby's at the sink, thank the stars. She reapplies her blood-red lipstick and raises her eyebrows when she takes in my rumpled state.

"I'm so glad I found you," I say.

"What happened?" She talks with her mouth open, lips barely moving.

"Turns out Nick is not the one. And Anders just kissed me."

Her grin starts slowly and builds to a full-on smile. "Finally."

"No, not finally. This isn't good news. I'm here with someone else, and Anders is my boss."

"Do you even like Nick?"

"I... not really."

She gives me a look. "Aren't you tired of being nice to people who don't deserve it? You've gone out twice, it's not serious."

My alcohol laden brain likes her logic and I nod slowly. "You're right."

"Of course, I am. Tell Nick it's over and be done. You should let loose and enjoy the rest of the night."

"And what if Anders kisses me again?"

She laughs. "One night won't hurt anything."

Ruby's wrong. One night can hurt everything, but instead of arguing my point, I ask, "How's mission 'Avoid Theo' going?"

Ruby groans. "Well, now that my wing woman is back, it'll be better."

"You know, there's a fine line between hate and love."

"I'll stay on the hate side of it," she says, glaring at me.

"Come on, let's dance and hide from Anders."

"And Nick?"

"No, I'll break it off with him first."

We shimmy out of the bathroom, through the dance floor, and to the bar. I scan the space for Nick, but I don't see him. My phone buzzes.

Nick: It's not going to work out. I'll see you around.

I HOLD it up for Ruby to see and she laughs. "You dodged a bullet with that one."

I grab two orange cocktails with a huge sphere of ice inside each glass. I pass one to her and keep one for myself.

"Cheer to that," I say.

She clinks her glass against mine and we down it like a shot. Vanilla, macadamia nut, and a hint of orange explode on my tongue. It's a cool twist on an Old Fashion.

"This is really good."

"What do you expect?" Ruby rolls her eyes. "We're at Grave Digger."

"True. Come, let's dance."

After dancing to a few songs, I'm sweaty and needing some water. I yell to Ruby that I'm going to get some, and she demands I also bring back alcohol for her.

I laugh and push my way through the crowd of people

to the bar. Plopping down on the stool, I'm relieved to not be standing anymore. I order water from the bartender and debate if I should massage my feet right here in the middle of the bar. They're so close to falling off after being on them all day and now strapped in heels.

I smell him first, before the heat of his body sears my side. Anders settles into the stool next to me, and the bartender places my water down before asking what Anders wants.

I drink greedily before placing the cool glass against my neck, trying to cool down. I glance at Anders, who's watching with rapt attention. His cheeks have just a hint of redness to them, and he's the most relaxed I've seen.

"Where's your date?" he asks, not taking his gaze off the glass on my neck.

I place the water back on the bar and half turn toward him. "He left."

"Good. He listened."

"To?"

"Me."

I glare at him. "Don't tell me you ran my date off."

"You deserve better than that douche."

I should be mad, and I wait for the outrage to hit. But it doesn't. Nick wasn't the right person for me. If he got scared off by Anders, he'd dig a tunnel across the country to get away from my family and their contempt.

I sigh. "You're right."

He appears shocked by my admission, and I shrug in response. He slides me over a new cocktail, and I place it next to my water.

"The lunches?" I ask. I have to know why he did it,

why he took care of me. That's not the action of someone filled with hate.

He leans closer to me, so close our shoulders touch. "I didn't want you to get sick, and with the risk of cross contamination so high, I didn't want to take a chance."

I take a sip of the cocktail, needing the courage to say the next words. Words that make me question if I perhaps misjudged him. Without looking at him, I whisper, "Thank you."

"Anytime. Are you having fun tonight?"

I turn my face toward him. "Isn't that what I'm supposed to ask you?"

He snorts and wraps his hands around the legs of my stool before dragging it closer to him. I grip his biceps to avoid falling over. The alcohol in me rebels against my body making sudden movements.

I snap, "A little warning would've been nice."

"I quite like how we ended up."

It takes a moment to realize that my hands are still on his biceps.

Uh oh.

I pull away slowly, sad to not be up close and personal with his delicious muscles. "I blame it on the alcohol hands."

"The what?"

"You know, when you reach a certain point in the night where your hands become grabby little assholes who have a taste for hot men."

"Hot men, you say?"

I freeze, realizing my mistake a gazillion seconds too

late. "Did I say hot? I meant a taste for assholes. Like attracts like and all that."

I pick up my water and chug it.

"Do you want to dance?"

I blink at him, and blink some more. Did he ask what I think he just did? I'm not prepared to be all up on his delicious self, but my damn mouth moves without synching up with my brain and I find myself saying, "I think I can spare one dance for the birthday boy."

"How magnanimous of you."

I laugh, completely free and unchecked. He stares at me and it's his turn to blink like he's shocked.

"What?" I ask. "Do I have something on my face?"

"You're bewitching."

I don't have time to react to that compliment before he grabs my hand and leads me to the dance floor. The song switches to one with a sultry beat and is all about sex. I look to the DJ booth to find Ruby there, giving me a two-finger salute. I flip her off in return and can almost hear her cackle over the music.

Anders drags me close to him and begins to move his hips. Oh my stars, did my underwear just disintegrate at how hot he dances? He moves like he's part of one of those male striptease shows, but without it being overdone or cheesy. I can't help but imagine how he'd use those moves in the bedroom.

I drag my hands through his hair before looping my arms around his neck and straddling one of his legs to dance closer to him.

He stares deep into my eyes, and it's too much. Too

intimate somehow, as if he's trying to tell me something without saying it aloud.

I spin around and grind my hips into his erection, his huge erection. I toy with him, and he groans before squeezing my hips. He trails a finger over my hip, down my ass crack, and back. I suck in a sharp breath and shiver at the sensation.

He leans down to my ear. "Two can play that game."

He spins me back to face him, and it's the worst thing he could possibly do. A bead of sweat runs down his neck and disappears into the unbuttoned neckline of his shirt. I've never been jealous of sweat before, but here we are.

"What game?" I give him a coy smile.

He grins before crossing the metaphorical bridge between us. His nose runs along my neck, and he inhales deeply before placing a kiss on my skin.

I close my eyes and lean into the kiss. He licks my neck and kisses me again, below my ear.

A voice in the back of my head screams at me to abandon ship, but I can't remember why this is a bad idea. Not when it feels so good, and the alcohol pumping through me makes me brave. Maybe a onetime fuck is a good idea? Get it out of our systems and all that.

He tugs on my earlobe with his teeth. "Follow me."

I gulp. This is it. I've got to make a decision. Do I follow him and explore whatever is happening tonight, and maybe get an orgasm, or do I refrain?

I think back to my horoscope for the day and for once, it's an easy decision to make. The stars are promising something spicy for me today, and I'm going to take it and live for once without second guessing everything.

If Zodiac Way of Life gets me an O tonight, I've got to find a way to thank them.

He tugs on my hand, and I follow him through a dark corridor and to an elevator. He presses the top button marked with an R. When the doors open, it reveals a rooftop terrace.

Fake grass covers the ground, and it has a beachy theme. Complete with outdoor furniture, shells, a makeshift bar with sand surrounding it, and tiki torches.

He lights the torches and turns on a few heaters next to the couches and bar.

"What is this place?" I ask.

"Theo owns the building and lives on the floor below. This is his terrace, and we use it for intimate parties." He goes behind the bar. "Drink?"

I should say no, that I've had enough, but the bite of the fresh air and dancing has diminished my buzz. And I'm having too much fun to stop. Too much fun letting go of my worries, even if it's for one night. "Whatever you have back there."

He grins and pulls out multiple bottles.

"Don't tell me your drink making skills also include cocktails," I say.

He arches an eyebrow. "Who do you think helped Theo make his menu?"

"Is there anything you can't do?"

That earns me a scorching look.

"Nope." He pops his P.

Fuck me sideways and call me Susan. I'm jealous of his bottom lip with that move.

I walk behind the bar and ask, "Teach me?"

He grabs my hand and positions me ahead of him, my back flush against his front.

"Is this really necessary?" I ask.

"Definitely."

On the counter sit a bottle of bourbon, cherry liquor, lemons, and a container of maraschino cherries. He leans further into me and grabs the shaker and a measuring device.

"What are you making?"

"A cherry blossom. Cherries are my favorite."

"Really?" I grab the jar of cherries and remove one from the container. "Can you tie a knot in the stem with your mouth?"

He turns me in his arms so that I'm facing him and leans forward. He closes his mouth around the cherry between my fingers.

Oh, okay. Wow.

Is it hot out here, suddenly?

He swirls his tongue around my fingers before biting into the fruit and pulling back. All I'm left with is a stem in my hand and a burning desire to kiss him.

He chews and raises an eyebrow at me. "Can you?"

My gaze is glued to his mouth. I don't know where I was going with my question, but it's fun and flirty. It's like my old self is making an appearance tonight.

My Leo sign shines bright. To be honest, it's been shining all night and I'm only now realizing it. It's the first time since Addie died that I've caught a glimpse of who I was before grief and betrayal dimmed me.

I can't hold back now. Even if I'm playing with fire by doing something with Anders, my boss. That's a problem for tomorrow. I'm jumping back into my number sixty slutty era with two feet and, fuck, does it feel good.

I grin. "Maybe. Care to wager a bet?"

"And what would the terms be?" His gaze sparks.

"If I win, you owe me a favor."

"Agreed." He doesn't even think about it for a millisecond. "And if I win, I get to kiss you."

I flush with desire so strong, my knees almost forget to function and stop carrying my weight. My voice comes out breathier than I care to admit. "Deal."

We each hold up our stems. He counts us down from three. On go, I place the stem in my mouth and move it around. I have no idea what I'm doing, but he looks like he does. He doesn't take his gaze off my mouth the entire time. In seconds, he's removing the stem from his oh so kissable lips. It's perfectly tied.

I remove my straight one and place it on the counter.

He grins when he sees it unknotted. "You don't know how to do it, do you?"

"Maybeee."

"And yet you made the bet and agreed to the terms, knowing you'd lose."

I remain silent, not giving him the satisfaction of that admission. That once he said the terms, I was totally and completely okay with losing.

"Interesting." He licks his lips and pushes me until my back hits the bar. He sucks on my earlobe before skating his lips across my cheek and chin. I dip my head to catch his lips and he pulls back with a laugh.

"Ah, ah, ah. You're giving me one kiss and I refuse to waste it."

"Well, get on with it."

He chuckles against my skin before kissing his way down my neck, across my collarbone, and to my cleavage. I suck in a breath as he breathes over my nipples, but he drops to his knees and straightens my right leg. He drags his lips across my skin, his beard tickling, and nips my thigh.

I'm so wet, I'm afraid my dress is going to be soaked with my arousal. This is the most erotic moment of my life, and he's barely touched me. I grip the bar with both hands. He lifts my dress oh so slowly up, giving me all the time in the world to deny him.

His gaze drills into me. "You like me between your legs, don't you?"

"Depends." I lick my lips.

"On?"

"If you're any good."

He nips my clit right over my thong in reprimand, and I jerk into his mouth. "You'll grade me afterwards, so pay attention."

He rubs his nose along my inner thigh and trails a finger over the edge of my thong. "How drunk are you?"

"Don't you dare stop." I lift my hips, begging for more with my body. "I'm sober enough to give my consent. But it can only happen once, and you can't fire me because of it."

He growls, honest to fuck growls. "Once?"

"Yes, but I need to hear you say you won't fire me."

"Of course, I won't fire you. You have my word. But I disagree with the onetime condition."

"What are you, a fucking lawyer?"

He puffs out a breath, the hot air brushing against where I need him the most. "It's called compromise."

My hormones bitch-slap my brain into submission. "Fine, just don't leave me hanging."

"Don't worry. I'll take care of you." He grabs my thong and slides it down my legs so slowly I'm about to combust. He lifts the material to his nose and inhales deeply before stuffing my thong in his pant pocket.

"You're so beautiful." He slides a finger through my wetness and circles my clit before sucking his finger clean. "Tastes like cherries."

He dips his finger inside and then holds it out for me. "Taste for yourself."

I've never done something like this before. Eric was only about his own pleasure, not mine. I had to finish myself off while he cleaned up in the shower more times than I can count. And oral? Out of the question.

Without thinking it through, I lean down and suck his finger as if it were his dick. I meet his gaze and suck harder.

He squeezes my hip. "Later, first I need to give you the kiss I owe."

Holding my breath, I can't take my gaze off him as he lowers his head. My craving for him intensifies the closer he gets to my pussy.

He teases me with light kisses and nibbles on my thighs, on my lips, basically everywhere but where I need him. I lift my hips, searching for more.

He laughs. "Feeling needy, hmm?"

"If all you're going to do is tease..." I try to close my legs, but he stops me with his hands on my thighs. He grins and throws my right leg over his shoulder. The move opens me further, and he dives in, no longer playing.

He feasts on me as if I'm the best thing he's eaten all day. There's a ferocious intensity to his technique, and it's hot as fuck. He sucks with just the right amount of pressure and then spears me with his tongue.

Holy shit.

He nips at my clit, hard enough to sting, but when he laps at it, the pain turns into the best kind of pleasure. The one where it hurts so good. I'm close to seeing the stars I follow when he inserts two fingers and curls them. He does something magical with his tongue, and I'm there.

I grip his hair and shove him closer, unable to control myself.

An orgasm barrels toward me, and I'm helpless to stop it. Two point five seconds later, I come so hard my backs bows off the bar. He laps at me while I come down from my high.

I grab for him and drag him to stand. "Wow."

He grins. "I don't know how I've lived my entire life without tasting something so delicious."

I lick my lips, needing to taste him and myself on his tongue. He's so in tune with my body, he knows exactly what I want without asking. Winding his hands into my hair, he pulls me in for a kiss. He takes control the second our lips touch, deepening the kiss.

Our tongues move like a wave, in sync with each other. Tasting the mixture of myself and him turns me on even more. I never thought I'd be into it, but oh my, am I.

He pulls my bottom lip between his teeth and pulls

until it's forced to be released from his mouth. I dive back in, demanding more. Needing more.

He leans into me, and I wrap my legs around his waist. His hands automatically pull my lower back closer to the erection straining his pants. I'm so wet, I'm probably leaving a trail on his pants, but he doesn't seem to care. I undulate my hips, craving more friction.

Craving him.

He tears his mouth away from mine. "We can't. I want you completely sober when I fuck you."

"Don't make me wait."

"I want every inch of you to remember our first time. I don't want alcohol clouding your judgment."

I pout. "But I need more."

His hips move sharply against my core, as if he can't help himself. "I like you needy and begging for me."

"Then let me beg." I push him back and drop to my knees.

I reach for his zipper, but he stops me by covering my hands with his.

"You don't have to. I'm the one who lost the bet."

"But what if I want to?"

"I don't want you to regret this tomorrow."

I don't even remember why this is a bad idea, but I want to erase all memories of Eric. "Birthday blow jobs are a thing, you know."

"Are they now?"

I grab his hands and place them in my hair. "Uh-huh. And it just so happens to be your birthday. I also didn't get you a present." I unzip his pants and look him in the eye. "So, happy birthday."

His glorious dick springs free. He doesn't wear under-wear, and that knowledge makes my core clench. The thin material of his pants was the only thing separating us from joining. He's thick and long. I don't know how it's going to fit inside me, but I can't wait to try.

I kiss his tip and lick down to his balls before sucking them into my mouth. His hands work their way into my hair, but he doesn't pull my head and take over. He just holds me while I suck his length down and swallow him until he's in as far as I can go. I gag and come up for air before doing it again and again.

"You're so beautiful with my dick in your mouth. Look at you, struggling to take my length. I can't wait to take you in every way possible."

I moan at the image he presents, and he lets out a whispered fuck. I moan again and suck him as if he's the best dick I've ever sucked. And he is. I hated giving Eric oral, was always waiting for it to end. But now? I want to stay here forever.

"I'm going to come." He tries to pull away, but my hands go to his ass and pull him closer to me.

"Are you sure?" he asks.

I hum my agreement.

He groans, "That's it. Swallow all of me. Don't you dare miss a drop."

His hips surge forward, and I do as told and swallow everything he gives me. The second he's done; he pulls me up and sits me back on the bar.

He kisses the life out of me, and I melt into him. But eventually, the cold of the metal bar seeps into my bare ass. So cold it burns.

I can't keep my teeth from chattering.

"Fuck." He wraps me in his arms and lifts me as if I weigh nothing.

He brings me to the couch, points the heater directly to me and piles fuzzy blankets on me. My shivers stop and he looks far too pleased with himself. He sits next to me and silence springs between us.

It's awkward as fuck. I just had the best sexual experience of my life... with my boss. The same boss who maybe hates me but also does sweet things for me?

It's confusing as fuck, and now I don't know how to act around him.

"Do you want that drink?" he asks.

I need a billion bottles of liquor, but instead I say, "Sure."

He makes the drinks we abandoned and settles next to me.

"Happy birthday." I clink my glass against his.

"This is shaping up to be the best birthday I've ever had."

"How so?"

"Because you're here."

I laugh. "You did not just say that."

"It's true, though," he says seriously.

"Yeah, right."

He sips his drink, and I copy his movement to avoid the still serious look in his eye. He can't be telling the truth, right?

"This is so good," I say, trying to break the tension between us.

He takes another sip. "I've tasted better." He gives me a

heated look and stares directly at the junction between my thighs.

I hit his chest. "I could report you to HR for inappropriate behavior."

"Might as well add to the report that I'll be dreaming about your taste on my lips and the sounds you make when you come."

I cover my eyes with a hand and groan. "Don't tell me you've lost your filter now that we gave each other an orgasm."

He pulls my hand away and kisses my wrist. "Did I ever have a filter?"

"No, you haven't." I clear my throat. "We should go back to your party, I'm sure they're missing you."

"If that's what you want."

No, it's not really what I want. But regret is starting to rear its asshole head and I'm nothing if not good at fleeing when shit gets tough.

I stand and he guides me to the elevator with a hand on my lower back. Once inside, I lean against the wall, and check the time on my phone. Fuck, work starts in three hours. I should sleep. I don't think I can make it through a full day after pulling an all-nighter.

"Any chance you'll close Amore tomorrow?" I ask.

He presses the button for the bar and leans against the wall next to me, so close our shoulders touch. "I should. But I only close on Christmas."

"Really?"

He nods.

"Why?" I ask.

He cringes and looks away from me to the wall. He's

silent so long I'm about to tell him to forget I asked, but then he whispers, "I'm afraid it'll fail."

My heart squeezes at his admission. It's exactly the kind of pressure Addie put on herself, probably the same type of sustained pressure that caused her heart attack.

I grab his face and kiss him hard. Once. Twice. I'll definitely regret this, but I can add it to the list of regrets I'll be making in the morning. It feels wrong somehow to stop celebrating right now and end the night on such a morose note.

So, when the elevator doors open to Grave Digger, where half the people are still dancing the night away, I pull Anders into the fray and make him smile again.

CHAPTER 15

"The stars are playing nurse and advising some TLC advice today, Leo. Take care of your health and take a break, or else you're going to be down for the count. Don't be afraid to lean on a friend so they can help you through it all. Here's to a speedy recovery. Love always, ZWOL."

THE ALARM BLARES through the room, and I jolt awake and sit upright. An arm pulls me back into what I thought was a pillow but turns out to be Anders's chest. His bare chest.

Oh fuck.

I look under the sheet covering us and yup. We're both naked and hello there massive erection. It's like a honing beacon, begging for my attention.

How we ended up in the same bed together, I don't remember. I don't even know where we are.

But okay, this is okay. I'm sure we didn't have sex. He said he wanted to wait until we were both sober, and I only accepted because I knew I wouldn't agree if I were sober.

I reach down between my legs and only my arousal coats my fingers. Whew, that's a good sign.

"Getting started without me?" Anders squeezes my hip and opens one eye. He's adorably rumpled and sleepy.

"I... did we have sex?"

His eyes widen. "You don't remember?"

"It becomes hazy once we rejoined the party. Just tell me, did we?"

He flips our position, so he's hovering over me. My legs go around his waist.

What the fuck legs?

He flexes his hips, and his morning wood brushes against my core. "Trust me, if I'd fucked you, you'd feel it for days."

I let out a breathless noise, part moan, part relief. My pussy has rejoined my slut era in full force. Unfortunately, she only wants Anders.

Traitor.

I unhook my legs and push against his chest. He rolls off me instantly.

"What's wrong?"

I search the ground for my dress, but I can't find it. "Where are we?"

"Theo's place, just above the bar." Anders gets out of bed and hands me my dress. "How about we try that again? What's wrong?"

I duck my head and busy myself with getting the dress on. "This was supposed to be a onetime thing, and onetime only. Sure, we didn't have sex, but we can't take it further. You're my boss, and I can't jeopardize my income because my hussy of a pussy wants more."

He grins. "I'm glad your hussy of a pussy is on my side."

"This isn't a time for jokes."

"I agree, but whatever's between us isn't over." He pulls me into his arms and kisses me like it's a promise. Like now that we've crossed over into sexy times, he has the right to make such statements.

I blink myself out of a daze and say, "We're... almost friends? What if we focus on becoming real friends first?"

"Friends?" He snorts and hands me my shoes and purse. "You could never be just a friend."

I flinch at his words. They hurt more than I expected. Of course, he won't be my friend. I'm messy Zoey to him. A spoiled princess and burden.

I make a beeline for the door. I need to be out of here ASAP. Hell, I'll take a fire escape if it will get me out faster than the elevator.

"Zoey," Anders bellows from the bedroom. "Don't you dare get into that elevator."

Ha, at least he's got to get dressed before following me. That'll give me enough time to make an escape. Ruby tiptoes out of a room down the hall and rushes to my side.

I raise an eyebrow and look from her to another closed door down the hall. "Did you..."

"Nothing happened," she says quickly. Too quickly.

Nothing happened, my ass. I press the down button a million times, chanting, "Come on, come on."

Ruby fidgets and chants with me. Looks like we're both escaping Watson men this morning.

Finally, the doors open, and I hit the close door button nonstop. Anders jumps into the elevator just before they close.

I sigh at the ceiling. Really? Can't a girl catch a fucking break, stars?

"Morning," Anders murmurs to Ruby before backing me up until I reach the wall.

"I'll just pretend I'm not here," Ruby quips.

She turns her back to us and puts her hands over her ears.

I'd laugh, but I've got more important things to focus on. Like the asshole in front of me.

I snap, "Don't pretend to care all of a sudden now that we've swapped some O's. As you just confirmed, we aren't even friends."

He places his forearm over my head and leans against it, caging me in. His other hand sneaks up and wraps around my throat in a sexy as fuck, dominant move. "I've been caring this entire time. Be serious, we can't be just friends when we have this much chemistry between us. We're more."

As if to prove his statement right, he leans down and kisses me so hard, I forget the argument I wanted to make. Hell, I even forget my own name.

He only pulls away when we reach the ground level for the bar. I'm gaping like an idiot when Ruby exits with a low whistle.

"As hot as that just was," Ruby says, "we need to get to work."

Anders glares at her, and I'm over here trying to

pretend like my brain didn't just rewire itself with that kiss. I duck and sneak under his arm and go to Ruby.

Anders says to Ruby, "Stay together, let me know when you've arrived at Amore." He turns his gaze to me. "I'll be seeing you later, we have an appointment."

Oh fuck, I forgot we're supposed to bake the first ideas for the menu. I don't respond and speed walk away from Grave Digger like my ass is on fire.

Ruby rushes to catch up to me and says, "Well, well, well."

"We're not discussing this."

"Oh yes we are."

"Fine, then let's discuss what you were doing last night."

She glares at me. "Okay, so last night is off limits. But tell me one thing, though. What appointment was he talking about?"

"We're working on a concept together for the new shop."

"Why didn't you tell me?" She stops walking. "Why didn't he tell me?"

"I… shit, you're right. I'm sorry. I've been so caught up in working on it that I didn't think." Really, I was following Anders's lead. It seemed like he wanted to keep it a secret, but I never intended to hurt Ruby.

"I accept your apology, but don't keep something like that from me again."

"Agreed," I say easily.

"So, what's the concept?"

"Zodiac signs paired with food."

She laughs. "No shit."

"Seriously." I spend the rest of the walk to Amore describing the idea and Ruby bounces on her feet in excitement.

"I can't believe Anders agreed to it," she says.

"I know, but it didn't take much convincing."

She gives me a look I can't decipher. "Hmm."

"What?"

"Nothing."

I glare at her. "Just tell me."

She laughs and unlocks Amore. "Anders has never been one to rely on other people, well anyone besides his family."

Her statement echoes what Anders mentioned before. Why does he have such a hard time relying on people? I want to ask her about it, but she's already handing me a spare flannel to cover our outfits from last night and changing the subject. Damn. I guess I'll need to get info on him the old-fashioned way—by actually talking to him, which is lame.

"Please tell me I'm not the only one still drunk," she says.

"Of course not. I think we've drunk enough to keep us tipsy for the next week."

The sweet and sickly scent of alcohol coating my pores makes me slightly nauseous every time I move. I'm seriously debating rubbing some coffee beans all over myself to help.

We half-ass getting the shop ready, but it's fun to open while drunk rather than hungover. So that's a win. Ruby makes me a coffee and demands I drink the entire thing to help me through the day. I need food, but I'll have to wait until lunch to get something.

An hour after my lunch break and a sandwich from a food truck, my hangover descends. Every second after that hurts. My head from all the noise in the shop. My body begs for more sleep. My liver raises an angry fist in the air for treating it so poorly. And lastly my stomach and intestines, who want me to throw up and have alcohol shits all at the same time, also striking me with nonstop cramps.

Lovely.

Ruby doesn't look hungover at all but keeps shooting me concerned looks after every customer we serve.

After ten minutes, she texts furiously on her phone for a few minutes before saying, "Why don't you go home early?"

"It's fine, I'm just hungover."

"You're scaring the customers away. I've got it, seriously. You can always owe me one later."

"But—"

She points to the door. "Now."

I nod, grab my things, and leave.

The cold air does nothing to help my nauseous state. With cramps knifing through my abdomen, I hunch over. I stumble up the stairs of my apartment and collapse onto the couch.

Hangovers have always hit me hard, but this might be the worst one. Maybe it's due to the lack of sleep, but it's like my body is shutting down. Exactly like I feel when I've been glutened.

Oh shit.

Lunch.

I knew the food truck was a bad idea, but I haven't gotten sick since moving here and I thought it would be okay. But I'm realizing now that might because Anders made all my food, or I ate prepackaged certified gluten-free things.

This isn't a hangover.

Shit, shit, shit.

Today will be the worst. I'll oscillate between nausea and diarrhea until it levels out to only diarrhea. The diarrhea will hang around for a few days and it'll look like I'm eight months pregnant for at least a week after this.

I squeeze my eyes tight. Why stars, are you doing this to me now? Is this the mysterious sickness ZWOL alluded to? Because fucking hell it would've been nice to know before I got lunch. I just thought it meant I was going to be hungover.

Taking deep breaths, I try to keep the nausea at bay. Thank the stars I'm alone. It's what I'm used to when dealing with this. My parents never tried to comfort me, they just left me alone to deal with it all.

Hours pass.

Between the nausea and diarrhea, I'm wiped out. I've just got to wait until my body finishes rebelling against me.

There's a banging on my door.

I ignore it and curl into a ball.

"Zoey, open up."

Oh fuck, it's Anders. I forgot to message him and cancel. My phone's still in my purse by the door, probably dead by now.

I groan and shuffle to the front door. I talk through the closed door. "I'm really sick right now, I'm sorry for not cancelling sooner."

There's a pause.

"What's wrong? Do you need a doctor?"

"No, I'll be fine. I just need some time for it all to pass."

"Can I come in?"

I jerk back from the door. "Why?"

"Because I want to make sure you're okay. I can run to the store and get some medicine?"

There's no medicine that'll help, but I could use some crackers for whenever I can eat again. I run my hands over my face and unlock the door. Anders immediately helps me back to the couch.

"How can I help?" he asks.

"You can't. I've been glutened."

"This is from eating gluten?"

I nod and close my eyes. "The worst has passed. I need to sleep it off."

He grabs the kitchen towel and wets it before placing it on the back of my neck. It feels like heaven. I'm not sure how he knew that trick for nausea, or even how he knew I'm nauseous. But it doesn't matter, not when such a simple thing can feel so good.

He gets up again and hands me a glass of water. I take a couple sips and he rubs my back.

"You don't have to stay," I say. "We can meet tomorrow. I should be okay by then." Well, okay enough.

He cocks his head to the side. "You don't like people taking care of you, huh?"

"I guess I'm not used to it."

"What about your parents? When you were young?"

I shake my head. "They just left me to it. Never really accepted my diagnosis and if I did get glutened, they'd blame me. Said it was my fault for not being careful."

Same with Eric, but we didn't live together during our relationship. When I said I needed a couple days to deal with my sickness, he left me to it. Anders probably thinks the same thing as them. I'm stupid for trusting the food truck, it's my fault. I let out a shaky breath.

"Well, you're not alone anymore."

I swallow down the emotion building in my throat. "I did this to myself. I deserve to be alone."

"No one deserves to be alone."

"But it's been ingrained in me to triple check. And yet I didn't. I was distracted and—"

He cups my cheek with his hand. "It's okay to make mistakes. You don't have to beat yourself up over them."

He's right. I'm an asshole to myself. Anytime I make a mistake I dwell on it for weeks, months, or even years. Worst of all, it's become so ingrained in my personality that I've never questioned it. It's just part of who I am. But he talks like not being an asshole to myself is possible and that there's another way.

"Do you beat yourself up over mistakes?" I ask.

"I used to. But I've been getting better at focusing on the learnings from them and moving on."

"You might have to teach me how you do that."

"Anytime." He gives me a soft smile.

His phone buzzes in his pocket and he takes it out. "Where's your phone? Ruby's been trying to reach you."

"Purse. By the door."

He gets it and hands it to me. It's dead. I plug it into the charger and wait the few minutes for it to turn on. There are twenty messages from Ruby, all asking if I'm okay and threatening to send Anders if I don't answer.

There are three from Anders, asking where I am.

I look up at Anders. "Did Ruby send you?"

"Of course, she was worried and so was I."

> Me: I'm fine. Sorry my phone died. Thanks a lot for sending Anders while I'm having explosive diarrhea.

> Ruby: It was an emergency, you weren't answering. Are you okay? Can I get you anything?

> Me: Anders is refusing to leave.

> Her: He's so whipped.

> Me: You must not know him very well, then.

> Her: *voice note*

I press play and it's her cackling like what I said is the funniest thing she's ever heard.

> Me: Oh, fuck off. Just wait until you get sick next time. I'll send Theo over to help you.

Ruby: That'll never happen, I don't get sick.

I SEND her a voice recording of me cackling. Anders laughs and our gazes catch and hold.

"Let me run to the store and get some things for you before it gets too late. Do you need anything in particular?"

"Some crackers would be great."

"Can I take your keys?"

"Yeah, they're on the counter."

"Be right back."

He lets himself out and I scroll on my phone to pass the time. When he returns, he sets down a bundle of plastic bags on the counter.

He pulls out a bouquet from one of the bags and brings the flowers to me. They're sunflowers dotted with white carnations.

I inhale the scent and say, "They're beautiful."

"Do you have a vase?"

"No, but you can use a cup."

He nods and prepares the flowers. He keeps them on the kitchen counter, and it's the first sign of life in this place besides the Christmas tree.

He brings more bags over and places them on my lap. "I did some research, and every site recommended bone broth, sauerkraut, Epsom bath salt, and peppermint tea to support healing after getting glutened."

I peek in the bag and oh wow. He got me everything

he just named as well as loads of gluten-free food. Everything from crackers to cereal to readymade meals from a brand recognize as safe.

I'm speechless. No one has ever done something like this for me, not even Addie, and she's the baseline I compare all relationships to.

I swallow back the building tears and take a steadying breath. "I… thank you. This is too much."

"It's nothing." He brings the bag back to the kitchen and unloads the new food into the pantry and refrigerator.

"Did you do anything fun today on your day off?"

"Had lunch with my family, took it easy." After he finishes unloading, he comes back to the couch with one more plastic bag. "I bought one more thing when I was out. But I want you to close your eyes first."

I roll said eyes. "Dramatic much?"

He grins. "Very."

"Fine." I close my eyes and hold out my hands.

There's a rustle of a plastic bag and he places what feels like a cable in my hand. I snap my eyes open and stare down at the string of Christmas tree lights.

"I thought your tree could use a little something."

"Thank you." I clutch the lights. "But no more. You've bought way too much."

"Why are you uncomfortable?"

"Because I have literally nothing, and this just reminds me how far I've fallen." And it feels more than friendship and straight into relationship territory.

"Fine, I promise to not buy you anything for a week."

He says it so seriously, I laugh. He smiles.

"Are you willing to reconsider my friend request?" I ask.

"Are you willing to reconsider being more than friends?"

"I can't be in a relationship, not right now."

"Why not?" he asks.

"Because I need to work on me. My last relationship ruined my life in every way possible. I need a break from men."

He doesn't even miss a beat and says, "That's fine, I can respect that and wait."

"No, you're not getting it. I'm not worth waiting on. I'm a failure."

"Hey, don't talk about yourself like that, especially when you're wrong. When I see you as..." He pauses and his gaze roams my face.

I mentally fill in adjectives like messy, stupid, a waste of space. But instead of any of those words, he says, "I see a woman who's clever, intelligent, funny, and kind. Oh, and let's not forget gorgeous."

I blink, and blink again, shocked he said something nice while sober. "Are you sure you didn't hit your head between yesterday and today?"

He snorts. "If it makes it easier to hear, than sure, pretend that happened."

"Why do you hide this side of you from everyone?" The question pops out and I lift my hand in the air. "Wait, forget I asked that."

He stares at my Christmas tree and says, "It keeps people away. No one ever stays, so there's no point in letting them in."

My heart aches for him. I'm about to ask more, but he stands. "I should get going, but to answer your question, I accept being just friends... for now."

His words, his little disclaimer, does something to me. It feels an awful lot like hope, but I don't want to look too deep into it.

"Deal," I say.

"See you tomorrow?"

"Definitely."

"Good night, Zoey."

"Good night, and thanks again for well, everything."

"Anytime."

After he leaves, I lay back down on the couch.

I lost everything because of Eric, and I don't want to go through something like that ever again. It's a special kind of torture to want someone but not let yourself have them due to fear. It's not as simple as snapping my fingers and getting my way. I wish it were, but that's not real life.

And I need to remember that.

CHAPTER 16

"*T*he stars are playing therapist today, Leo. It's time to reach out to your family, hug it out, and let go of any lingering feuds. This could be your chance to work through past conflicts and misunderstandings to get that warm fuzzy feeling back in your heart. Good luck. Love always, ZWOL."

ANDERS TEXTS me first thing to take the morning off and to come in after lunch.

And thank the stars, because today is a doozy of a horoscope.

No matter how many times I reread it, it remains the same. There's also no wiggle room in its interpretation.

Fuck, I'm going to have to do this.

I spin my phone on the couch and debate if I should try Lilly or mom. Lilly would be the easy choice because I can always ask about the wedding. And if Lilly doesn't answer, she most likely won't call me back.

Mom on the other hand... I don't know what to say to her. What to talk about.

So, Lilly it is. I pull up her contact information. My finger hovers over the call button for so long that it begins to shake. Ugh, this is ridiculous. It's my sister. I can manage a sixty second call.

Squeezing my eyes shut, I press the button. Part of me hopes she doesn't answer.

"What is it?" she asks.

I clear my throat. "Hey, didn't think you'd answer."

"Didn't think you'd call."

"I... how are you?" I wince at the question. It's stupid of me to ask that and give her an opening to berate me for destroying her dreams. Again.

"Fine."

She doesn't elaborate.

"Excited for the holidays?" I push on, at this point praying this conversation ends quickly. Christmas is always a big deal in our family, and I'm devastated no one invited me.

"Sure." She says it with sarcasm.

"Come on, Lilly." I groan. "I made one mistake and you've cut me out of your life? We're sisters. Family. How is it so easy to hate me?"

She scoffs. "How is it so easy for you to pretend nothing happened?"

"I'm not pretending, but it's also not entirely my fault. We all trusted Eric. It's not like you didn't all love him too."

"You should've known, should've seen him for who he really was before it was too late. Before we all suffered for it. You're sorely mistaken if you think mom and dad can bounce back from this. They lost their retirement fund because of you. How could you be so stupid?"

I suck in a sharp breath. Each word crushes me into the couch, but I take the beating. It's what I deserve.

I whisper, "I'm sorry. I don't know how to make it up to you all, but I will."

"Don't bother."

"How can you say that?"

"You made it easy to not want you around. I would've uninvited you from the wedding, but it'd take the spotlight away from me. Everyone would be talking about you and want to know where you are. But it's my day. You've already taken so much; you don't get to take that too."

Ouch. I'm a pity invite to keep the attention on her. I shouldn't be surprised. I've seen Lilly cut people out of her life for chewing too loud, but I never thought in a million years she'd direct that toward me.

"I understand." But I don't, not really. I need to find a way to pay my parents back their retirement fund.

She sighs. "I've got to go."

She hangs up on me before I have the chance to utter another word.

I need more money, and there's no way I can earn that at the coffee shop. My parents were planning to retire next year, and now it's not possible. There's no way they can earn back everything they lost, even if they continue working for another ten years.

They had plans with that money. Travel they've been putting off, a wedding to pay for, or two if I ever found someone, and to enjoy doing nothing. They deserve it, and it's all gone now.

Because of me.

But worst of all, I didn't just lose their retirement fund, Lilly's wedding budget, and my own savings, but also money we got from Addie's death and selling her bakery.

I lost her life's savings.

I lost it all.

* * *

WHY ZWOL WANTED me to reach out to Lilly, I'll never know. But I've been in a funk all day thanks to that call and now I've got to spend the evening with Anders working on the menu idea. At least I'll get to bake.

Anders waits for me on the sidewalk and comes to my side when he spots me. He lives in a two story, Victorian home four blocks away from Amore. It's cute, with a wraparound porch in the front. But it's the color that causes me to cover my mouth to contain my giggle.

His house is lilac. Which is pretty, but not something I'd ever expect of his house.

He gives me a sideways glance when we walk up to the front door. "Are you laughing at my home?"

"I would never. Just wasn't expecting the color."

"It adds character."

"That it does."

He removes his shoes by the front door, and I follow suit. I take a moment to get my bearings and I'm shocked. It's an open floor plan. The kitchen, living, and dining room flow into each other so seamlessly. I wouldn't be surprised if it was custom-built. He went for a rustic feel inside and took advantage of the wooden floors to complete the look. It's all creams and browns, and it's gorgeous.

"Oh, wow," I say, taking everything in.

But how does he afford such a place? I didn't think Amore was this lucrative.

He turns to me. "You like?"

"Um, I love. You might have to force me out of here."

He mumbles something under his breath, but I don't catch it. Before I can ask, he goes to the state-of-the-art kitchen and waves a hand at the counter where all the baking ingredients I asked for are displayed. It's the kind of kitchen I'd love to have. It even outdoes my kitchen in Atlanta, which I was proud of.

Anders grabs a mixing bowl and passes it to me while I open up the bag of sugar and gluten-free flour.

"Which one do you want to work on first?" I ask. "Crêpes or the blood orange pastry?"

"My mom always told me ladies first. So, let's start with your sign and the crêpes."

"Right." I open the photo app on my phone and find the one I took of Addie's recipe.

I haven't been able to stomach baking much this past year. A pie here or brownies there. Eric discouraged it, saying it was too unhealthy and that we'd both get fat if we ate desserts regularly.

And now, I get to bake, to return to the one thing that's always been there for me besides numbers. I haven't made her crêpes in a year, not since she died. But as soon as I crack the eggs into the bowl, the recipe comes back to me as if it never left. I don't even need to look at my phone.

Anders starts preparing the bacon and asks, "Have you ever made this recipe before?"

"Just every week for years."

"Your mom's?"

"No. My aunt's. She owned a bakery, and we'd make them every Sunday morning together for the family when I was growing up."

"In Atlanta?"

"No, in a small town near Charlotte. That's where my family still lives."

"I'll need to visit her bakery one day," he says.

"That'll be hard." I duck my head and focus on mixing the ingredients.

"Why's that?"

"Because she died."

The only sound in the kitchen is the oven kicking on and my whisk hitting the sides of the bowl.

"It happened on Christmas Eve." I slam my mouth shut after saying that detail. There's no need to get into it or how I don't want to think about how the one-year anniversary is coming up or that I'll be alone for it.

"But you're not taking Christmas off—you won't be with your family?

"Definitely not. We're not... we don't..." I take a deep breath and search for the right words. Finally, I settle on, "They hate me, so there'll be no more invites to the holidays."

Anders pauses at the oven with the sheet pan in hand. "I find it hard to believe your own family hates you."

"You have no idea."

"Okay." He turns to me. "Try me. What could they possible hate *you* for?"

The way he emphasizes "you" doesn't escape my notice. Like he finds it inconceivable that someone could hate me, which is ironic coming from him.

"My sister's getting married in the middle of the week because it was the cheapest day. I did that." I point at my chest. "I ruined their lives and crushed their dreams. Kind of hard not to hate someone after that."

"That's a lot of blame to put on one person."

I brush off his words. "It's well deserved."

"I somehow doubt that. Wait, does this mean you're going to spend Christmas Day by yourself?"

"You don't have a crêpe pan by chance, do you?" I ask, avoiding his question.

I expect him to pull out a frying pan, not a crêpe pan, along with a wooden T-stick to spread the batter out. Oh wow. Okay, he doesn't do things half assed.

I pour the first batch on the pan and ask, "Can you whip some heavy cream into stiff peaks?"

He places a bowl in the freezer for a few minutes before getting to work.

When he's done, and the mixer turns off, he asks, "Why don't you come home with me?"

I freeze and look around. I say slowly, "I thought this was your house?"

If he is trying to pawn this house off as his and it's really someone else's, I'm going to kick him in the balls.

He snorts. "I meant to my parent's house. For Christmas."

Oh. OH.

"Are you inviting me out of pity?" I don't want to be a charity case, and this is totally a pity invite. He hears my sob story and boom, Christmas invite with the fam.

"Not at all. It'll be fun, and my mom loves cooking."

A family gathering, fun? Yeah, that must be an exaggeration. They're bearable at best. Or at least they used to be when Addie and I would just get drunk and chat in a corner. While dad watched TV and mom and Lilly would fuss over the meal. A completely gluten meal. Even though Addie hated cooking, she'd always come over with a plate full of food just for me.

"Is this a friend invite? Wait, do you normally invite friends to Christmas?"

"I do, and this invite is me being a good friend, at the very least."

"And at most?"

He turns serious. "You're not ready to hear that."

I lift my eyebrow, unimpressed with that statement. "Oh, really? Well, I'll have you know—"

"Just say yes."

"But—"

"It's not a big deal, and if you hate it, we can leave at any time."

"Will Ruby be there, too?"

"No, she's visiting her sister in San Diego."

"Oh." I carefully lift the crêpe off the pan and onto a plate.

"Come on, you know you want to come."

I never needed a friend to invite me to a holiday

dinner. Until now. I was hoping I could spend the day with Ruby but looks like that option is not possible.

If this is really him being a good friend, then why now?

"Okay, fine. But if it's awkward, I'm going to blame you."

He laughs. "I wouldn't expect anything else."

Each crêpe has a different filling for us to try. Once it's all cooked, I place them on different plates, and we sit at the counter in the middle of the kitchen.

Anders places an affogato, topped with whipped cream, in front of me and says, "Let's start with a dairy free vanilla ice cream."

"Can you get us a knife and a fork?" I ask. We're going to need to cut these in half to share.

He grabs one knife and one fork from the drawer.

I roll my eyes. "Seriously?"

"What?" He smirks. "Everything's in the dishwasher."

He cuts a piece of the first crêpe, the one with bacon and jalapeño jam, and holds it out for me to bite.

I close my lips around the fork, and he doesn't take his gaze off me as I chew and swallow. I take a sip of the drink to experience how all the flavors work together.

The hot crêpe and cold ice cream make the best sensation in my mouth. I love it. I don't even need to try the others to know this is the one.

He waits until I'm finished before taking his own bite. He takes a sip of my drink, his gaze never straying from my own. There's something sensual about sharing food with him. About having our gazes locked while we try the food we made.

When he's finished, he cuts me a bite of crêpe number two and feeds me again. And we repeat the process for number three. Neither of us speaks, lost in the moment.

Well, he might be lost in the food, but I'm lost in him. In the way his throat bobs when he drinks. Or how the remnants of ice cream make his lips oh so lickable. Or how he likes to feed me first and watches my expression with rapt attention.

"What do you think?" he asks once we finish all three options.

"You first."

"You're so fucking talented. I'd never know these crêpes are gluten free."

"I earned those seven fingers, huh?" I say, reflecting back on when I was listing all the reasons I should work on this and said I was an amazing person.

"And more." He grins. "My favorite is number one."

"Same."

I stare longingly at the leftover food, and he laughs and says, "Eat whatever you want. I'll finish what's left."

I grab the rest of number one to eat and push the plate with two and three toward him. "Shall we work on your pairing now?"

He nods and eats two while going to the fridge and shows me some pre-made, gluten-free pastry. "Thought we could use this as a shortcut."

"Good idea."

Anders helps me peel and section the blood orange and gets out three small pots for us to use. I want to season them differently. One with just sugar, one spiced heavily, and one spiced lightly. He takes over stirring duty for two of them and I stir the last one.

Our shoulders brush every time I stir. Okay, distraction needed, because right now all I can think about is Anders.

"You have a fully stocked kitchen," I say.

"I like to cook."

"Because of your mom?"

"Yeah, she's obsessed with all things cooking, but keeps it as a hobby. We've all tried to convince her to open a restaurant, but she insists she's happy owning the Christmas tree farm you visited."

Ahh, so that's why he was working there that day.

"Does Theo help out, too?" I ask.

"Nature's not his thing, but Hayden's there regularly. He's the youngest."

"Have I met Hayden? I don't remember meeting him at your birthday."

"He was in Singapore on my birthday, but yes, you've met him. He helped you with your tree."

"I see." Because that means he was either watching the security footage or it was notable enough for his brother to mention it to him. I'm not sure which would be better.

"What about your sister? Is she younger or older?" he asks.

"Younger by four years."

"How long has she been with her fiancé?"

"Too long."

He laughs. "Not a fan, I take it?"

"There's nothing wrong with him per se, just seems like Lilly likes him more than he likes her."

"He's not the man you'd chose for her." He says it like a statement of fact, and he's right.

"She seems happy. So who am I to judge?"

He frowns. "Seems happy?"

I used to think we were close, but after she cut me out of her life like it was the easiest thing in the world, I'm not sure if we ever were or if it was all one sided. Instead of explaining any of that, I say, "I'm not the best judge of character, so don't take my word for it."

He opens his mouth to say something, but I cut him off and say, "Let's have some of these with a hole cut out to show the filling and others where the pastry fully covers it."

He gives me a look, like he knows that I'm trying to distract him from the conversation, but I don't care. He turns on some music while we fill the pastry and put them in the oven.

I go to the sink to start washing the dishes, but he places his hand on my arm and says, "Leave it. I'll take care of it later."

"You sure?"

"You want something to drink? I've got gluten-free beer, cocktails, or wine."

"I'll have whatever you're having."

He grabs two beers from the fridge and passes me one. He definitely didn't have gluten-free beer lying around for himself. He bought it for me, and I should be surprised, but I'm not. Now I know Anders makes all my lunches to ensure they're gluten free.

"You still hungry?" he asks.

I shake my head, my stomach too full of butterflies to

want more food. I also don't know how to spend time around him if we're not working or kissing.

"Relax, I'm not going to bite." He spears me with a look. "Unless you ask."

I gulp. "Want to watch something?" I wave my hand toward the TV.

His lips twitch and he says, "Get comfortable. I have a surprise for you."

I scoot back on his brown suede couch and chug the beer. It's a good couch. Deep enough where there's space to bring my feet up on the cushion and be comfortable.

Anders returns and lifts something to my mouth. "Try this."

My lips close around the food and his finger. "Oh, wow." Layers of caramel and peanut butter surround a nut stuffed date. "That's better than sex."

His gaze heats with a hunger so deep it borders on starvation. "Then the guy's not doing it right."

"And how would you rate your skills?" Ugh, filter where have you gone? "Wait, forget I said that. That was inappropriate."

"I think we threw inappropriate out the window on my birthday." He runs his thumb under my bottom lip. "And if I remember correctly, we made a deal to have sex while sober."

"We did no such thing."

"Hmm." He grips the nape of my neck and massages the base of my skull. "You sure about that?"

"I…"

I blame it on the bacon. He must've put something in it because I'm turning into a sex crazed person who can't control myself. Sex has never been anything to write home about, and maybe years of being unsatisfied are boiling to the surface at the worst fucking time in human history. That must be it. It's just been too long since I've had the D.

My brain screams at my body to abort mission, but my body doesn't get the memo. Instead, I lean back into his hand, loving how he touches me. Loving everything he does.

He tilts my face up to his. Our gazes lock and hold.

Sex with him would be the definition of mind blowing. But sex will also blur the lines between us, well, more than they already have. I can't risk getting involved with him. My heart is full of so many holes at this point, I don't have much to give. He deserves more.

There's a magnetism to him I can't quite explain, an allure that beckons me closer with every interaction. He's full of dichotomies and maybe that's what draws me to him. He's in the service industry but doesn't love people. He's modest, but super talented. He's disciplined in his work and thrives on routine, but spontaneous in his free time and travels the world. He's so interesting on so many levels, it's no wonder I'm hooked.

I break our gaze and straighten on the couch. "Maybe I should go."

"Don't you dare walk away right now."

I raise an eyebrow. "Or what?"

"I'll punish you."

I squeeze my thighs together at the threat. "You think that's a deterrent?" I motion for him to come closer, and he does. "That's an encouragement."

He waves a hand toward the door. "By all means, walk away then."

I laugh and he lifts his hands in a placating motion. "If I keep my hands to myself, will you stay?"

"And your lips."

"Maybe you're the one who should have the nickname Killjoy Zoey," he pouts.

"I guess so." I laugh.

"Fine. Let's watch a movie and relax. We still have thirty minutes before the timer goes off."

"Fine." I may or may not say it like a petulant child. I'm happy he's respecting my new boundaries, but also... not.

"Don't be afraid to show your excitement."

"Movies don't get me excited," I say, to cover my disappointment.

"And what does?"

"Food, alcohol, and sex."

"Noted. I'll be sure to add all the above to the day we have sex, and blow your mind."

I hit him in the chest, but he grabs my hand and holds onto it. "You never said I couldn't talk about sex or all the things I want to do to you."

I sigh and look at the ceiling. "You're insufferable."

"You love it."

And yeah, I kind of do.

CHAPTER 17

"*H*ey there, Leo! Time for a cosmic dare. Drop your sorrows like a hot potato and dive headfirst into a day of unadulterated fun with your beloved crew. Take an amusement park ride for your soul. Life's too short for tears when you can create memories that make your heart roar with joy. So, put on your party hat and show the universe how to embrace pure, unbridled fun like the true Leo you are. Love always, ZWOL."

ANDERS and I slip into a rhythm. Work at Amore in the day and recipe pairing at his home in the evening. We follow the baking up with movie nights that always seem to linger too long. At first, he'd walk me home after the movie, but the past few nights we've fallen asleep on his too-comfortable-for-its-own-good-couch. No stolen kisses. No swapping of O's.

He was serious when he said nothing more would happen besides flirting. Which is fine. Grand. Nice, even.

Now that I know he follows through on his promises, it's a little less scary to consider exploring what's between us. If he says I won't lose my job, then I shouldn't. But starting a relationship with him would be a distraction from my goal—to repair my relationship with my family. And I'm confident I'd drown in him and never resurface, which means getting involved with him would be risky.

But none of that matters today. Not when it's Christmas Eve and the anniversary of Addie's death. I'm regretting the promise to go to Anders's parents, especially when all I want to do is curl up on my couch and cry.

When we're ten minutes away from the house, according to the navigation, I ask, "You sure it's okay I come?"

Even though my horoscope today is in line with spending time with friends, I'm still nervous as hell.

Anders says, "Yes."

"Maybe I should—"

"No."

"But you don't—"

He glances over at me before returning his gaze to the road. "You're coming. It'll be fun. Just relax."

Of course, my body does the opposite and I tense. I've got to get it together; I can't be an emotional wreck when we arrive. So, I tie a tourniquet around all thoughts of Addie and pull it as tight as possible until I can manage some semblance of normality. If I think about her, I'll break down and that definitely doesn't scream "thanks for inviting me."

I grip the flowers I bought his parents tighter and the cellophane cringles under the assault, giving away my emotional state. He must sense my turmoil because Anders grabs my hand and holds it for the rest of the drive. His touch calms something in me, grounding me. More than words ever could.

His parents live near the Christmas tree farm they own. The gray house is set back in nature, with a perfectly landscaped front yard. There are steps on the right and left leading to a front porch. It's all angles and windows, making it look even bigger than it is.

Or maybe it's Anders's casual mention of it having six bedrooms on the way over that cements the idea. It's the type of home I'd have saved on my Pinterest page for a vision board entitled Life Goals.

Who knew owning a Christmas tree farm could be so lucrative?

I climb out of Anders's truck, and he takes my hand and leads me up the steps. Probably to keep me from running away. The front door opens to his mom wearing a festive sweater, and an apron filled with tiny reindeer and Santa's on it.

She immediately engulfs me in a hug. "Thank you for coming. It's lovely to see you again."

"Thanks for having me, Mrs. Watson." I pass her the flowers.

"Oh, call me Liz. Mrs. Watson is way too formal." She releases me and gives Anders a side hug.

"You have an amazing home."

She smiles and kisses Anders's cheek. "My sons are generous with their money. At least I can now live in my dream home."

I imagine her as an eighty-eight. Holds up the entire family, always ready for a hug, and stable. I give Anders a confused look and he mouths "later" to me. Who is rich enough to drop millions on a home for their parents just because they can? Is it Hayden? Did he buy Anders's house for him, too?

Once inside, I ask, "Do you need any help?"

"Nope. Go enjoy yourself." She waves me toward the living room and disappears into what I assume is the kitchen.

It's full of hardwood floors, grays and whites, but all broken up with ruby red couches and chairs. It's gorgeous and contemporary. The modern fireplace is ablaze, and Hayden's sitting next to his father on the couch while Theo is in a plush chair. There's some kind of action movie playing in the background.

Liz yells from the kitchen, "Anders, get your girlfriend a drink."

"Mom," Anders groans. "I already told you she's just a friend."

"Give the guy a break," yells Theo. "He just wishes she was his girlfriend."

Anders closes his eyes and takes a breath before saying to me, "Welcome to my ridiculous family." He raises his voice for the last two words, just so his brothers and dad can hear.

His brothers immediately yell back.

"Who you calling ridiculous when you've got

eyebrows like yours?"

"Remember that time—"

"Boys calm down," his dad says. "Anders, do me a favor. Next time you look in the mirror, say hello to the clown you see there for me, would you?"

"Burn!" Hayden high-fives his dad.

Theo laughs and lifts his beer in the air. "Welcome Zoey."

"What did I get myself into?" I ask the room.

His mom yells from the kitchen, "I ask myself that every day."

Anders hands me a glass of wine, then leads me over to the empty three-person couch and we sit next to each other. I make sure there's a space between us, there's no reason to make his family think we're dating any more than they already do.

"I hope you both brought your A-game today," says Hayden.

"Always," Anders and Theo say at the same time.

"I'm Jack," Anders's dad says to me.

"Nice to see you again," I say. "Care to explain why we need our A-game?"

He laughs. "I always forget our traditions aren't so traditional in other families."

"Yeah." Theo grins. "Especially when no one ever joins our festivities besides Ruby."

I take a large gulp of the wine. "What do you mean no one ever joins?"

"Mom and dad were only children, but we've never brought friends or"—Hayden waves a hand to encompass Anders and me—"whatever you are to him."

"They're not normally like this," Anders groans.

"What Hayden's trying to say, in case it wasn't clear, is you're the first person any of my boys have brought home for us to meet," Jack says.

"I take that back," Anders says. "They're normally like this. Want to leave yet?"

"No, I'm good," I say. "But let's revisit the whole 'I bring my friends over to Christmas all the time' convo we had."

His lie was the only reason I accepted the invitation. Now it's awkward as fuck. I didn't sign up for a night of interrogation about our relationship, or lack thereof. What did Anders get me into?

Jack shakes his head at Anders. "Amateur mistake. You should've at least clued us in on the lie before coming."

Theo nods. "I taught you better than that."

"Assholes, the lot of you." Anders glares at his family. "Way to out me like that."

"Aww, you still love us," Hayden says.

"I think it's time for that tour I promised you." Anders widens his eyes in a "get me out of here" expression.

I debate calling him on his lie and having his family lay into him. Again. It's fun to watch and his brothers and dad are more fun than I expected. Nineties are playful numbers. I already numbered Hayden from the Christmas tree farm as a ninety-one, and it still fits. Theo gives off an underlying caring vibe, so he's a ninety-three. Threes are like half a hug and half an ear, so he can listen to all his customers in his bar. And Jack, the most surprising of all, is a ninety-eight. Stable but playful.

But as fun as it'd be to watch the nineties in action, I

need to have a talk with Anders before this goes any further.

"Sure, let's go on that tour." I can't help but infuse the words with sarcasm.

We leave to Theo and Hayden making kissing noises and Jack telling Anders to "not do anything he wouldn't do." Anders leads me past the front door, up the stairs, and down a hallway.

When the sounds from below are muted, I stop and cross my arms. "You lied."

Anders winces. "I'm sorry. I shouldn't have, but I couldn't stand the thought of you being alone on today of all days. If you want to go home, we can leave now."

Is it okay to lie to someone even for their own good? Being here is better than being alone, especially today. But he still lied, or at least stretched the truth. Eric lied to me for half our relationship, and I was too stupid to realize it until it was too late.

"I can't stand liars," I say. "My ex lied to me for months."

He softens. "I get it. My ex lied to me, too. I promise not to lie again. But there are things you don't know about me yet, not because I lied, but because they never came up."

"Fair enough. I'd like to stay."

"Promise me one thing? If my family gets to be too much, or their jokes go too far, let me know immediately. They can be full on."

"I promise, but they're fun."

"They're something all right."

I grin. "So how about that tour?"

He grabs my hand and guides me around the house. There's a gym and a movie theater. True to his word, the six bedrooms are spread across the first and second floor.

"This place is huge," I say in awe.

"It was Mom's dream to have a home like this. But don't worry, she uses the size to guilt us all into spending the night randomly."

I thought Anders was a struggling small business owner, but it doesn't look like he's struggling at all.

"What did she mean earlier? Which one of you bought it for her?"

"All of us did. I'll explain it all later, I promise. Dinner will be ready soon."

"Which room do you normally stay in?"

"We don't have set rooms, more like whatever one we feel like."

That's the kind of thing Addie would've done. She would've fit in with his family perfectly with her easy-going and quick-witted nature. The thoughts slip through the emotional tourniquet. It's depressing to face the reality that she'll never experience these things with me.

"Hey, are you okay?" he asks.

"Yeah, sorry just thought about Addie there for a minute."

"One day, I'd love to hear more about her. When you're ready."

"Yeah, one day."

Mom refuses to talk about Addie since she died. Maybe it wouldn't be the worst, to share all the happy times I've had. Maybe someone else can appreciate her like I do.

Anders closes the distance between us. He's close enough to be inappropriate and yet not close enough at all. He tucks a stray piece of hair behind my ear. "Zoey, I—"

"There you are," Theo says.

We break apart, as if he caught us with our pants down rather than talking.

Theo grins as I smooth down my hair. "Food's ready."

Anders shakes his head at Theo and grabs my hand again. He doesn't let go the entire way to the dining room, not even when his entire family zeros in on our joined appendages. I try to release his hand, not wanting to give the wrong impression to his family, but Anders tightens his grip and refuses to let me let go.

Anders pulls out the empty chair next to Hayden and gestures for me to sit. When Hayden doesn't move from his own chair, Anders smacks Hayden on the back of the head. "Get out of my seat."

Hayden laughs and says, "You snooze, you lose."

Their mom deposits creamed spinach on the table and then swats at Hayden. "Move, or you're on dish duty for the next three Christmases."

"You wouldn't."

"Try me," she says.

Hayden grumbles and moves down to another seat, apparently his own. Once he's settled, Theo gets up and smacks him in the back of the head.

"Ow." Hayden rubs at the now sore spot. "Would you all stop? My poor head."

Anders looks to Theo. "It's like Slapsgiving, but for Christmas. Slapsmas?"

"Slapsmas." Theo nods in agreement. "A new tradition, thanks to Zoey."

"Thanks a lot, Zoey," Hayden grumbles.

"I've never started a tradition before," I say with a grin.

Jack raises his wineglass in the air. "To new traditions and new friends."

Liz adds, "And I better not have any leftovers. I outdid myself this year."

We all raise our glasses and take a drink. Anders's dad plates a dish and passes it to Liz.

I take in the amazing spread of food and hesitate. I don't want to be rude, but I also don't know what's safe to eat.

Anders leans into my side. "Everything is gluten free, so you don't need to worry."

"Everything?" I say, shocked.

"Even dessert. Mom really outdid herself."

"Wow."

He scoops some mashed potato onto my plate, and I give him a helping of the creamed spinach. The food reminds me of Thanksgiving, with the roast turkey and side dishes. It's like I'm celebrating both holidays at once, and since Thanksgiving was ruined, it's almost like a do-over.

Liz can't keep the smile off her face as she sits back and watches everyone enjoy her food.

"This is so good," I say to her after a few bites. "Thank you for making everything gluten free."

She smiles. "Wait until dessert."

"I have a feeling I'm going to win this year," Theo says.

"Win what?" I ask.

"The dessert competition," Hayden says. "We each make something and rate the dessert. Winner gets a bottle of Hibiki whiskey. Loser does all the dishes."

"Do you know ahead of time who made what?" I ask.

Anders laughs. "Nope, not since Hayden cheated when we were ten. Now mom only knows which dessert is which."

"I can't believe you didn't tell me." I give Anders a sidelong glance. "I would've totally made something."

"It slipped my mind."

"Uh huh," I say. "More like you didn't want the additional competition."

The table roars with laughter and Anders grins.

Liz says, "You can make something after dinner if you want? I've got a stocked pantry."

"I'd like that," I say. "And I can't wait to take that bottle of whiskey home." I'm probably the only person at the table with experience baking gluten free, which is way more difficult than swapping out the flour cup to cup.

"You talk a big game," Theo says, "but you're going to need to back it up."

"We've got years of practice," says Hayden.

"I've already accepted my defeat," says Anders. "Zoey is the best baker I know."

"And you'd know this how?" asks Hayden.

Everyone looks between the two of us.

"She's helping me with the menu for the new shop," Anders says.

There's a collective pause.

"Since when have you been working on the new shop?" Hayden asks. "And why didn't you tell us?"

Anders glances at me. "It's recent but I think we'll make it on time."

"What's the concept?" Theo asks me.

"A pairing of food and coffee to the different zodiac signs."

"That's brilliant," Theo says.

"I know," I say. "It was my idea."

The table's silent for a full minute, everyone giving each other looks. I thought they'd laugh, but now it's just awkward. I don't know why they're having this kind of reaction.

I look at Anders and whisper, "What's going on?"

"Nothing." Anders shakes himself. "They're just shocked I'm actually working on the new shop."

"It's not like Anders to accept help." Liz clears her throat. "We're just surprised, that's all."

Jack moves the conversation along, and everyone joins in and acts like nothing happened. I'm still confused, but I'll have to ask Anders about it later.

The rest of the dinner passes in more banter, and before I know it, it's time to bake. Liz brings me into her kitchen, and it has all the ingredients and tools I could ever ask for.

Should I go simple and bake brownies? Or more complex like a cake or a pie? I'm not sure what the others have made. I stare at the walk-in pantry, and nothing comes to mind. No recipe, no real idea. Just panic at having to now live up to being the best baker Anders knows.

Why did I agree to this again?

"Don't overthink it," Liz says. "Just go with your heart. That's when the best baking happens, anyway."

She's right. Addie always said she baked because it was what her heart demanded of her. To share that joy with others.

I close my eyes and all I can think of is my favorite dessert. Bourbon chocolate pecan pie with bourbon whipped cream. My family would complain that I'd make my favorite pie every year for Thanksgiving and Christmas, but Addie loved how much I loved it. She'd insist on having two pieces every holiday, even though she hated pecans.

She did it for me.

I put together the ingredients using my favorite pie crust recipe, one I've memorized over the years. His mom stands guard at the door while I work. All the men try to peek, but she shoos them away the second the door starts to open.

"Did you also bake something?" I ask his mom.

"Nope. I make the main meal, but dessert is all theirs."

I roll out the pie dough. "That's smart. To divide up the work."

"It was their dad's idea to turn into a competition when they were younger. It kept the complaining at bay about having to bake. But they loved it so much they begged for us to do it again the next year. Before we knew it, it was the highlight of the day."

I smile. "You're a great mom."

"It helps to have a great husband to support with everything."

I continue to work on the pie, but Anders's mom isn't

the type of person to enjoy silence. She enjoys talking and being in motion. A bundle of energy.

"So you and Anders, huh?"

"It's not like that. I'm his employee and friend."

She smiles kindly. "You must be a special kind of friend to bring here."

"I think he just didn't want me to be alone. On today of all days."

"You're always welcome here, on any holiday."

"Thank you, really. I didn't realize how much I'd be missing out on by being alone. Until now."

Anders was right, but it's hard to know what you're missing until you experience it. Being around a family who truly loves each other helps to fill the gaping hole left behind after Addie's death.

The relief is temporary, but I'll take it.

"Wait until after dessert." She grins.

I place the pie in the oven to bake. "What's after dessert?"

"Games. We split into teams and compete against each other."

"I've never played any games on Christmas."

"It's another way to keep them coming home for the holidays. No matter where they are in the world, we always spend Christmas together. Traditions help tie us all together, even silly ones," she says.

"I like that."

Her phone rings, and she looks at me. "Oh, I've been waiting for this call. It's a friend from Japan. You okay alone for a moment?"

"Of course."

"Yell if someone tries to enter and cheat." She pushes through the door with the phone already to her ear.

I start the bourbon cream and use the mixer for it to whip. A memory, buried with time, pushes to the front of my mind. One of Lilly and I playing a card game with our grandparents after Christmas dinner. Our grandparents, on both sides, loved cards and we learned to play their favorite game, Hand and Foot.

It was convoluted, but we wanted to sit at the adult table and join them. And they let us, even if we struggled to keep up with the rules.

But all our grandparents died by the time I turned thirteen. After that, Lilly and I would play card games together, but never Hand and Foot. It was an unspoken rule that once everyone died, we'd never play it again.

But I miss it.

I pull out my phone, and text the dead group chat with Lilly and Mom before I can talk myself out of it.

> Me: Do you remember Hand and Foot?
> It's been ages since we played…

I STARE AT THE MESSAGE, waiting for some acknowledgement. The app indicates they read it. I wait ten more minutes, but no one responds. So I write one more message.

Me: Merry Christmas Eve.

No one responds or reacts to the message.

The door opens and Anders pops his head inside. "It smells amazing in here."

"You can't be here." I rush to him. "Your mom will kill you."

He grabs me by the hips and pulls me out of the kitchen.

"Better?"

I steady myself and grip his shoulders. "Yeah."

"You good?"

"Yeah, actually I am." Even though my family didn't respond to my message, it's not like I expected anything else.

"You okay to spend the night here?"

"I don't want to impose…"

"I can stop drinking now if you want and drive you home whenever you want to go. The games after dessert are drinking games. It's part of our tradition."

"I can order a taxi or something."

"You're not getting into some stranger's car in the middle of the night on Christmas Eve. No, I'll drive you."

I don't want him to leave his family. Not when Liz has an entire evening of activities planned and made these traditions to keep everyone together. I also don't want to go; I want to experience these traditions. ZWOL said to have fun and make new memories. I have a feeling the rest of the evening will be a big part of that.

"Are you sure your mom won't mind?" I ask.

"She'd be fucking thrilled. It's not like we don't have enough space."

I mentally run through the items in my purse. At least I have my makeup, so I can reapply in the morning. I can also sleep naked, so that won't be a big deal. There's nothing stopping me from saying no, so I say, "Okay."

"Thank you." He pulls me in for a hug and kisses my hair.

I sink into his warmth, and a throat clears behind us.

We pull apart, and Theo's there, grinning. "I keep interrupting, huh?"

"Maybe next time, keep walking on by," Anders says.

"But where's the fun in that?"

"I got to get back to my dessert," I say. "It's time to take it from the oven."

"Hmm, you used the oven." Theo's gaze sharpens. "Did you make a cake? Or cookies? I bet it's brownies."

"No cheating, asshole." Anders slaps him in the back of the head.

"Where's the fun in that?"

I grin and go back into the kitchen.

His mom is there warming the other desserts up in the second oven. I pull out the pie, and it's perfect.

She asks, "Can you let the guys know we'll start in less than ten minutes and for them to set up the table? I'll finish up here."

"Sure."

I push through the door and slow my steps when I hear the guys talking.

About me.

CHAPTER 18

Times eavesdropping has gone well: 0
Amount of drinks I've consumed: 3
Oh, fuck it. Stop with the lists and pay attention.

"So?" Anders asks.

"She fits in," Hayden says.

"Yeah," Theo says, "and best of all, she's not like Courtney."

Courtney? Who's Courtney? I remember that name. Anders mentioned her before he called me messy. The last time I was eavesdropping. I take a step closer.

"I like her too," his dad says.

"I'm worried—" Anders stops talking when he spots me.

They all turn to me, and I paste on a wide smile and step into the room, acting like I didn't hear a thing. Acting like I'm not dying to hear what Anders was about to say.

Worried? About me? Something else? "Dessert competition starts soon."

Theo rubs his hands together. "Finally."

Hayden goes to a cabinet and takes plates out to prepare the table.

"You ready to lose?" Anders hands me a full glass of wine.

"I don't know what I'm up against, but I'm proud of what I made," I say.

He leads me to the table, and we all sit down. There are five folded cards, numbered one to five, in front of each setting. A piece of paper with a rating system from one to five for texture, taste, and design lays to my right with a pen on top.

Whoa. They're a lot more serious about this than I originally thought. A sudden case of nerves strikes, causing my palms to sweat. I want to impress them, especially if I'm helping Anders with his menu for his new shop.

If I come in last, will he still trust me to help him?

I should've thought this through before baking a pie. I should've taken this more seriously. It's not just a competition, but a way for me to leave an impression on them.

"You okay?" Anders bumps his knee into mine.

I wipe my sweaty hands on my green velvet dress. "Oddly nervous?"

"It's just for fun." He covers my hands with one of his. "You'll see."

I give him a nod as his mom brings in a tray and places a plate in front of each number. I'm number two.

"This year," Liz says, "all the desserts are gluten free.

Number one is a chocolate reindeer cookie with peppermint icing." The reindeer is lopsided and doesn't look like much of a reindeer at all, which makes it all the better. "Number two is bourbon chocolate pecan pie with bourbon cream. Number three is chocolate cupcakes with spiced rum frosting in the shape of a snowmen. Number four is a yule log dusted in powdered sugar and fresh berries. And finally, number five is a mini lemon cheesecake."

She doesn't elaborate on number five, but it just might be the prettiest dessert I've ever seen. It's way more than a cheesecake. There's a snow globe of gelatin with the shape of a Christmas tree somehow inside.

How did they do that? Who did that?

My pie looks so sad in comparison. There's nothing Christmassy about it. I had no idea that design was part of the process. I may know how to bake, but presentation isn't my strong suit.

What did I get myself into?

"Of course, you're number five." Theo shoots Anders a glare. "You asshole, how'd you managed that? You get zero stars for presentation."

A laugh bursts out of me, and Anders flicks his gaze to me for a moment before leaning back in his chair, all cocky.

I lift up my burnt reindeer cookie just as Hayden pokes at his own. "Best presentation so far. Ten stars."

I look down at my paper and ask, "I thought the rating system was out of five?"

His mom laughs. "I try to keep some order to these hooligans, but it never works. They rate it however they want and base it on the most random things. Last year, Theo gave one hundred stars to a dessert with red frosting, just because it was his favorite color."

I shake my head at their antics and taste the desserts. Number five is the best in all categories compared to the others, even though the crust is a little too grainy. The reindeer cookie is dry and burnt. The yule log looks amazing, but is too sugary, as if the person who made it dumped in one cup too many. The cupcake is okay but has a weird texture from the gluten-free flour. However, the frosting is out of this world. I'm going to have to steal the recipe from whoever made it.

Theo and Hayden rate the desserts based on whether it smells like Christmas or not, whatever that means, and whether it pairs well with what they're drinking. It's hilarious.

Anders remains quiet the entire time, hiding his ratings with a receipt he produced from his pocket. Hayden tries to swipe at Anders's paper, but Anders is faster.

"No cheating." Anders laughs at his brother's frown.

"Zoey, help us out here." Hayden begs.

"Time's up," Liz says. "Pass me your papers."

We all pass her the papers and she sets them to the side, without looking at them.

She gets up and places the whiskey on the table in front of me. "The winner, by a clear margin, is Zoey."

"What about the rating system?" I ask.

Liz laughs. "I'm the real judge. It keeps things fair since *some* people"—she shoots a look at Theo and Hayden—"can't handle using a simple star system."

"How the hell did you make such an amazing pie so quickly?" Hayden asks.

"Never underestimate Zoey," Anders says. "She's the most talented person I know."

My cheeks heat at the compliment and how everyone turns to stare at me. Theo looks at Anders with a contemplative expression, and Hayden wiggles his eyebrows at me.

Theo pulls Hayden into a heated argument on how the rules need to change for next year, and Anders throws an arm around my shoulder and whispers in my ear. "Did you like my dessert?"

"Number five, right?" I ask, and he nods. "I thought you'd win. How did you get the tree inside the gelatin?"

"That's top secret."

I can't help but stare at his oh so kissable lips. Lips that not so long ago gave me the best compliment ever.

Anders's gaze darkens. "Hold that thought."

He pushes away from the table and grabs the whiskey in one hand and mine in his other. "We're going to get some glasses for this bad boy." He calls to his family, but he doesn't wait for their response.

He drags me out of the living room and into the kitchen so fast that I'm out of breath. The door closing behind us punctuates our relocation. He sets the bottle on the counter and stalks toward me.

Closer and closer, until I'm backed against the wall.

"I can't think when you look at me like that," he says.

"Like what?"

He leans his forehead against mine. "Like you're

seconds away from kissing me. Please, lift your kissing ban."

His lips hover so close, I swear I can feel them ghost mine. All it'd take is one small movement, and we'd be kissing. No matter how many times I tell myself this isn't a good idea, my body can't seem to get on board.

Because I want him.

More than I've wanted anyone.

Would it be so bad, to give in?

"Promise I won't lose my job, no matter what happens between us," I say.

He pulls back. "I can put it in writing if it helps."

"Or just seal the deal with a kiss?"

"Are you sure?"

I grip the back of his neck in answer and pull his mouth down to mine, needing him. His hands tangle in my hair, and he quickly takes control of the kiss.

He still kisses me like he's starved for it, like I'm the best dessert he's ever had and has been waiting years for another taste.

Far too soon, he pulls back, both of us breathing hard. "We need to stop, or else you'll be naked in my mother's kitchen."

I shiver at his statement and give him a nod. It's all I can manage when my voice isn't working from being kissed stupid.

He grins, as if he knows exactly how his kisses make me feel, and runs a thumb across my lips. "Shall we open the whiskey?"

"Sure."

Anders pours a shot for everyone in red plastic cups. I

would've thought he'd pour the drinks into something more expensive, given the quality of everything in this kitchen. Strange.

I smooth down my hair and run my fingers under my eyes. I open the freezer and stick my face inside. Is two minutes enough to calm my body down after a kiss like that?

Probably not, but I've got to look somewhat presentable when I go back out there. Anders swipes the tray from the counter and leads the way back to his family.

They don't comment on our absence or my blush. Instead, his mom claps her hands twice and asks, "Ready for the games?"

The entire family whoops in response.

"Okay, first up, we've got Anders's favorite. Flip cup. Pair off into two teams and let's get started."

"Your family plays flip cup? On Christmas?" I ask Anders.

"What better time than Christmas?" he asks, grinning.

Huh, what better time indeed? Anders takes his place across the table from me. We're both second in line. His mom is starting on my side, and his dad is on his side. Instead of beer, we're playing with whiskey. They're not messing around.

Theo, the last person on my team, whistles to get everyone's attention. "Ready? On the count of three. One, two, three."

His mom slams back her shot of whiskey and flips her cup as if this is an Olympic sport and she trains five times a day. I'm so shocked at her performance that she has to nudge my shoulder and yell at me to drink.

I throw back the shot and line the cup up, only for it to fall to the side. Shit. I grab it again and make it the second time, just as Anders's cup lands.

I cheer on Theo while he goes head-to-head with Hayden. I'm invested one thousand percent into this game. Maybe it's the alcohol talking, but there's something about competitions that gets my blood hot.

Theo wins with a millisecond to spare, and his mom and I jump in the air and engulf him in a hug. We all jump around and shout that we're the winners, like the good sports players that we are.

Anders has a soft expression on his face before he huddles in a team meeting with his dad and brother.

His mom looks at both Theo and me. "We've got to win one more time to be declared champions. It's best out of three."

"We've got this," I say with an air of confidence, as if I can play flip cup in my sleep.

Theo puts his fist in the middle. "Winners on three. One, two, three."

"Winners," we shout and break into a laugh.

We reshuffle ourselves, with his mom going to the back of line and me starting against Anders. This round, they pour two shots in each cup, upping the ante.

"Ready?" Anders asks me.

"I wasn't the one who lost last time."

He grins, and this time, his dad does the countdown. On the go, I chug the whiskey, but when I try to flip the cup, all the alcohol I've consumed catches up to me and

I'm sloppy. There's always that moment in drinking, where I swing from being super skilled and amazing games to uncoordinated-can't-believe-I'm-an-adult-and-am-allowed-to-drink.

Unfortunately, it hits at the worst time. My team keeps shouting encouragements at me, and I keep laughing. Anders is having as much trouble as me in landing his cup.

With a concentration I didn't think I was currently capable of, I finally flip my cup correctly and Theo chugs his whiskey.

While staring at me, Anders flips his cup, and it lands with ease. Did he… allow me to win?

If so, that might be the most romantic thing my drunken heart has experienced. I'm not the type to get mad about someone letting me win. I'll take any win in life lately, even in the form of a game for fun. Even if someone cheated to let me win.

I turn from Anders and watch as my team wins again.

We all cheer and parade around the living room. I swipe a pen from the table and offer to sign my autograph on Anders's cup. He passes it over and I sign my name in a flourish with an XOXO at the end. He tucks the cup behind a vase, and I laugh at his hiding spot.

"Let's take a break and rejoin in thirty," his dad says.

Thank the stars. I can't get face-down, black-out drunk at someone else's house. That's bad form.

Anders appears at my side and hands me a glass of water. "Need some fresh air?"

"Yeah." It's exactly what I need to sober up before the next round.

He leads us to the back doors and the crisp, wintery air cools my heated cheeks. I take a deep breath, the air so fresh out here.

Anders drapes a heavy blanket across my shoulders and guides me to sit on the couch outside.

"It's beautiful here," I say.

The dark woods seem so endless, the neighbors must be miles away.

"It is."

I lean into his side. "Your family is amazing."

"They are. You holding up okay?"

"Yeah. What's the next game?"

And I am okay. Anders's family is fun, and they're treating me like I'm another family member. It's easy not to dwell on Addie being gone, and to just enjoy the moment when there's so much happiness around me.

"Probably charades, and then my parents will go to sleep. My brothers and I normally play cards after that."

I don't want to move, but tipsy me will turn into sleepy me in two point five seconds if I stay here.

"Shall we head back inside?"

Anders helps me up. "I'm so glad you came tonight."

"Me too," I say. "Thanks for forcing me to come."

"After tonight, everyone will be forcing you to join us at every holiday, even Washington's birthday."

I laugh, and Anders keeps his arm around me as we head back into the house while his family sets up charades. We break off into two teams, but this time Anders, Liz and I are on a team together.

His dad brings out some tortilla chips, dips, nuts, fruit, and the rest of my pie for snacks. Anders cuts himself a huge slice of the pie and eats it while Hayden pulls the first card.

He starts to sway side to side while unbuttoning his shirt.

His dad says, "A drunken man trying to use his shirt to catch a cat falling from a tree."

"I got it," Theo yells. "You're walking a tight rope a thousand feet in the air on a windy day to save the cat from the other side."

Hayden grins and simply says, "Correct."

He throws down the card on the table, and it reads strip tease. I giggle at the outlandish guesses and how the more outlandish they get, the more correct they become. I love how they don't play by the rules and make it all about having fun and laughing.

If my family were to play, dad would read the rules to everyone and enforce them at every turn. I'm not sure if I'll ever follow game rules again after today.

Anders and his family have a connection and closeness that doesn't seem real. Perhaps it was born from moving around so much, and only relying on each other, or maybe his parents are just amazing at keeping their family tight knit. Either way, it's impressive and I'm so lucky to be able to experience it.

The rest of the game is full of laughter and fun until his parents say goodnight to us all. His mom gives everyone a hug and kiss on the cheek while his dad waves from the edge of the room.

After they leave, Theo shuffles a deck of cards. "What are we in the mood for?"

"Asshole," Hayden says.

Theo and Anders nod.

"You know how to play?" Theo asks me.

I nod. "Yeah, played in college."

"Want to make it a drinking game?" Hayden asks the table.

No one answers at first, but Anders looks at me before shaking his head. "Nah, just have a drink on the side if you want one."

The brothers accept that easily and I'm relieved I don't have to drink any more alcohol tonight. I would've said yes to fit in, but I'd pay for it tomorrow.

Theo deals the cards, and we begin passing our cards to one another while Theo asks me, "How's the menu for the new shop coming along?"

"Good. We've got the pairings down, but we need to figure out either how to pre-make the food or if we should make it to order. Do you happen to know a chef looking for work?"

"We don't need a chef." Anders stiffens next to me.

"It would free up more time if you hired someone to help you." I glance at him. "Even if we go with the pre-made option, someone still has to make it and prepare it all. You can't do everything by yourself."

"I wouldn't be by myself. I'd have you."

"And if one of us gets sick? That's not a sustainable business model."

Anders crosses his arms across his chest, clearly annoyed. "I've made it work before. At Amore, it's only Ruby and me."

It's at this moment, with Anders's agitation clear for everyone to see, I realize I may have overstepped, especially in front of his brothers. Even if it's true, and his stubbornness has the potential to hurt the concept. I should've brought it up in private. But even knowing this, I still say, "You don't need to work yourself into an early grave."

Like Addie did.

Anders pushes up from the table. "I need a moment."

He storms out of the room, and I'm left horribly embarrassed that there was an audience for this. That he got so mad he had to leave... because of me.

"Sorry," I mumble, placing my cards down.

"You didn't do anything wrong." Theo places a hand on mine. "He has a hard time trusting people since Courtney."

"Who's Courtney?" That's the second time I've heard her name tonight.

"An old business partner..."

"And?" I ask, the suspense killing me.

"It's his story to tell," Hayden says. "Ask him."

I blow out a breath. "I doubt he'll tell me; he can barely talk about hiring someone without blowing a fuse."

"You're the only one who's able to talk to him." Hayden gives me a sympathetic smile. "Hell, you're the only one who got him to start working on the shop. We've all been trying to help since he bought the building, but he's shut us all down at every turn. For some reason, he responds to you."

Huh, maybe that explains the awkwardness from earlier and their reaction to finding out about us working on the shop. They were shocked.

"I do have someone in mind," Theo says. "To help you out with the cooking. I'll message you her details."

"You should go to him." Hayden lifts his chin to where Anders went.

I chew on my cheek. "It's pretty clear he doesn't want me around."

"He does," Theo says, "he's hurting and stressed, even if he doesn't want to admit it."

I sigh and head down the hall Anders disappeared to.

"Anders?" I whisper shout. I wait a beat and walk further down the hall. "Anders?" I repeat again.

"In here," he says, and I follow his voice to a bedroom with the soft glow of a bedside lamp illuminating the space. It's all dark wood, grays, and whites.

Anders is perched on the side of the bed, but his body is hunched, defeated.

"I'm sorry," I say, and sit next to him.

"You've got nothing to be sorry for."

"Can you tell me about her? Courtney?" I grab his hand in mine.

He jerks his head up. "How do you know about her?"

"I don't. Your brothers mentioned her name. I also overheard you say her name with Ruby."

"When I called you messy?"

I nod.

He blows out a long breath. "You have to know when I said that I was talking about myself, not you. I'm the one who's a mess. I can't stand to hire someone to help at Amore, even if Ruby and I are working ourselves ragged."

"What happened?"

"I had a startup with my brothers before Amore. That's

how we can afford this house and our businesses. When we sold the company, I needed a change. I was close to burnout, and the promise of Amore was what helped pull me out of it. It was the idea of going back to my roots and love for coffee that drove me. That's when Courtney stepped in to help. She worked in our startup in the marketing department and promised to take care of everything. She wasn't my girlfriend by any means, but we did hook up a few times. I trusted her, especially when I couldn't handle it on my own."

He hangs his head in shame and shakes it. "Turns out she was setting me up to fail. Apparently, her brother's company lost out on an investment because it went to us instead. She wanted to bring down Amore from day one, and she almost succeeded."

"I'm so sorry." The words feel inadequate, but it's all I've got.

"She would undermine the business every step of the way. Theo caught on first when we were losing money that first week we opened. Hayden helped correct the business and pushed Courtney out."

He spears me with a look, one filled with an emotion I can't read. "My entire life, people have been temporary. We'd move every few years, and I learned the only people I can rely on are my family. When I relied on Courtney, I almost lost everything. That's why it's hard for me to trust anyone with my business and why I can't bring myself to hire more people at Amore. The new shop brought back all those feelings and I've been frozen, unable to decide on anything. Scared I'd fail. Until you."

"I hope you know I'm here for you. I only want to see you succeed."

He pushes some of my hair behind my ear. "I know that now, and I'm so sorry for how I treated you when you started. It felt like history was repeating itself, but it was so much worse because of my attraction to you."

"Attraction, huh?"

He closes the distance between us until our noses almost touch. "You have no idea."

"I'm still scared," I whisper.

"Me too. I don't want to get hurt. Courtney betrayed my trust and nearly broke my business. But with you? You have the power to break my heart."

His heart?

I swallow hard at his admission, at how it makes me feel. If his heart is on the table, then that means he's falling for me. It means love, or at least the potential for it. My own heart yearns for him, the beat like a war drum. It's so strong it's about to burst through my ribcage.

We're both wounded by our past and our exes. But I'm tired of letting Eric have control over me. He's probably happy, rolling around in all the money he stole, and yet I'm left dealing with the aftermath.

This wonderful man is right in front of me, ready for me to claim him, and him me. And what, I'm too scared to try? Because of Eric? Eric's not a good enough reason to keep denying the possibility of something with Anders.

I close the distance between our lips. It's my confirmation that I'm ready for this, to at least try.

He kisses me like he's cementing my actions into words. This kiss is different from all the others. We stole kisses in moments of passion, passion we couldn't contain. It just spilled over into our lives, and we were unable to control it.

But this kiss? It's intentional and slow, as if we have all the time in the world. It's a declaration that we're together. It no longer matters if someone catches us. There's no longer a push and pull between us. We're now perfectly in sync.

His tongue tangles with mine. I pull back and bite his lower lip. He groans at the movement and returns the favor. His bite causes my core to pulse in time with the tinge of pain. I moan into his mouth, and he swallows it down. He grabs my hips and pulls me on top of him. My legs fall on either side of his and I grind down on his erection without thought, driven by pure need.

Need for more. For all of him.

He groans at the contact and grips my hips tighter. His hands run under my dress and scorch a path up my ribcage to my breasts. He pulls down my left bra cup and rolls my nipple between his thumb and forefinger.

I want, no need, to see him touch me. I rip off my dress. He chuckles at my neediness, and it turns into stunned silence as he takes in my black lacy bra and matching thong. He stands and brings me with him, his arm under my ass.

I sputter, not sure what's going on. In two strides, he makes it to the door, closes it, and locks it.

I'm glad he's got the foresight to take care of that, because my brain is in a haze of lust. All for him.

He pushes me against the door and pulls down my other bra cup.

He nuzzles my chest before sucking a nipple into his mouth. The suction of his mouth, the scrape of his beard, his teeth teasing me... I'm nosediving into pleasure.

The wooden door cuts into my back, but I'm in a cocoon of Anders, his body pressing into mine and restraining me. It's all too much, and not enough all at once. I squirm, needing more.

Needing everything.

"Please," I whimper.

"I know. I want to take my time."

"Don't you dare." I arch my back, seeking more suction from his mouth.

His laugh caresses my nipple, causing it to pebble even more. He swings me around and throws me onto the bed. I've never seen a man undress so fast, but Anders is naked in one second flat. He ripped his shirt off. The buttons still rolling on the floor as he covers me with his body.

I love the weight, the feel of his skin against mine. I lift my back off the bed, needing no barrier between us.

"Bra." It's all I say, and one-handed he undoes the clasp and throws it off me.

I want my thong gone, but he's in no rush. No, he pulls at the top of the material and the thong digs into my aching pussy. My hips press down into the mattress on their own accord, loving the ache. He pulls harder, and the thong teases my entrance. My entire being is focused on what he's doing to me, at how a simple piece of fabric is making me ache for him.

Anders runs his hands and mouth down my entire body. He licks the skin at my waistband and down my thong until he reaches my entrance. I open my knees and he lifts one leg over his shoulder.

He moves the thong to the side and makes one long lick from slit to clit. "I could eat your pussy every day and it'd never be enough. Your smell." He inhales and runs his nose across my inner thigh, a thigh that's quivering. I'm strung tight with need, ready to break. "Your taste." He sucks on my clit and my hips rocket off the bed. "You."

He climbs up my body and kisses my lips, caressing my tongue with his.

"Don't tease," I beg. "I need you."

He works his way back down my body, licking and biting my nipples. Still teasing.

"Anders," I moan.

He bites my clit, hard enough to sting, and thrusts two fingers inside. Finally, he's doing more than teasing. And holy shit, I could come just like this.

"Patience," he demands. "I refuse to rush this. Not when I've been dreaming about it since I first met you."

"No. Rush now. Next time we can go slow."

The grin he gives me is all evil. He pulls hard at my thong, and it snaps at the sudden force he exerts.

He balls it up and places it in my mouth. "You'll need this to muffle your screams."

I huff, outraged I've got my thong in my mouth, my juices coating my tongue. He adds another finger to my pussy and goes back to sucking and nipping at my clit in such a way that I thrash from side to side. The pleasure builds so suddenly, I barely have time to take a breath before I break.

Stars explode behind my eyelids. My thong barely

muffles my screams. He rides my orgasm with me, not stopping his movements. Only when I start to come down does he lighten up. He laps at me like he's savoring me.

I toss the thong to the side and grab at his shoulders to draw him up to me. I kiss him with everything I've got. His dick presses against my entrance and I lift my hips. The tip enters me before he pulls out and does it again and again.

It's pure torture.

It's pure ecstasy.

I lift my hips again, trying to chase him. I need him deeper, but he withholds.

"Condom," he says, pulling back.

I grip him tighter, not wanting him to move. "I'm clean and have an IUD."

"I'm clean, too. Are you sure?"

"Yes," I breathe.

Just when I'm about to cry in frustration, he thrusts and seats himself fully. I suck on his neck and moan. He frames my face with his hands and stares at me as he stretches me. His gaze is locked on mine, and he finds a rhythm that causes my eyes to roll back in my head. Where pleasure and heat coil inside me.

This moment right here means something more. More than any sexual encounter I've ever had. It's deeply intimate to look someone in the eye while being fucked senseless. To connect on every level during sex.

"I'm close," he says.

"Me too."

He drives into me as if crazed. He lifts my leg and pushes deeper and hits a new angle. Pleasure builds until I can't take it anymore. Until I get so high, there's nothing left to do but fall. He follows seconds later.

I manage to keep my eyes open, for us to hold each other's gaze through it all, as pleasure contorts both of our faces.

He remains inside of me as he rolls to his back, holding onto me so now I'm lying on top of him.

I try to maneuver to his side, but his arms band around me, forcing me to straddle him. I lay my head on his heart, the beat steady.

"I'm too heavy," I complain.

He snorts. "You're perfect."

He's still inside me, semihard. I don't want to lose the connection between us, so I relax. He runs his fingertips up my back and ribs, an exploration of my body.

I run my fingers over his chest, shoulders, biceps, and forearms. The hard ridges of his body are so fascinating.

"What do the tattoos mean?" I ask.

"Most represent a place I've lived." He runs his finger over an intricate tree made of elephants, longboats, and tigers on his shoulder and down his arm. "For Thailand, where I learned about adventure and mindfulness." There's a coffee cup with flowers, hearts, and the name Nonna written for the handle of the cup. "For Italy, and the first coffee shop I worked at. There was a little old lady who only went by Nonna to everyone there. She taught me everything I know. I'm not sure why she took the time to teach a teenager and foreigner the art of coffee, but I'll be forever grateful for it."

They flow into each other so effortlessly, and are so beautiful, I feel like I could study them for hours. I lift my head to look at his other arm, but he laughs and says, "Relax for now. You'll be able to look your fill later."

"I'll hold you to that."

"I look forward to it."

With his heartbeat under my ear, my body settles. He's still inside me, and I love it. I don't want to move, to be anywhere else but here. But when my eyes begin to droop, I force myself to push off his chest.

"What's wrong?" he asks.

"I should pee."

He shifts and lifts me with him while he stands.

"What are you doing?" I shriek.

"Taking care of you." He pulls my head back down to his shoulder. "You were about to sleep. Let me help."

I yawn, punctuating his point. "I don't need help to pee."

"I can at least offer you a ride, so you don't have to walk."

I've never had a guy even care about that. They normally fall asleep, and I'm left to do the cleanup myself.

I give him a small smile and he sets me down in the ensuite bathroom. I reluctantly let him go and close the door to do my business. The second the toilet flushes, he opens the door and grabs a washcloth. He runs the warm cloth over my body and between my legs.

Goosebumps spread over my skin, and he helps me into a black T-shirt. When he's done, he lifts me back into his arms and deposits me gently on the bed. He pulls the covers up to my chest and heads to the bathroom himself.

Being taken care of is something new. I never realized how much Anders liked to care for others until he started thawing toward me. Even when I thought he hated me, he took care of me. And now that he's told me he likes me, it's like he refuses to hide it.

He returns in a pair of black sweatpants. He pulls me into his body, my head on his chest, my legs tangled in his.

"Goodnight," he whispers and kisses my head.

"Night."

I close my eyes and wait for dreamland to take me away.

Anders was right. I forgot about all my problems while here. Instead of grief and sadness, I'm filled with happiness.

Thanks to him and his family.

I wish Addie could see me now.

CHAPTER 19

"*B*race yourself, mighty Leo, because it's time to face the music. Yep, even the queens of the zodiac need a reality check once in a while. So, put on your big-girl crown and open those regal ears wide. It's time to embrace the message you've been avoiding like the plague. Sure, it may sting a bit, but trust me, honey, it's for your own damn good. Love always, ZWOL."

"Merry Christmas." Anders's mouth latches onto my clit right after he says it.

It takes me a few seconds to fully waken, and oh wow. What better way to wake up than his mouth on my pussy? I could get used to this.

I grip his hair and ride his face. He wrings every ounce of pleasure from my body in an embarrassingly short time.

I gasp and catch my breath as Anders smiles at me as if I just gave him the best present. "You are magic. I never orgasm so quickly."

"Maybe your ex just didn't know what he was doing."

"That's a given. He refused to go down on me."

"Seriously?" Anders scowls.

I nod and look down at the duvet. "Yeah, he didn't like anything about it. Wouldn't even try, just vetoed it from the start."

"Looks like you're owed a lot of orgasms. His loss, because your pussy is the best I've ever had the pleasure of getting acquainted with."

I huff out a laugh, then head to the shower. Anders follows me and fiddles with the dials. A stream of perfect temperature water, hot but not too hot, falls on us. I lean into him and kiss him stupid, before trailing my fingers down his abdomen, followed by my lips. His abs clench the closer I get to his dick. Every inch of him is beautiful. Especially his dick.

I take his heavy erection in my hands and suck on his balls before licking my way from base to crown. He splays his hands on the dark blue tiles and leans back. I hum when I take him in my mouth and his hips jerk forward, shoving him farther down my throat.

I swallow him down and start to suck him off in earnest. He fucks my mouth and I gag. It's the best feeling in the world. To see him come undone because of me.

He increases his pace, and I squeeze his ass. Pulling out suddenly, he lifts me to my feet and spins me around. My hands grip the tiles before he takes me from behind.

He slaps my ass, not hard enough to leave a mark, but enough for me to drench his cock.

He grips my hair and turns my head to the side. Sucking on my neck, he asks, "You like when I spank you?"

I moan out a yes, loving when he takes control of my body. When he's a bit rough with me. I'm never thought I'd like it, but apparently, I like everything that is Anders.

He increases his pace and squeezes my breasts in his hands before slapping my ass again. I arch my back and he hits the perfect spot before his hands pinch my nipples. I explode the second his fingers touch me.

My screams bounce off the walls while he shouts out his own release.

He turns me in his arms and kisses me oh so slowly. My knees grow weak, and he holds me up with his arms around me. Arms meant to take care of me.

"Merry Christmas," I say.

He laughs. "Best Christmas morning of my life."

"Mine, too."

He turns me around and washes my hair and body. I return the favor, savoring the feel of his skin against mine. Once we're all soapy, it's too tempting not to fuck him again.

"We'll be late for breakfast," he says, pushing me against the wall. My legs go around his waist.

"Then I guess we've got to make it fast."

"First one to orgasm wins." His gaze sparks at the challenge.

I smirk. "Good luck."

He thrusts into me, and we both cling to each other. How can it still be this good? We just had sex, but it's only getting better. With Eric, it plateaued real fast. The first two times were okay and after that, it went downhill.

But Anders? Fuck, I don't think it could ever be bad.

I swivel my hips, and he groans, "Do that again."

I repeat the gesture and lean into the wall while we lose ourselves in each other.

When we finish, he makes sure we're all clean and wraps me in a fluffy white towel. "We need to hurry. Breakfast starts in"—he checks the time on his phone—"two minutes."

I nod. "No problem."

I scrape my wet hair back into a cute topknot and apply basic makeup. I slip into the dress from last night, only this time without any underwear since my thong got destroyed. We slip out of the room, and Anders grabs my hand and leads me to the living room.

Christmas music drifts from a speaker. The scent of bacon, bread, and eggs greets me. I would've thought my stomach would reject food this morning after drinking so much, but it's the opposite. It rumbles in appreciation.

Theo and Hayden stand and give us a hearty round of applause when they spot us.

Hayden grins. "That bedroom is all yours from now on. You're not allowed to stay anywhere else."

"Yeah, we'll make sure to stay upstairs when you two spend the night. There's nothing like waking up in the morning to..." Theo wiggles his eyebrows.

"To what?" Liz asks, clearly confused.

Jack laughs. "To the birds chirping."

"Fuck off," Anders says. "No wonder you're both single. You couldn't please a woman if you tried."

Oh my stars. I slap a hand over my eyes, completely mortified his brothers heard us and that he confirmed to his parents what we just did. At least his parents didn't seem to hear anything.

Anders removes the hand over my eyes, turns my face to his, and kisses me on the lips. In front of his entire family.

It's a short kiss, but one full of ownership.

Liz's eyes widen, as if she's now understanding everything her sons have been suggesting.

"It's a Christmas miracle," she cries and rushes to us before holding us tight in a hug.

"Merry Christmas," I say.

"Come on, I'm starved," Jack says.

Liz laughs and dabs at her eyes. "Yes, let's make sure it doesn't get cold."

We all sit in different seats than yesterday, and Liz says, "Everything is gluten free."

"Even the pastries?" Pastry is difficult, even with wheat. To make it gluten free requires a ton of work.

She smiles. "Especially the pastries. I've been practicing baking them ever since Anders took an interest in gluten-free cooking."

She's so thoughtful. It's more than my family has ever done for me and my disease. Mom would never take the time to experiment with recipes to adapt them to my needs. Only Addie.

Fuck, I miss her. She would've loved Anders and his family.

"Thank you," I say through the lump in my throat.

Anders pulls me into his side for a hug.

"So are you official?" Hayden asks.

"Yeah, Zoey and I are together," Anders says.

"About damn time," Theo says.

"Good things come to those who wait." Anders pushes Theo in the shoulder playfully as we head to the table.

"Said no one ever," says Hayden.

His mom smacks the back of his head. We all laugh and eat the amazing spread laid out before us. It's the best Christmas I've ever had, thanks to Anders. They don't open presents, and it's freeing to have it not be about the actual gifts but about being together and enjoying everyone's company.

Time passes too quickly and before I know it, we're in Anders's car heading back to the city.

I fiddle with my dress, trying not to worry about how everything will change now that the bubble we're in is gone and returning to real life.

* * *

ANDERS KEEPS HOLD of my hand during the entire drive back to the city and takes us to his house.

"I should check on my apartment," I say.

"No."

"No?"

"It's supposed to snow tonight. I don't want you to freeze in your place."

"It's not that bad..." Even I don't believe the lie.

"Just stay tonight. If nothing else for my comfortable bed."

I roll my eyes. "It's still going to be cold tomorrow."

"And you can also stay tomorrow, too," he says.

"I can't stay here all winter."

He glances my way. "You could."

Panic builds in my chest. We just made it official. It's too soon to move in together. My life is quickly becoming entwined with his, and it's too much.

"I'm not ready for that," I say. "It'll be too hard..." I can't complete the thought, the words sticking in my throat. When we end, I won't be able to extract myself if we're living together. It'll be a thousand times more difficult than what happened with Eric.

His lips purse in annoyance. "Because you're only thinking about what will happen if we break up."

I soften my tone, not trying to hurt him, but needing to protect myself. "I'm being realistic. Not so long ago, we didn't like each other. It's moving too fast if we also move in together."

"Let's stick a pin in this discussion and revisit it later. Can you at least spend the next few nights here, though?"

He's right, a snowstorm in my place would be horrible. "Fine, but I do need to get some clothes."

"Sure, want to go now?" he asks.

"You like to strike when the iron's hot, huh?"

"I don't want you to change your mind."

When we arrive at my apartment, I grab my backpack, but Anders shakes his head and pulls out my lone suitcase instead. The one I used to move myself here.

He begins to fold some of the clothes hanging on my rack.

"Anders," I say with a warning to my tone at the size of the suitcase. At the implications.

"I want you to have options for the next three days." He's the picture of innocence, but I know better. He's planning to move me in, one suitcase at a time.

"You're the first person to want to live with me," I mumble.

He hears, of course he does. "Good. I want to have the rest of your firsts."

I reach for one of my favorite dresses, and cringe at the possibility of wrinkles from the folding, but I take a steadying breath and fold it, anyway. It's depressing that these clothes and my still-unrepaired car are all I have to my name. The only things worth any money. Everything else is temporary.

If I move in with him, will I be permanent in his life? Part of me wants permanence and stability like my next breath, but another part, small but loud, is scared and clings to the fact that I could leave tomorrow with a single suitcase and never look back. Right now, I have the freedom to walk away if I need to.

My life isn't normally rainbows and sunshine, but right now it is. And it's so scary I can barely breathe. Something must be on the horizon that will tear this all away from me.

He silently watches me fold another dress and cringe as I lay it in the suitcase.

"What's going on?" He covers my hand with his.

I'm close to tears, overwhelmed by everything. It's

annoying I can't be happy that he wants me. I'm too burned from my past to believe this is real. Instead, I say, "I'm folding designer dresses like a psychopath."

He pulls me into his arms, brushing a kiss across my lips, as if sensing it's not at all about the dresses. "We can use a garbage bag to cover them. It's just during transport and they'll be as good as new."

Why does he have the perfect solution for a problem I didn't really have? It gives me a glimpse of what life would be like with him by my side. He'd be there helping me through all my ups and downs and never waver. It makes me want to hold on to him and never let go.

When did he worm his way into my life so deeply?

He unfolds the dresses and returns them back to their hangers while I grab some garbage bags. I pass the bags to him in silence and bring the suitcase to my bathroom to grab my toiletries. The suitcase is far too big for the few items I have, but I place the shampoo, conditioner, and skin creams inside anyway.

My belongings barely fill half of the suitcase. I add the empty backpack and hope it'll add some volume to it and zip it shut before he can peek inside.

Anders, being Anders, takes the suitcase from my hands and raises his eyebrows at the weight.

I give him a look. "Not one comment."

He frowns before nodding slowly. "No problem. Come, let's get back home before the storm."

Home. The words passes through his lips so easily, as if he really sees me as part of that word. And part of me likes it, even if I'm scared.

After we return to his home and unpack the groceries,

he hangs my dresses in his closet and clears out a dresser drawer for me.

"Hungry?" he asks, once he finishes.

"I ate so much at your parents. I can't be hungry?" It comes out as a question, and my stomach protests that declaration with a loud rumble.

He laughs. "I'll make us some lunch."

"Let me help."

"Nope, but you can park your gorgeous self there"—he points to the bar stool at the counter—"and keep me company."

I sit and watch him cut chicken and prepare a marinade. My phone pings with a text from Lilly.

My heart trips over itself as I swipe open the message.

> Lilly: I need to know if you're bringing a plus one.

I CHEW on the inside of my cheek. I'd like to bring Anders, but I'm not sure if I should subject him to my apology tour.

"Who is it?" Anders asks.

"My sister. She wants to know if I'm bringing a plus one to her wedding."

"And do you want to? Bring a plus one?"

"It would be nice, but it's not going to be a fun wedding. It'll consist of me apologizing every other sentence."

"Because of your ex?" he asks.

I nod.

"What if I come with you?"

"I'd love that… but it's not realistic."

"What's the worst-case scenario?" he asks as he washes his hands and cleans up after placing the chicken and marinade in the fridge.

I snort. "I bring you and they're horribly mean to both of us. You don't deserve to be treated like that."

"Neither do you." He says it so simply that it throws me off balance. "What happened with your ex?"

He has a right to know, especially if he wants to be my boyfriend, but what if he doesn't want me when he finds out?

"I… I'm scared you're going to hate me or not trust me," I say.

"That's impossible."

I blow out a long breath. "I met Eric in college, but we didn't hang out in the same circles. Right after Addie died, he reached out and asked me on a date. It helped to focus on something other than my grief, and he was one of the smartest people I knew. When he wanted to create a startup, I invested in his company. He made it sound like the risk was low, especially when his figures were solid. I fell for his lies so easily and unfortunately convinced my family to invest as well. Four months after we invested, he disappeared."

That saying "don't shoot the messenger" really lived up to its name when I told my family what happened. They placed all the blame on me for convincing them to invest. They trusted me and thought if I was smart enough to run a division in a billion-dollar company as my job, then I'd be smart enough to determine if Eric's idea was worthwhile. I thought I was smart enough too. The kicker is, it was a good idea—an app to help people with their mental health—with a solid business plan.

"Disappeared?"

"Yeah, he ghosted us. When you give someone money, apparently you have three months to claim it as fraud, but after that time is up, the bank or police can't really help. We made contracts and everything, and I thought we were secure, but I was wrong. I was so stupid."

He's by my side in an instant and pulling me into his arms. "We all make mistakes."

"Not like that."

"How much did you lose?"

"Every single cent from my parents, myself, and what Addie left behind. We went all in. That's why they hate me and can't forgive me. But it's fine because I can't forgive myself."

"But it's not your fault," he says.

"Did you hear a word I just said?"

"Yes, did you? Because what I heard is Eric took advantage of the fact you were grieving and wormed his way into your life with the sole purpose of stealing from you, to con you."

I lift my head from his chest and frown. "What are you talking about?"

"Don't you think it suspicious he approached you right after Addie died?"

"I…" Was it? All I remember is the pain and anger over losing Addie, but Anders has a point. Why wouldn't Eric reach out to me in the years between college and Addie's death? Why did he wait?

He presses his advantage. "You weren't thinking clearly, and he took advantage of that. It's not your fault. It's his."

My world tilts on its side and everything I thought I knew gets rearranged within a millisecond. Eric targeted me.

Holy shit.

"You're a victim of a crime, Zoey. You're not the perpetrator."

My next breath comes as a gasp, and so does the next. I can't get enough air in my lungs no matter how many times I inhale.

Anders guides my head down between my legs. "Shh, it's okay. I've got you."

He rubs my back while I struggle to breathe. After a minute, I take my first deep breath since Anders spoke those words.

I sit up and wipe my face. "Am I a victim, even if I missed all the signs?"

"Even then." He says it so confidently, as if it's ridiculous I'd think otherwise. "I'm so sorry that happened to you, but it's not your fault."

"I think I'll need some more time before it really sinks in. I've spent months blaming myself..." Is this what ZWOL was referring to? Because if so, it's eerie how accurate the app has been.

"Well, good thing you have me to remind you."

Warmth spreads through my entire body at his declaration, the certainty in it. That he'll be by my side, supporting me. My hesitation at inviting him to the wedding disappears. He's more than capable of handling anything that comes his way.

"Will you come with me to the wedding?"

"Of course. I'll always have your back."

"We're going to have to miss work."

"You're more important than work. Ruby and Theo can run things when we're gone."

I laugh. "And not kill each other?"

"Maybe they need to get it out of their systems."

I move closer to kiss his cheek, but he turns his face at the last second to catch my lips.

"Smooth," I say, and he grins in response. "Let me text her now while I have the courage."

I head to my purse and type out a quick response to Lilly, letting her know that my plus one is my boyfriend. While there, I grab the gift I packed when we visited his family. It's remained in my purse since they didn't exchange gifts during the festivities.

The blue and silver wrapping paper is perfectly done, thanks to years of wrapping all the Christmas presents in my family. Mom hated to wrap, so I took over that task.

"Merry Christmas," I say and pass him the present.

His eyebrows shoot up. "You got me something?"

"Yeah, it's small, but..." I shrug, awkward.

He turns the package over in his hands a few times before opening the paper carefully, reverently, as if he's never received a present. When he reveals the new sketchbook, he traces the molasses-colored leather cover with his name engraved on it. There's a leather tie that he undoes and tests the paper inside. I got it on sale at a used bookstore and spent some extra money on the engraving.

But it's worth it to see the look of awe on his face.

"This is amazing," he says. "My old one was running out of pages. Thank you."

"You're welcome."

He sets the gift to the side. "I also have a present for you."

He produces an envelope from the kitchen drawer and passes it to me silently. It's thin and long. I carefully open it and a flight ticket is nestled inside. Well, a placeholder for a ticket, as if he made it on the computer to represent the real thing. On it states my name and the destination.

Helsinki.

I gape at him. "You can't be serious."

"I know Addie isn't here to join you, but I'd like to."

"Why?" Why would he do this for me? This might be the most meaningful gift I've ever received.

"Because it means something to you. You think I didn't notice your sadness when we talked about it? Maybe it could help…"

He doesn't finish his sentence, but he doesn't need to. Maybe it could help me heal after Addie's death.

"This is too much." I swallow down the emotion choking me.

"The cost is insignificant, and summer would be the perfect time to go…"

He's making plans for the future. For us, as a couple. And I'm not going to lie and pretend it's not significant. "Summer sounds good."

A blinding smile lights up his face and he lifts me in

the air. My legs go around his waist, and I close the distance between us and kiss him. I use my lips to show him how grateful I am, and how much his gift means to me.

Words are inadequate at a time like this.

Especially because I think I'm falling for him.

CHAPTER 20

"*I*t's time to let your hair down and have some fun! The stars are encouraging you to embrace your playful side and let loose without worrying about the consequences. This is the time to live in the moment and enjoy all that life has to offer. Keep shining bright, Leo, and remember to have fun along the way. Love always, ZWOL."

I WIPE down the tables at Amore while Anders makes us drinks. Last night felt so natural to spend the night with him. It'd be easy to become addicted to waking up with his arms wrapped around me.

Ruby still has off for the next few days, so it's just Anders and me manning the shop during the awkward week between Christmas and New Year's.

But no matter how hard I try to ignore it, his statement from last night runs on an endless loop in my mind. Was I really a victim of a crime?

It's a perspective shift that's beginning to take root, minute by minute. One that shines a whole new light on what happened. If we were victims, then the only person at fault was Eric. Not my family. And definitely not me.

Hope blossoms, and the promise of forgiveness suddenly feels within my grasp. The wedding is going to give me a chance to explain all the details I was too shocked to explain on Thanksgiving. I stayed silent during their attacks, and maybe they thought that because I wasn't defending myself, I was guilty. But when I explain everything, they'll for sure forgive me and accept me back into the family with open arms.

"Here's your hot chocolate," Anders says.

I jump. "Thanks."

He slaps my ass when he passes behind me.

"You can't slap my ass while we're here," I say.

"I want to do more than that." He runs his fingers down my ass and between my cheeks. "Do you know how much I've dreamed about fucking you over this counter? This ass has been teasing me from the first day you walked in here."

My core clenches and I push further into his touch. "I'm not going to be able to concentrate on anything if you keep that up."

"Good. Now you know how I've felt for weeks." He gives me a wicked grin. "We could always play a game to make the day go by faster."

"What kind of game?"

"A game in restraint, in teasing. Whoever breaks first and needs sex during the day loses."

"What do I get if I win?" I ask.

"Anything you want."

"Anything?"

"Anything."

"Done." I close the distance between our lips and kiss him.

He grips my ass and pulls me into his body. My leg goes around his waist, and he runs a finger over my slit.

I break away and catch my breath. "You play dirty."

"No, I play to win." He spears me with a heated look. "Which I will. My terms are the same as yours."

Oh fuck. Playing with him just might be the best-worst thing I've done today, and it's not even seven in the morning.

I pluck my hot chocolate, now more like lukewarm chocolate, off the counter and take a sip. He laughs and drinks his espresso in one go.

For the rest of the morning, he becomes an expert at teasing me whenever there's a lull in the customers. Which is more often than not.

He touches me everywhere but where I want him. Who knew my ribs were so sensitive? And my ear lobes. And my collarbone. And my calf, which he ran his hands up and down when he pretended to tie his shoe.

I'm rapidly losing this game. I should've adopted his strategy, but instead, I went with the straightforward approach and grope his ass and dick any chance I can get. But fuck, he doesn't appear to be close to giving in.

By lunch, I'm ready to break. My thong is soaked through and so are my leggings.

Maybe it's the fact that my dry spell is officially broken, and my vagina is looking to make up for lost time, but I feel like a sex fiend. I made it months without sex. I can totally make it through one workday without it.

But no, my pussy begs to disagree.

Anders sends me to the break room to eat first. I give myself a pep talk as I finish his homemade chicken curry. If I can get my hormones under control, I could win this.

But I wouldn't mind losing and finding out what Anders would request from me. Would it be sexual in nature or something else?

Once done, I heat up Anders's food for him.

Firm hands grab my hips, and I jump and spin around with a shriek. "Oh my stars, you scared me."

He doesn't say anything, but kisses me like he's waited years to kiss me. I fall into it, losing all sense of time and place, lost in a cushion of bliss.

The microwave's beep brings me back to the room.

I blink out of the daze and say, "I need to go take care of customers."

He smiles a knowing smile and pulls me into a hug. I take a moment to soak him up. His warmth, his presence.

If he wouldn't lose out on customers by leaving the counter unmanned, I'd give in. But I don't want to do that to Amore, especially after finding out about Courtney and what she did.

"You okay?" he asks and kisses my hair. "You ready to break yet?"

"Nope, not even close." I lie through my teeth.

He grins. "Keep telling that to your body."

It's two hours before closing and no one new comes through the doors. The remaining customers slowly file out. I clean the tables and counters to keep my mind off Anders.

But no matter how hard I try to have an Anders free moment, it doesn't happen.

I rub my thighs together, searching for any kind of friction to relieve the endless ache that he caused. Shit. I'm totally going to lose.

Anders takes in the empty place and grins when he notices my expression. He catches me by the waist and reels me into his body.

"Do you admit defeat?" He runs his nose along my neck. "I promise it'll be worth it."

I shudder. "Yes, please. I can't take it anymore."

He bends me over and my elbows rest on the countertop. A tug and my leggings and underwear end up just past my ass. He positions my flannel shirt to cover my backside. He enters me in one thrust and grips my neck, pulling me up a little.

"How fast can you come?" he demands.

I moan in response. "I... I don't know."

"Count." He chuckles and presses a finger against my clit. "Let's find out."

"Wh-what?" I keep my gaze glued to the door. Equal parts scared and exhilarated that someone can walk in at any moment.

"Start counting. Out. Loud."

I begin to count, but stumble over the numbers when he circles his hips. I barely finished saying the number sixty by the time my orgasm barrels into me with the speed of lightning. I come so hard I scream. He slaps my ass, and my pussy spasms around him. He shouts his own release, and I sag against the counter. My body needs time to reboot after that mind-blowing orgasm.

One minute. That's all it took for me to shatter.

Anders corrects my panties and leggings and tucks himself back into his pants. I'm still hanging onto the counter for dear life, not yet recovered.

When he finishes, he spins me in his arms and brushes a kiss across my lips. "Worth it?"

"I'd say I won our little bet with that orgasm."

He smirks. "I can't wait to claim my prize."

A group of people enter before I can respond. Holy shit. We were seconds away from being caught.

Anders moves me to the side, in front of the machines, while he greets them. I retie my shirt and run my hands through my hair, trying to tame the "just fucked" look I must be sporting.

And yet I feel no shame. Huh, maybe I'm a bit of an exhibitionist?

The remaining hours pass with me in a relaxed, dazed state. That orgasm must have messed with my brain because I'm still mush after it.

I don't think I've ever had so much fun on a shift. I crave him in a way I thought was only reserved for fictional characters. Eric and I never had this phase when we first started dating. Hell, I've never experienced this with anyone.

Anders doesn't stop smiling, and when Theo walks through the door thirty minutes before closing, he does a double take when he takes in Anders's smiling face.

"Hi," Theo says when he sees me.

"Hey, what can I get for you?"

"Nothing." Theo leans against the counter of the almost empty shop. "Just came to say hi since I was bored."

"More like you were looking for Ruby," Anders says.

Theo straightens. "Now why would I do that?"

"Ruby's off the next few days," I say.

Theo gives me a grateful look, and Anders says, "Actually, I was wondering if you could help us out."

"What is it?" Theo asks.

"We need to go to Zoey's sister's wedding in a few weeks. Can you cover for us and work with Ruby?"

"Yes." He says it so simply, not even needing to check his calendar.

I guess that's what it's like with family, close family. They're supportive and show up when someone needs help.

I wonder if Lilly or mom would be so open to the idea if I were to ask them. I somehow doubt it. They'd most likely make an excuse or make me feel guilty for even asking.

"Been busy today?" Theo asks.

I shake my head. "Not really."

"Maybe next year you can close the day after Christmas, too." Theo glances at Anders.

"I think that might be a good idea," Anders says, looking at me.

I ask Theo, "Do you have any plans for New Year's?"

"We have a big party at the bar that night, so I'll be working."

"Can we get tickets? Ruby too?" asks Anders.

"Of course, you don't even have to ask."

"I can't wait to see what cocktail specials you have planned." I haven't even thought about New Year's, but now I'm excited.

Theo grins. "You'll love it. I've been working on the menu for a month."

"A month? Just for this one occasion?"

"Tickets are five hundred a pop. My customers demand perfection."

My mouth hangs open. "Five hundred?"

He shrugs. "I'm the best bar in town. I can set my prices."

"Holy shit."

Anders throws an arm around my shoulders. "It's also the best New Year's party in the whole town."

"Well, now my expectations are through the roof."

Theo and Anders laugh, but don't try to manage my expectations or backtrack. They're so confident. I'm now even more curious about the party. After Theo leaves, I'm so excited about the prospect of getting dressed up and celebrating New Year's. I've never had a fancy New Year's.

It's not just getting dressed up and drinking cocktails, but I'm excited to go with Anders. For us to be together for real, without trying to hide how much I like him.

I'd like to buy a new outfit, but I've got to use the money I've made to buy a new dress for Lilly's wedding now that I'm not her maid of honor. It's something I've been putting off since I don't know what sort of dress would represent the apology I want to give them. Maybe Ruby can help me pick something out.

When we exit Amore after cleaning up, snowflakes fall

from the sky. I stare up at the dark clouds and smile as they caress my cheeks and melt on impact.

Anders brushes his hand against mine and I look over at him with a wide grin.

"You like the snow?" he asks.

"Only in short doses, it's too cold, but the first snow? It's my favorite. It feels magical after months without it."

He grabs my hand, holding it as he looks up at the sky and closes his eyes. I squeeze his hand. It doesn't matter if we're blocking part of the sidewalk, we're just enjoying the simple pleasures in life. Something I never used to do in Atlanta. If it snowed, it was a burden. I never enjoyed the beauty, the peace.

We make it back to Anders's house and he makes me a hot chocolate just the way I like it, so thick it's like a milkshake, with a splash of bourbon and lots of whipped cream.

I snuggle on his couch with the drink in hand. He sits next to me and arranges a fuzzy brown blanket over our legs. I lean into his side, and we watch the snow coat his backyard.

"I thought of a name for the new shop," I say.

"Oh?" Anders turns towards me.

"A Cup of Zodiac."

He remains silent and I turn to him fully. He's smiling broadly. "I love it."

"Yeah?"

"Yeah." He leans closer to me. "Just like I lo—"

His phone rings, stops, and rings again.

"Shouldn't you answer that?" I say, but what I really

want is for him to continue what he was going to say. Was he about to say love? What does he love?

He sighs and glances at the screen before straightening. "Hello?"

Whatever he hears, it causes him to tense. He pushes up from the couch and walks to his bedroom and shuts the door.

I could snoop and listen in on his conversation, but that'd be breaking his trust. He'll tell me if he wants to, though I'm dying to know.

After ten minutes, he returns.

"Everything okay?" I ask.

"Yeah." He turns on the TV and doesn't elaborate.

"Who was it?"

"Hayden."

When he doesn't continue, I say, "Not going to lie, you're acting mysterious in a bad way right now."

He sighs and throws his arm over my shoulders, and I snuggle back into the nook in his arm. "Sorry, we're in the middle of a deal to buy another company and it's falling apart. But I'm sure Hayden will figure it out."

"When did you start investing in other companies?" I ask.

"A few years ago. Remember I told you I did a startup with my brothers?"

I nod.

"We sold it for millions and reinvested most of it to fund new ventures and became investors in other companies."

I look at him. "I knew you were doing well with Amore, but I didn't think you were a multimillionaire."

"Does it change anything?"

Does it? Not really. I used to earn six figures a year and was on track to becoming a millionaire myself if I had invested my money wisely. That clearly didn't happen, and even if I'm poor now, it's not like I'm dating him for his money.

"No," I say. "But I am surprised. You don't act like a millionaire."

He arches an eyebrow. "What's a millionaire supposed to act like?"

"I don't know, someone who's more lavish in their spending?"

He laughs. "I don't have time to spend my money."

"Who does what in the company with your brothers?"

"Hayden basically runs the company for us. Theo and I chose to have smaller roles and do other things that we're more."

"Well, knowing this does take some of the pressure off A Cup of Zodiac. I thought it was make or break for you."

"It's not about the money, but I aim to succeed in every venture I embark on."

That statement causes me to respect him more. He's not just flippantly going into business knowing he's got millions to fall back on. No, he's determined to succeed.

"Said like a true entrepreneur," I say.

He chuckles and kisses my cheek. "Shall we watch a movie?"

"Okay, but we really need to work on A Cup of Zodiac now that I've got a CEO to impress."

He throws back his head and laughs. "Deal."

CHAPTER 21

"Psst, Leo. Listen up. It's time to stop playing second fiddle to someone else's ego trip and letting them trample all over your majestic self. Show 'em what you're made of and give them your best sassy side-eye that says, "Try me, I dare you." The universe is on your side, so don't settle for being a doormat when you were born to rule the damn jungle. Love always, ZWOL."

I smooth down my gold sequin dress and take one last look at my appearance before stepping into the living room. A living room that's become my own over the past week. Neither of us has mentioned the fact I've stayed longer than our original three-day agreement. We've found an excuse every night for me to stay, and I don't hate it.

Anders buckles his watch and glances up when I enter the room.

He does a double take and says, "I think my heart just stopped. You're breathtaking."

He crosses the room in a few steps and runs his finger across the hemline hitting high on my thigh. I shiver in response, and he lifts his fingers higher until they reach my thong. He traces over the edge of the silky material near my thigh.

I push against his burgundy suit, and he takes half a step back. "I spent way too long getting ready for you to mess it up."

That color suit would look ridiculous on someone else, but on him? It's perfection. Fitted like a glove and emphasizing all his muscles. His dress shirt has the top two buttons undone, and damn. Can he get any hotter?

"Fine, but later you're mine," he promises.

He helps me into my coat and wraps my arm through his as we walk to Theo's bar.

There's a line around the block of partygoers, but Anders bypasses it and heads straight through the door, nodding to the security guy.

Theo has decorated the inside with streamers and black balloons. The atmosphere is like a gothic New Year's celebration. Black roses paired with skulls, black balloons, blood red streamers, and banners saying "The End is Nigh" populate the space.

It's awesome.

It's already packed with people, and the hostess brings us to an empty table for three, the same one we used last time Ruby and I were here.

Apparently, it's the best one in the house. The nearest

table is a good distance away from us, but we're still in the middle of the action at the same time.

Theo's wearing a tux with a blood red shirt. He approaches us the minute we sit with two martini glasses filled with pitch black liquid, streaked with silver.

"Welcome to the party of your lives," Theo says.

He eyes the empty chair and raises his eyebrow in question.

I take one of the drinks and say, "Ruby just messaged. She's on her way."

Theo nods. "The menu is on the table. I'll come back over in a bit."

I take a sip of cocktail and am bombarded with the flavors of walnut, bitters, whiskey, and a hint of something silky.

It's delicious.

I lick my lips and Anders tracks the movement. He grabs my thigh under the table. "Careful, keep that up and we won't make it until midnight."

"Is that supposed to deter me?"

He squeezes my thigh again, but whatever he's about to say is cut off when Ruby slams her red clutch on the table.

We jump apart and she says, "I'm going to need all the cocktails to get me through this night."

She's wearing a black pantsuit but with no shirt underneath. Her jacket is open and somehow covering her breasts, though it looks like she may flash someone at any second.

"How was your trip?" I ask.

She lifts her shoulder. "Annoying. My sister wanted to

spend the entire time with her new girlfriend. I was the third wheel, and it was annoying as fuck."

Anders and I glance at each other. We've kept our contact with Ruby to a minimum over the past week, too wrapped up in each other. We planned on telling her we're together tonight.

Anders clears his throat. "Well, speaking of girlfriends..."

Ruby snaps her gaze between the two of us and raises an eyebrow. "When did this happen?"

"Christmas," I say.

Hurt flashes across her face. "And I'm only finding out about it now?"

"I'm sorry," I say. "I wanted to tell you in person and not over text."

"Is there something in the water?" Ruby asks. "Because everyone and their mother is in a relationship these days."

"Hayden's single... as well as Theo," Anders, oh so helpfully, says.

Ruby rolls her eyes and Theo arrives with a drink for her.

"Ruby," he says in greeting.

"Theo." She glances at him briefly before taking a sip of the offered drink.

He looks at her as if she's the only person in the room, but she pointedly ignores him, looking anywhere but at him. He continues to stare at her until Anders nudges him in the shoulder.

Theo glares at Anders and says, "I'll be back later."

Ruby continues to ignore him, and he stomps away with a huff.

I nudge her shoulder with my own. "What is going on between you two?"

"Nothing. Nothing at all."

I can't tell if Ruby's happy or disappointed about that fact. Before I can ask her about it, she steers the conversation back to us. "You better not make me a third wheel when we're all together."

"I promise," I say.

Ruby glares at Anders and he sighs. "Yes, fine. I promise, too."

Ruby nods, apparently satisfied with our responses, and lifts her drink in the air. "To new beginnings."

We all raise our glasses and drink to her declaration. We spend the next hour catching up, and it's the first time we've all relaxed around each other. Anders and I are in a good place, and we no longer have that push and pull thing going on.

It's an amazing feeling.

When Ruby and I head to the bathroom together, I say, "I really am sorry I didn't tell you earlier and that I've been MIA. I just... it feels too good to be true. It's hard to trust that, you know?"

"I get it. But just so you know, out of all the years I've known Anders, I've never seen him as happy as he is now."

"Yeah?" It's comforting for her to confirm this. That I'm not imagining my feelings or his, even if we haven't said anything out loud. Even if I've only known him for a month.

"I may not believe in relationships for myself, but happiness sure does look good on you."

"Thank you," I say, hugging her.

She hugs me back for a moment before releasing me. "Okay, I'm all hugged out. Let's go party."

As we head back to the table, my phone buzzes with a new message.

> Lilly: You've got to be kidding me. You're not bringing some random guy as your plus one to my wedding.

I STARE at the message in disbelief. It's been a week, and she's only writing back *now*? Well, ZWOL said I should stick up for myself, so I write back doing just that.

> Me: I can bring whoever I want. If you didn't want me to bring someone, then why give me the option?

> Lilly: Given your track record, being with a guy should be the last thing on your mind.

I WINCE. Okay, sticking up for myself lasted two point five seconds. It's not easy to do when I'm trying to make amends with my family, and when I'm reminded of my failures every other sentence.

"Who are you messaging?" Anders asks.

280

"Lilly. She's just now responding to my message from a week ago."

"About bringing me?"

I nod. He gestures to my phone, and I pass it to him.

"What's going on?" Ruby asks.

I summarize as briefly as I can, and she asks to see the phone as well.

"I don't know maybe it's easier if you don't come," I say to Anders.

"Easier for them, but not for you," he says. "There's no way you're dealing with them alone."

"But—"

"No buts."

"Yet—"

"Or yets."

I glare at him. "Fine, however—"

"Or howevers." He pulls me into a hug. "Lilly doesn't scare me, and neither do your parents."

I lay my head on his chest. "You're really coming?"

"Of course. Tell her that and stand your ground."

He's right. I can't keep ignoring my wants and needs because of them.

Shaking out my hands, I take the phone from Ruby and type in my response.

Me: I'm happy with my decision. He's coming. See you in a few weeks.

My heart races as adrenaline floods my system. One message and I'm filled with the flight or fight response. On one side, I'm proud I did it, but on the other, I'm freaking the fuck out. I can't help but worry about the implications. At how this'll influence my apology tour.

I reread the words of my message twenty times, as if confirming I really hit send. I wait for her response, but nothing comes.

"If it helps," Ruby says, "your sister sounds like a bitch."

I chug my drink. I have a choice: to panic and ruin the night or to let it go and enjoy the now. But my family has ruined enough. They don't get to ruin tonight, too.

"Let's dance," I say.

The rest of the night is filled with drinks, dancing, and laughter. Thirty seconds before midnight, when the countdown clock begins, Anders pulls me into his arms. Bodies press into us from all sides on the dance floor, but all I feel and see is Anders.

He cups my cheek before saying, "Happy New Year's. Here's to a year of love, happiness, and adventure. Together."

"Together," I repeat.

The crowd chants the numbers, all staring at the screen, but Anders doesn't care. With ten seconds to go, he kisses me like he's a dying man and I'm the cure.

Confetti sticks to our skin as it falls from the ceiling, and people cheer around us, but we don't stop kissing. I'm as lost in him as he's in me.

When we finally break apart, everyone is back to dancing and celebrating. I cling to his arms, disoriented from that epic kiss. His gaze softens as he takes me in and he kisses me one more time, short and sweet.

A final taste before we rejoin the real world, even if I would prefer not to. I want to stay wrapped up together, in our own bubble. And why not do something about that? No one is forcing us to stay and party.

"Do you want to get out of here?" I ask.

He nods and searches for Ruby. She's with a guy and Anders talks to her for a bit before Ruby gives me a thumbs up. I barely have time to wave back before he's pulling me out the door.

My skin heats every time he touches me on the walk home, which is constantly. The walk itself is foreplay and I'm about to combust, my desire crashing into me with the subtly of an eighteen-wheeler.

When we arrive, he closes the door and flips the lock. He turns around to face me, as if suddenly he has all the time in the world.

He takes measured steps toward me and spins me so that my back is to his front. He oh so slowly lowers the zipper on my dress one tooth at a time. My dress pools around my feet when there's nothing left to hold it up.

He doesn't speak, and why is that so hot?

He palms my breasts before tossing my bra to the floor. My thong is next, but he doesn't let it drop.

No, he pockets that shit like he's going to build a shrine.

He brushes my hair to the side and nips and licks at my neck before making it to my ear.

"You know I respect you, right?" he asks.

I nod, confused as to where this is going.

He leans closer and whispers, "Good, because I'm about to fuck you like I don't."

Aaannnddd that's it, I'm toast.

Words.

That's all it takes to cause a mini orgasm.

He picks me up, throws me over his shoulder, and slaps my ass on the way to his bedroom. His clothes brush against my skin with every step.

I'm tossed on the bed, and he arranges me on all fours. In the next second, he slams into me. He yanks my hair back, and I arch to accommodate the force.

He pulls out so slowly, it's torturous, and crashes back in.

With every thrust inside, I'm jolted forward. He wraps my hair around his hand, keeping me in place. My scalp stings, but it's not enough for me to stop.

"Do you like when I fuck you like this?" he asks. "When I take everything for myself and don't concern myself with your pleasure?"

"Yes," I moan.

And I do because I know I'll never truly be left without pleasure, like with Eric.

I ache for him, for more, for everything he has to give.

He pulls out again, and I wait for him to re-enter me.

And wait.

But nothing happens.

I turn my head to look over my shoulder, but he grabs the back of my neck and nips my shoulder.

"Don't move," he says.

My whole body is hyperaware of him as he shuffles around the room. Stopping is its own form of torture. My arms shake as I wait, for what I'm not sure. The sounds of him undressing, opening and closing a drawer, and the pop of a plastic cap opening fill the air.

He positions himself behind me again and rubs his thumb over my other hole. "You ever had something in here?" he asks.

I tense and nod. Never with a partner, just me experimenting while alone.

"Did you like it?" He dips the tip of his thumb inside my ass and rubs my clit with his fingers.

"Yes," I whisper, "but I've never had anal sex." And I don't think I'm ready for that.

"Do you trust me?"

Do I?

Trusting someone after Eric's betrayal used to seem unbearable. But with Anders? It's a real possibility. He's someone I can rely on and has been there for me nonstop since moving here. Even if we started out all wrong, I can at least trust him with my body. And maybe, just maybe, eventually with my heart.

I nod, and he hums with his approval. "I'll only play with you here with my fingers tonight." He moves his thumb deeper inside. "Okay?"

I nod again, but he pulls me up to my knees, so my back is flush against his front. "I need to hear you say it out loud."

"Okay, but can you fuck me now?"

He pushes me back onto my hands and knees and bites my ass cheek. "I'll fuck you when I want to."

I push my ass back, searching for more, for him.

He slaps my pussy. "Naughty, naughty."

I force myself to remain still, even though the wait is killing me. If I listen to him, maybe he'll must give in sooner.

But the wait drags out endlessly, and I'm hyper focused on every movement he makes.

He runs a finger down my spine and toward my ass, but he skips over everywhere I want him to touch. His fingers jump to my toe and lazily draws them up my foot, my calf, my thigh. They jump again, this time to my ribs, my hips, my stomach.

I'm so focused on his fingers tracing my shoulder blade that when he thrusts into me, I scream.

He chuckles and pours lube over my ass. He keeps a steady rhythm while he teases my forbidden hole with his fingers. Circling, teasing my entrance, circling, inserting the smallest amount of his finger before retreating.

It's driving me insane. Ecstasy and torture weave through my body. It's not enough, and yet it's sensory overload.

"Please," I beg.

With one last slap of my ass, he finally inserts more of his finger and picks up the pace.

I grip the covers and hold on. It's all I can do. Pleasure builds until it crashes over me in a wave so strong, my soul leaves my body for a hot minute. He follows me into the land of bliss.

We're both breathing hard as he gently lays me on the bed.

"Are you okay?" he asks.

"Better than okay. That was…"

"Epic?"

I laugh. "Yes."

I cup his face in my hands and pull him into a kiss. It's gentle, slow, sweet. The exact opposite of our sex, but still amazing.

Damn, having sex with him will never get old.

He pulls back before peppering kisses across my cheek, down my neck, and to my breasts. "Let me draw you a bath and make you feel good. So you can start your new year right."

I grin. "Happy New Year to me."

"To us."

"To us," I repeat.

And why does that sound so good?

CHAPTER 22

"*L*eo, the stars indicate you need to learn a difficult lesson today. It's time to ditch those rose-colored glasses and see things as they really are. No matter how hard it may be to accept, the truth will come to light today. Remember to trust your own inner strength and resilience. Good luck, you'll need it. Love always, ZWOL."

ANDERS'S HAND rests on my bouncing thigh as the pilot informs us that we'll be landing in twenty minutes. We took the night flight to Charlotte, and I'm exhausted. Even though Anders bumped us up to business class, I couldn't sleep.

Since the holidays, Anders and I have spent every second together. Working at Amore, working on A Cup of Zodiac, learning about each other. And everything I learn about him, every moment we're together, solidifies my feelings for him. Anders reminds me daily that I'm worthy of forgiveness from my family, that I'm not responsible for Eric's actions, and that a crime was committed against us.

Since New Year's, he started writing down all these beliefs on sticky notes and sticking them to his bathroom mirror, to random surfaces in my apartment, and to the wall in the break room at Amore. Ruby also started writing her own sticky notes. But those are all about me being a badass.

My confidence is at an all-time high, even if there's still a nugget of guilt that my family got caught up in the mess with Eric. With Ruby, Anders, and his family around, I'm the happiest I've been since even before Addie died.

And I'm ready to face my family. I'm ready to tell them what happened with Eric, so they realize I didn't have any part in it. How he approached me when I was at my most vulnerable, and we all fell for his lies. Not just me.

I'm one thousand percent sure they'll forgive me once they hear me out.

In about six hours, I'll see them for the first time since The Event That Shall Not Be Named, aka Thanksgiving, aka the moment they discovered Eric fooled us all and the money we invested in his business disappeared along with him.

"You okay?" Anders asks for the millionth time.

"Sure."

"Don't lie. Not to me."

I blow out a long breath and say, "It depends on the minute. One minute I'm confident, the next I'm freaking out a little."

"It'll be okay. A shower and a quick nap will make it all better."

"That's some solid life advice there."

He laughs. "Of course, it is. It's coming from me."

* * *

BABY PINK THREW up all over the room. Lilly always loved the color, but to have it on the tablecloths, carnations, napkins, and name cards is a bit cringe. It reminds me of a child's birthday party rather than a wedding. Though with that kind of history, it wouldn't be somewhere I'd want to use for a new beginning.

Instead of the estate, we're in the event room of the local hotel. Instead of hardwood floors, we have a drab, multicolored carpet of an average two-starred one.

There are two adjoining rooms for the wedding. One is set up for the meal with tables and centerpieces, and the other for the ceremony with a stage and aisle. My father is shaking everyone's hand as they come through the door to sit for the ceremony.

I tighten my death grip on Anders's hand when I see him. He's combed his dark hair to the side and gelled it into place. His black suit fits him without a wrinkle in sight and his shoes are polished to perfection.

We wait behind a couple, friends of my parents from their college times. They probably only invited them to show off that Lilly found a husband.

After too many congratulations to count, they move on to find their seats. I step forward, my slate gray A-line dress brushing my calves.

"Zoey." His tone is curt. I never expected my name to sound so disgraced on his lips, but here we are. His heart clearly hasn't warmed toward me these past months.

I let his disappointment and anger wash over me. It's okay, he doesn't know the truth. "Dad. Please allow me to introduce my boyfriend, Anders. Anders, my dad, Chris."

Anders holds out his hand for a handshake. My dad can't stop his eyes from rolling. He doesn't lift his hand to shake Anders's hand and instead glares at it as if it's poison. Anders drops his hand and uses it to wrap around my hip, pulling me closer into his body, as if to shield me from the hurtful words building on my father's tongue.

I brace myself when my father straightens his shoulders. "You have some nerve bringing a boyfriend here. I can't believe you didn't listen to Lilly when she told you not to bring him. Are you trying to ruin her big day... well, more than you already have?"

A hundred responses form, but I'm not about to make a scene. No matter how I respond, my father won't listen. Not right now, when people are watching. I need to talk to him in private.

It doesn't help that one of his biggest triggers is money. He's been so frugal his entire life, and it was going to pay off for him. My parents were set to retire, to enjoy all the money he had carefully saved away. They wanted to travel to all the places they put off because of life, but life just got in the way yet again.

He's now got only a few thousand dollars to his name, and his dreams of retirement have disappeared because of Eric.

I paste on a smile. "Good to see you too. Hope you enjoy the wedding."

I tug on Anders's hand and guide him to the bride's side. I sit four rows back, close enough to the front, but not close enough to offend my parents. I snag a place next to the aisle so I can see Lilly clearly when she makes her appearance.

"So that's your dad," Anders says.

I snort. "Yeah…"

Anders doesn't say anything in response, probably picking up on how much my father's words hurt, and instead places his hand on my knee and squeezes. I place my hand over his and wait.

Wait for the right time to talk to my family. Anticipation is killing me, but it's not like I can ask for a schedule and have them pencil in a chat with me today.

But I'm dying from anticipation, of not knowing when I'll be able to talk to them. The older man sitting across the aisle from us adjusts his bow tie. He looks like a number fourteen. When he grumbles as a person slides past his knees and to the empty seats next to him, I smile.

"Ha, I knew he was a number fourteen."

"Did you just say someone is a number fourteen?" Anders glances at me.

I close my eyes briefly. "Please tell me I didn't say that out loud."

"You did." Anders tilts my face toward his. "What does it mean?"

"So, I kind of number people and guess their zodiac signs."

He raises an eyebrow. "Really?"

"Yeah, it was something I did with Addie at her bakery. It was fun."

"What number and sign did you guess for me when we first met?"

"I didn't… it was the first time I ever drew a blank."

He looks far too pleased with that response. "So, who's number fourteen and why?"

"The man across the aisle. Uptight, prickly. I don't know, it's just the number that somehow fits that description for me."

"So that would be what? A Virgo?"

I turn toward him so fast, I almost fall out of my chair. "What… how did you know that?"

"We're opening a zodiac-themed coffee shop." He grins. "I was bound to pick up some things along the way."

I lean toward him and steal a kiss. Even though he doesn't believe in horoscopes, he's learned about them. And not only that, but he's playing the same game I used to play with Addie.

"What about her?" He nods toward a woman with bleach blonde hair and a skin-tight red dress that wouldn't be appropriate at most weddings.

"Oh, that's easy. She's a sixty-seven."

"Why?"

"Slutty, but in a good way. She's on the prowl, but it looks like she'll turn on someone if they cross her. Perhaps a bit catty?"

"I'm not sure what zodiac sign that'd be?"

I laugh. "Let's go with Scorpio."

I lean into his side as my mother makes the announcement that the wedding is about to start.

When the music begins, I turn to the back doors and watch as the bridesmaids walk down the aisle. When the maid of honor comes, it's a stranger. It's a kick in the teeth to be replaced by a random person. It would've been easier if she'd chosen an old friend, but no. That's not Lilly's style.

The music swells and transitions into the traditional bridal march. My father beams as he walks Lilly down the aisle. Lilly looks like a princess in her puffy white gown. It's like something Cinderella would wear, and I can't help the emotion that overwhelms me. To see my younger sister looking so grown up.

Her gaze coasts past me, like she didn't even see me. Maybe she didn't. Maybe it's overwhelming to see so many people staring. Either way, I video the entire thing. It's something I'll replay repeatedly when I miss her.

The ceremony passes by slowly, but I savor every moment of it. This is what we dreamed of as kids. The moment when the person we love promises to be with us forever. To bind themselves to us.

There's something romantic about pledging your love to someone so publicly.

When it's over, the guests make their way to their tables while the photographer leads the wedding party away for photos.

Photos my family doesn't ask me to be part of. They've let me be here, but they're still ostracizing me, and they don't seem to care. Photos last forever, and I won't be part of a single one from today. It'll be like I died.

Even if we make up in a few hours or days or even years, I'll still not be in a single photo from Lilly's wedding. It'll be a scar that will last forever, and a reminder of how much they're punishing me for something that wasn't only my fault.

Anders passes me a glass of champagne, and I chug it in one go. He raises an eyebrow, but I ignore it. I set the flute down on a random table.

He stares at the door my family went through for a beat before gripping my hand. He pulls me in the direction they went. I clutch his hand too tightly, as if it'll contain my devastation.

"Where are we going?" I ask.

He doesn't respond and looks right and left through every open door we come across. When he spots a staff member, he stops them and asks, "Do you know where the wedding party went?"

"Sure, down that way and out the door." The staff member points to the door at the end of the hall that leads to a small courtyard.

"Thanks," Anders says and pulls me along.

"Anders," I warn.

"One photo, and then we'll go back to the reception."

"Why?"

"You think I missed the pain on your face when you watched them leave without you?"

I chew on the inside of my cheek. "Fine, one photo. If they accept that."

We enter the courtyard that has an arch decorated with pink flowers. Lilly and her husband are beneath it with their wedding party. My parents mingle with his parents off to the side and sip champagne.

My mother spots me first. "What are you doing here?"

Anders squeezes my hand in support.

"I'd like one photo with Lilly," I say.

My father snaps his gaze to mine. "No."

"One photo won't hurt." Mom shoots a pointed look at the people around us.

My dad turns his back on me and mumbles something to my mother.

The rest of the wedding party steps off to the side and Anders nudges my back. I approach Lilly under the arch.

"You look beautiful," I say.

"I know," she says. Just Lilly being Lilly.

The photographer directs us to do a few different poses, back-to-back, side-to-side, and facing each other with our hands entwined. The entire time, Anders watches me with a quiet intensity. Offering me support with just his gaze.

When the photographer lowers the camera, I say to Lilly, "I'm so sorry. For everything. I love you, and I don't want to fight anymore. I can't take it."

Lilly opens her mouth to respond, but my mom interrupts. "Are you done yet? We need to get a move on, so the guests don't have to wait hours before eating."

Lilly steps away from me, and the moment disappears. She says to the photographer, "What's next?"

I take it as my cue to leave and walk back to Anders with my chin held high. Once we're out of earshot and halfway back to the reception area, I tug Anders to a stop.

"Thank you," I say. "I'm so glad you insisted I do that."

Anders smiles. "You need a drink?"

"More like twenty."

"I can do that."

We make a beeline to the cash bar and both order whiskey on the rocks. Simple, but with a burn that works its way down my throat and into my empty stomach.

We walk around the room, hunting for our table. When we find it, it's filled with people Lilly isn't close to. The ones she invited because she had to, not because she wanted to. There's a neighbor we used to live next to when we were five but have not seen since, a frenemy of Lilly's who's now dating Lilly's old boss, and someone her husband works with.

It's another thing to add to the list of hurts I'm accumulating while here, ones I'll dwell on when I get back to Portland. But first, I need to make it through the night. Maybe I should turn it into a drinking game. The more I hurt, the more I drink. That seems perfectly reasonable to me.

I drain my whiskey and Anders passes me his full one without question.

The lights dim and an MC welcomes the new couple to the room. We all clap while Lilly and her husband enter. They stand behind their table and thank everyone for coming, crack a few jokes, and then inform everyone the buffet is open.

I don't move, and Anders asks, "Aren't you hungry?"

I sigh. "It's a buffet which means it's a cross contamination nightmare."

Anders remains seated next to me. "Whenever you want to leave, we'll leave."

I lift my glass to Anders and say, "Thank you. In the meantime, I'll continue with my soup diet."

"Soup?"

"Whiskey soup."

Anders chuckles and nuzzles my neck, dotting kisses up to my ear. "I'll join you on said diet."

The next hour drags by, and not in a good way. I'm so glad Anders is here to keep me entertained through the slideshow of baby pictures I'm not in, speeches that don't mention me, and cake cutting.

Once everyone finishes eating, the DJ begins to play music for people to dance to. Typical cringy wedding music pumps through the speakers.

I debate if I want to dance, or if I want to leave when Lilly takes the empty seat next to mine.

"Having fun?" I ask.

She lifts her shoulder. "It's okay, a lot of talking to random people rather than enjoying."

I smile, but she doesn't return it. Instead, she glares at Anders holding my hand on the table.

She swirls the champagne in her glass. "I see you've scraped the bottom of the barrel to find this guy."

I take a calming breath and focus on my goal. At explaining everything. "Let's not waste time talking about anything besides you and me. I need to explain what happened with Eric."

"And I'm not interested in listening."

"You should," I say, "because he conned us all. Targeted us when we were emotional and grieving the loss of Addie."

"No, he conned *you*. Not me."

"Only because you had no money of your own to invest."

She glares at me. "And you were stupid enough to fall

298

for his con and drag mom and dad into it. I told them they shouldn't invest, that it was too good to be true, but they trusted you. And you broke that."

"And I'm trying to make it up to them, to you."

"Really? Because from where I'm standing, you're not trying at all. You're off living your best life and jumping into yet another relationship. I was the one left to pick up the pieces and deal with the aftermath." She points to her chest. "Me. Not you."

"Living my best life? You mean being so poor I can barely afford food?"

"You're not any skinnier, so it can't have been that bad." She throws her hands in the air. "Just stop with your sob story. You're not the victim in this story."

"But I am, and so are you."

"No, I'm not. And whoever told you that you are is lying."

"Wait one minute," Anders says.

"What do you want from me?" I ask Lilly, talking over Anders.

"To pay mom and dad back. To stop ruining everyone's life with your issues. It's not that hard. Get it together."

"That's enough," Anders says coldly. "You've gone too far, and I will not sit here while you talk about Zoey like that."

"And you're just a placeholder in her life," she says. "Just wait, she'll ruin you too. It's her specialty."

I whisper, "Is that really what you think of me? That I ruin everything?"

"If the shoe fits…"

"It's time for you to leave," Anders says to her.

Lilly storms away and I hang my head and rub my temples. I refuse to cry in a room full of people. But everything Lilly says keeps swirling around in my mind. And it all comes back to the same thing—Lilly hates me. And it's clearly not a new feeling.

How did I not see it before? I really am the worst judge of character. First Eric, and now Lilly. Who else have I misjudged? Addie? My parents? Anders? Ruby? Fucking hell.

Anders rubs my back. "So, that went well."

"I handled that all wrong."

"Not from where I'm sitting." He reaches out and cups my cheek. "How can you not see how horrible they're treating you?"

"She's just mad..."

"Let me ask you this. How do you think my mom would react to me losing all of her money?"

"I..." I pause and think about it. "She'd be pissed but would probably work with you to find a way forward."

"Exactly. We'd figure it out together, as a family."

"But that's your family. That's not how it is in mine..."

"And do you think that's right?" he asks.

I whisper, "No?"

To admit aloud that my family isn't all that great feels wrong, like I'm outing them when I should be protecting them. But I was blinded by love and some imaginary loyalty to people who threw me away the second they got the chance. They've hurled insults my way and acted like I was less than, and reminded me of it anytime we talk.

Oh my stars.

My family really are treating me like trash. They hate me. Even if I messed up with Eric, do I really deserve that?

"Can we go?" I ask.

"Are you sure?"

"I can't take it anymore; I see it now. How they've been treating me."

He nods once. "I'll call our driver."

"Let me clean up in the bathroom first. Meet you outside in a few minutes?"

He nods and we worm our way through the dancing crowd and out the doors. He heads to the front of the hotel while I go to the restroom. When I come out of the stall, my mom is leaning against the sink.

"Hey," I say, my heart sinking.

"You looked cozy with that guy you brought."

"He's a good man," I say, trying to convince her of that, as if those simple words would be enough to influence her opinion of him. Part of me is still holding out hope that she's not as mad as Lilly and dad. That I didn't misjudge her, that I can get through to her.

"That's nice, dear." She says it in an automatic way, like she didn't hear a word I said. Like it's just a placeholder in the conversation until she can say what she really wants to say. "But why did you come?"

"Lilly invited me, and I actually wanted to talk to you. About what happened with Eric."

"Oh, so now you're ready to talk about him?"

"I've been ready," I say. You're the one who's ignoring me, who won't take my calls. The question is, are you ready to listen?"

"There's nothing you can say that'll make it better."

"Even if he was a con artist and took advantage of us? Targeted us right when Addie died and stole close to one million dollars?"

"What difference does it make? You're the one who let such trash into our home, into our lives," she says.

"And you were the one who welcomed him with open arms. You decided to invest. No one forced you."

"Because I trusted you," she yells, "and that trust has ruined my life."

"But you won't even let me try to fix it."

"If you really wanted to fix it, you wouldn't have moved across the country in the first place. You'd be here, repenting."

"I needed a fresh start to heal first. What I went through… it was too much."

"Was it? Because it looks like you didn't learn anything if you're in a new relationship."

And just like that, any hope for mom being on my side bursts. In place of the hope is anger. Anger at how they're treating me, how they've iced me out for months. How she doesn't think what happened was enough to learn some imaginary lesson she thinks I need.

Worst of all, she's dragging Anders into it. Making assumptions about him left, right, and center, and she doesn't even fucking know him.

Just like she doesn't know me.

"What do want from me?" I ask.

"I want you to repay what was lost. It's your fault, and you've got to fix it. Stop wasting your time with that stupid man and focus on what's important. Family is forever."

"Is it?" I ask. "Because from where I'm standing, it seems family is only temporary."

"One day you'll realize just how important family is. Soon, you'll be calling me in tears, and you'll come crawling back with your tail between your legs."

I huff out a laugh. "Thanks for the vote of confidence."

"You know I'm right, and that's why you're mad. Sometimes we're meant to be alone in life. Addie was, and I think you are too."

"Don't you dare bring her into this."

She snorts. "She was *my* sister, not yours."

"Well, she was more of a mom to me than you ever were."

The slap comes out of nowhere.

The sting in my cheek doesn't begin to register until Mom gasps and holds her hand over her mouth.

I cradle my cheek and stare at her in shock. I need to move, but my body isn't cooperating. The only thing working is my tear ducts.

Finally, fucking finally, my body restarts, and I burst out of the bathroom. I race down the hallway, through reception, and past the sliding glass doors that lead to the outside.

I barrel into Anders, who catches me easily. I'm a sobbing mess and his eyes widen in shock when he takes me in.

"What happened?" His gaze roams my face, and he touches my cheek before saying in a deadly voice, "Did someone hit you?"

"Can we please go?" I beg.

He stares at the sliding doors, as if he's going to go inside and hold up the wedding until he gets answers.

"Please." My voice cracks.

"Fine, but you will tell me. And there'll be hell to pay for whoever hurt you."

* * *

ONCE WE'RE inside the car, he gives directions to the driver before sliding the privacy window closed.

"What happened?" he demands.

"My mom. We said some horrible things to each other."

He passes me a cold bottle of champagne and motions for me to place it against my cheek. "That doesn't give the right to hurt you."

"Yeah…"

The bottle soothes the sting, at least on the outside.

"I'm sorry you're related to those people," he says.

I close my eyes and lean into the seat. "I'm so stupid. I really thought I'd waltz in and somehow turn everything around. And now? I'm not sure if I even have a family left after this."

It's agonizing to know it'll never be fixed, that all hope is gone. There's a fine line between hope and delusion and I must have crossed over it to even entertain the idea of them welcoming me back with open arms.

"Family is about who we choose to be with rather than who we're related to by blood. You have my family, me, and Ruby."

"How can you be so sure?" I glance at him.

"Simple. I'm in love with you."

"Wait, what?"

He looks me in the eye and says, "I'm in love with you."

Time slows, sounds stop, and my focus narrows to him.

To this moment.

To his declaration.

To the most meaningful words I've ever been told.

Tears roll down my cheeks and he wipes them away with his thumbs.

"How can you love me after knowing everything I've done?" I ask.

"Knowing all of that makes me love you more."

"But what if I fuck up A Cup of Zodiac?" And ruin him like Lilly expects.

"You mean if *we* fuck it up? If that happens, we'll find a way to fix it. Together."

"I..."

"Don't you get it? I can't not love you. That's like asking me to stop breathing."

I lean my cheek further into his hand. I may have been wrong about Eric and my family, but I can't be wrong about Anders. Right? Because if I am, how can something so wrong feel so right?

"I love you, too," I whisper.

His smile lights up the entire car, and he kisses me with so much tenderness, as if he's afraid I'll break after saying those words. I just might, but it doesn't make it any less true.

We settle back into the seats, and he refuses to let go of my hand.

I count the cars on the road, taking renewed comfort in the numbers I love so much.

How is it possible to experience boundless joy while simultaneously being consumed by profound anguish?

I mentally create a tourniquet around all my emotions concerning my family. They've taken up enough of my time and energy tonight. I refuse to give them more of me, not until I have time to process the implications of everything.

My stomach releases a loud grumble. "I guess I'm hungry."

"Don't worry, I've got the perfect place for us."

We pull up to a restaurant called Niche. I've never heard of it, but Anders leads me through the door and the hostess seats us immediately. It's cozy. The room is full of brown tables and booths, and the walls are cream.

Anders slides into my side of the booth and opens the menu.

"Everything in the restaurant is gluten free," he says.

"No."

"Yes." He laughs. "No risk of cross contamination here."

"How did you find this place?"

"I may or may not have searched for all the gluten-free restaurants within a thirty-mile radius of your hometown. It's brand new."

Ugh, can Anders be even more amazing? He just admitted to loving all the fucked-up parts of me, and now he's taking care of me. Being my buoy in the storm that is my life.

"What would I do without you?" I brush my lips across his in an almost kiss.

"Starve?"

"Probably." I laugh and swat him on the arm.

The menu has all the classic southern comfort food options I could ask for.

"I can't decide. I want to try it all."

Anders grins and waves down the waitress. "Can we have a tasting sized portion of everything on the menu?"

"Everything?" Her eyes widen.

He nods. "It all looks so good. We want to try everything."

"But we don't do tastings," she says.

"I understand." He smiles. "I'll happily pay full price. We just don't want to waste any food."

"Let me ask the chef," the waitress says.

She hurries to the kitchen.

I turn to Anders. "I can decide. I was only joking. There's no need to spend hundreds on a dinner."

"Why not? I can afford it and I'm curious, too."

Ever since he told me he's a millionaire, I've noticed him relaxing his spending around me. First with the business class tickets here, and now this.

"But—" I begin.

"Let me take care of you. After tonight, you need some happiness."

An unexpected wave of emotion rolls through me, and I get teary at his statement. "Thank you."

"You deserve it." He runs his thumbs under my eyes, catching any tears before they fall.

"The chef agreed with your request," the waitress says. "I'll bring out the items as soon as they're cooked."

We thank her and for the first time since boarding the plane, I allow myself to relax. To enjoy the moment with the only person in the world who loves me.

CHAPTER 23

"*H*old onto your hat, Leo, because with Mercury in retrograde, it's bound to be a wild ride. Expect miscommunications left, right, center, above, and below. But fear not. Clear communication is still possible if you choose your words wisely and listen actively. Don't jump to conclusions like a kangaroo hyped up on caffeine. Take the time to really understand others. Love always, ZWOL."

SINCE THE WEDDING a few weeks ago, something has changed between Anders and me. We're closer somehow. Maybe it's because I finally admitted out loud that I love him.

Or maybe it's because he tells me every day how much he loves me.

Life is good, amazing even, if I don't think about my family. They haven't reached out since the wedding, and neither have I. I expected my mom to apologize at the very least, but that hasn't happened.

So my doozy of a horoscope has put me on edge. Is it something to do with my family? Or my life here? We're under an immense amount of work pressure between Amore and A Cup of Zodiac opening in a few days. Theo connected us to Athena, a chef. We've been working nonstop to get her up-to-speed.

I get ready in Anders's bathroom for my girls' night with Ruby. When I returned from the wedding, she told me she has a surprise and demanded I clear my schedule for tonight. She guaranteed that her surprise is so good, I'll forever be in her debt. With a promise like that, I couldn't say no.

"Ruby will be here in five," Anders says from the doorway.

I spray on my perfume and say, "Are you sure it's okay I go? We still have to organize—"

He laughs and places his hands on my shoulder. "—the painters. I'll take care of it."

"And the—"

"—signboards."

I glare at him. "Are you psychic now?"

"Obviously."

"Then tell me what my horoscope means."

"You know, it could be something small that you're blowing out of proportion," he says.

"Hopefully..."

"Go. Have fun and take your mind off everything."

I lean in and kiss him. "Thank you."

A honk sounds from the front and Anders rolls his

eyes at Ruby's antics.

I grab my purse and when I'm at the front door, he says, "Keep me updated."

"Will do."

Ruby keeps up a steady stream of chatter while driving toward our destination, an auditorium.

"What are we doing here?" I turn to her and frown.

"There's a TED Talk you need to hear."

"Ohh, I love TED Talks. What's this one about?"

"The creator of the Zodiac Way of Life app is going to talk about their success and what they've learned from helping so many people."

I squeal with excitement. "You really are my favorite person."

She laughs. "Told you."

We filter into the multi-level venue, full of red chairs and spotlights. We're on the ground level and in the middle section, with a nice view of the stage.

After endless waiting, an MC takes the stage and makes the introduction.

"Tonight, we're doing something we've never done before at TED. The Zodiac Way of Life app has changed millions of people's lives in a short time. The CEO and founder, Beau Fellows, has a different philosophy in running the app. He prefers to maintain anonymity and doesn't want any specific name or face associated with the app. His intention is to keep the attention of the users solely on the stars, rather than on any individual. But we didn't want to pass up a chance to talk to him. Therefore, we'll only record the audio of this talk and not the video. Without further ado, please welcome Beau Fellows to the stage."

Beau walks out and waves to the audience, wearing a pair of khakis and a navy polo. I freeze when he turns fully and faces the crowd.

Because the person standing on that stage is someone I know all too well.

The large forehead that's covered by his mop of hair that falls into his eyes. He's got highlights since I last saw him, and it's now more tawny. His appearance is the perfect balance between not caring and caring that makes him cute but not quite hot.

When he smiles, the large screen zooms in on his face.

It isn't Beau at all.

It's Eric.

But that can't be right. There has to be a logical explanation for this. Maybe he's Eric's doppelgänger. I've read multiple articles about how we all have one in the world.

Yeah, that must be it.

The chance that my lying and stealing ex is in Portland giving a TED Talk would be too much of a mind fuck to even consider.

Beau thanks everyone for coming. He has the same voice as Eric. The slight Georgia accent with rounded and bouncy vowels. My breathing speeds up, almost to the point of hyperventilation. I cover my mouth and try to take a few calming, deep breaths.

Ruby grins at my reaction, thinking I'm freaking out in a good way. I wish, but no, this freak out is courtesy of an impending mental breakdown.

The harder I try to convince myself that Beau isn't

Eric, the more convinced I am that they're the same person. Eric refused to wear anything but Converses, and "Beau" has on a black pair. A watch exactly like the one I gave Eric, complete with a DIY solder kit and a plastic cover, sits on Beau's arm.

My nausea grows with every word he speaks. When he mentions Georgia Tech, I gasp. Ruby gives me a side eye but I wave her off and cover my reaction with a cough.

My brain whirls with all the possibilities, and then comes to a screeching halt at a sickening thought.

Did he steal from my family and me to fund Zodiac Way of Life?

I do a quick mental calculation, and the timing matches up.

"Most people ask me why I created a horoscope app," he says on stage. "And I always respond that horoscopes and zodiac signs have been part of my life since I was a teenager. I used to guess people's signs when I met them." He laughs and shakes his head as the audience joins in with him. "And I was good at it. So creating an app centered around horoscopes wasn't a far stretch."

That lying and stealing bastard. He hated horoscopes and was surprised when I casually mentioned Addie and I used to label people using their signs.

He's using my story, Addie's story, as his own.

And that's unforgiveable.

The crowd eats his words up, as if he were the stars themselves. He weaves his story so flawlessly. It'd be impressive if I wasn't so fucking angry.

He smiles. "From day one, our mission was to be the most accurate horoscope app in the world. We're unique in how we generate the horoscopes, but we had to verify the accuracy. In the first weeks, I wrote the horoscopes myself and checked them against our technology, as well as with astrologers. When our users confirmed the accuracy, the program learned how to develop the horoscopes itself with even more accuracy."

I'm too hot. Sweat peppers my brows and my vision tunnels. I have to get out of here. I heave myself up and out of the seat before forcing my way past the knees of what feels like hundreds of people. I run up the stairs and burst through the door, trying to understand something that can't be understood.

"Zoey?" Ruby calls out to me. I realize she's followed me out.

I hunch over and place my hands on my knees, trying to catch my breath. "Sorry, I feel sick. I need to go but stay and enjoy."

"Nonsense." She rubs my back. "I'll drive you home."

"No, really." I straighten. "I hate having people around when I'm sick."

"Fine…" She takes out her phone.

I wipe at the sweat on my forehead, not listening to the rest of her sentence. I wave and say, "See you later."

I stumble down the street and get into the first taxi I see. Robotically, I give an address.

If Beau is Eric, then there are too many open questions for me to process. Should I go to the police? Will anyone believe me?

I hardly believe it myself.

This can't be happening.

I've been taking advice from the person who ruined

my life. He confirmed it. Those first weeks he made the horoscopes himself. His words. Not an algorithm, not AI, not a computer.

Him.

And I followed it.

The first week or two of using the app came from him.

He infected my life yet again.

I stumble out of the taxi and dry heave on Anders's lawn. Everything I've done since arriving in Portland has been driven by that app. I must've made all the wrong decisions following it. There's no way Eric's advice would lead me down the right path. Not when I hate him so much for destroying my life in the first place.

I followed the app in the beginning, and at minimum, the first week would've led me astray. But that means Ruby, Amore, and worst of all, Anders aren't right for me.

I dry heave again and wipe the tears from my eyes. I curse the day I downloaded Zodiac Way of Life.

Eric is a poison that's infected millions of people. He's probably dishing out advice made to hurt people in the long run. He played me for a year. He's obviously a long-term planner. Quick wins lure people in and keep them reliant on the app, like me.

Worst of all, I've fallen for his con yet again.

A part of me, the part that was being rebuilt by Anders, fractures. And I'm not sure how to recover from this blow. The pieces are too broken to put back together. Maybe I should throw away the pieces and be alone forever. Mom and Lilly expect me to hurt everyone around me.

I need to rip all things Eric from my life and start

again with no trace of him. I stumble up the pathway to the house in a daze and push through the door. The second I enter, my knees crash onto the hardwood floor.

Anders rushes into the room and runs his hands over me, as if checking for injuries. "What happened? Are you okay?"

I remain silent and stare at him. I need space to think. I'm not even sure why I came here. My apartment would've been the better decision.

Spurred by that thought, I push to a standing position and head to his room. I grab my backpack and begin to shove clothes inside.

"What are you doing? What's going on?" Anders hovers behind me anxiously.

"I need to process everything."

"To process what?" Anders grabs the backpack from my hands. "What happened?"

"My life, my choices."

"You're scaring me. Sit." Anders places both hands on my shoulders. "Tell me what's happening right now."

"I ran into my ex."

"Eric?"

I nod. "He founded Zodiac Way of Life."

"Holy shit."

"He made the horoscopes himself in the beginning." I pick up the fallen backpack. "I've been taking advice from him, from the man who destroyed my life. Nothing good can come from that."

"That's not true." Anders frowns. "Something good came from it. *Us.*"

I remain silent, placing my makeup bag in the backpack. Because he's right, something good did come from it, but I'm too scared to admit that. By admitting it, Eric wins, right? He's still influencing my life, even though he's not in it.

My brain is a mess, struggling to follow the conversation.

"I see." Anders lets out a defeated breath.

My gaze snaps to his. "What?"

"You don't want to be with me."

"It's not that. I just need some time to process. To think."

"I don't care if a monkey made that app. How can this" —he gestures between us—"feel wrong?"

He stares at me, begging me with his expression to tell him he's right and that we're perfect. But all the words get jumbled in my head, past and present uniting, and all I can manage is a pained sound. A sound too close to a denial than what it really is. I want to agree. But my throat and tongue are locked against saying another word to explain.

The moment hangs between us, balancing on the tip of a knife. Either I make this right or it unravels before me. And yet, no matter how hard I try, nothing comes out.

He spins away from me. With his back to me, he runs a hand aggressively through his hair. "This is ridiculous. You're letting an app destroy us. Let's work this out together. I know you're scared, but you didn't do anything wrong."

"Can't you see?" I shout. "I do everything wrong. I make the wrong decisions and choose the wrong people.

My family? Eric? I couldn't even see them for who they were. I'll ruin you, too."

"Stop," he says. "Don't say that about yourself. You're not going to ruin anyone. You're in shock, and that's understandable. Let's sleep on it and we can work this out."

"I want to sleep at my apartment tonight."

"I don't think it's a good idea for you to be alone right now."

I level with him a look. "Well, that's what I need."

He pulls me into a hug, but I can't return it, not when I need to process everything.

"Will I see you tomorrow?" he asks.

"I don't know."

"Wait," he says. "Do you need space in general or space from us?"

At the moment, both of those things mean the same thing. So I say the worst thing imaginable. "Both?"

"I see. So that's it? You're dumping me?"

"I didn't say that."

"But you meant it. How can you leave me? After everything we've been through. I thought—" He breaks off and closes his eyes. "What about A Cup of Zodiac?"

"Maybe it's best if you finish it yourself." Until I can figure out which way is up and down or forward and backwards, I shouldn't be trusted with something so precious. I'll never forgive myself if I ruin this for him.

"What? You're going to stop working when I need you the most?"

"You'll be fine." He has a support system in his family and Ruby.

He stiffens. "I trusted you, more than I trusted my best friend. You're worse than Courtney ever was. You're setting me up to fail. On purpose."

I suck in a sharp breath, breaking at his words. But he's right, I'm pulling out when he needs me, when A Cup of Zodiac needs me. But fear stops me from correcting him. He's better off without me.

I'm like a form of cancer to the people in my life. I come on suddenly but kill them slowly.

"You're right," I say.

It's funny how, when you truly understand someone, you hold the power to strike at their deepest vulnerabilities. Relationships can be a source of solace or a weapon in disguise. And right now, I chose to use mine with Anders as a weapon.

But only to help him.

To save him and his businesses.

From me.

It's like a curtain covers the Anders I know, obscuring him, and replacing him with a stranger. This new version gazes at me devoid of warmth and familiarity, like he's returning to the Anders he was when we first met.

He storms to the front of the house, and I'm on his heels. He swipes his keys from the table and throws on a jacket. "I regret the day I met you. I regret hiring you and trusting you. But most of all, I regret loving you. I don't want you here when I return."

I gasp and bend over as if his words physically wounded me, as if he brandished a sword and ran it through me. Again. And again. And again.

He hardens further at my reaction and closes the door

softly behind him, which somehow punctuates our end more profoundly than if he were to slam it shut.

I collapse. His words have fractured every part of my soul. He struck true, wounding me as I wounded him.

Fear and regret crash into me like a tsunami. Drowning me, breaking me. But there's nothing that can be done except to pack everything as quickly as possible.

A voice in the back of my mind begs me to stay, to talk it out. To fix the wound I've just inflicted on him. But I mentally slap a piece of duct tape on the voice's mouth.

Propelled by grief, I somehow make it back to my apartment. It's so cold inside, my breath clouds with every exhale. The heater protests having to work after so long being dormant.

I dump the clothes in the middle of my living room and sift through everything for something to wear.

A flash of black catches my eye. I pick it up.

His sweatshirt.

I crawl onto the couch, as cold as literal ice due to not using the heater for weeks. It's lumpy and saggy and all wrong. Everything's wrong.

I bring his sweatshirt over my face and press down, half hoping I drown in his scent, and half hoping I suffocate to make this feeling go away.

This emptiness.

My lungs protest, but I don't pull away. Eventually, my brain overrides my actions and forces me to lift the material. I gulp down the fresh air and soak his sweatshirt with my apologies. With all the truths I had to hide during our final moments.

How much I appreciate him. How he makes me want

to become a better person. How he makes me laugh and pushes me out of my comfort zone. How loyal and caring he is.

And most of all, how much I love him with my entire being.

But he'll never hear those words because he's done with me. I did my job a little too well by pushing him away.

Though it kills me, it's for the best. It's about time I turn my cancerous ways on myself and protect everyone around me... from me.

I make a choking sound and sob harder into his sweatshirt.

My brain oh so helpfully highlights all my worst moments, and I drown in them over and over again, until I fall into a fitful sleep surrounded by all the mistakes I've ever made.

I hold them closer as a reminder.

As a warning.

CHAPTER 24

*N*o new notifications.

LET'S BE REAL, I deleted that toxic app faster than I could say "I'm a stupid bitch." It's been thirty-six hours and I haven't left the couch for more than water, crackers, and to use the toilet.

My phone pings, and my stomach clenches. Anders has called eight times, but I've ignored them all. This time, it's Ruby. Again.

I need to make a plan. I can't stay in Portland, not when everything reminds me of Anders.

I can't go home, I refuse to. Not after what happened at the wedding.

I could call some old classmates and ask if anyone's company is hiring.

Hmm, that's not a bad idea.

I bring up my social media and type in the names of a

few people I was close to. One doesn't work in engineering anymore, another just had a baby, but the last person, Daisy, works at Gutted. They're the hottest and most successful drink company specializing in gut health. The company is located in California.

It would be a good option, especially considering my experience at Spark, my old company. I rework my resume and write Daisy a message asking if she would mind passing it along to her company.

She writes back ten minutes later saying she's happy to help. The head of HR is a personal friend of hers and I should expect a call today. I can't believe it was that easy. One message and I could've had a higher paying job this whole time?

DROPPING BACK ONTO THE COUCH, I stare at the ceiling and the cracks that I've mapped out over the months. Cracks that didn't plague Anders's house.

My heart crumples at the thought of him. I miss him like I've never missed anyone. We were inseparable for these past months, and now it's like trying to function without my legs. Nothing is the same, but it's for the best.

For both of us.

Hours later, my phone rings. For a second, I think it's him.

But it's not. It's an unknown number.

I hate answering the phone, especially unknown numbers. I'm the type of person that rushes to input a number into Google to get an idea of who might be calling and still let it ring out to see if they'll leave a voicemail. If they leave a voicemail and it's important, I call back.

Sometimes.

Or more like I text them back.

But what if it's Gutted?

I swipe and say, "Hello?"

"Hi, is this Zoey?"

"Yes."

"Hi, this is Pam from Gutted. Daisy sent me your resume."

"Oh, hi, yes. Thank you for calling."

"Would you have time next Monday to come to San Diego for an interview? We have an opening that I think you'll be a great fit for."

"Yes, sure," I say mechanically. "Could you send me the job description beforehand?"

"Of course, I'll email that to you now. I'm looking forward to meeting you. Daisy spoke highly of your time together at Georgia Tech."

"Thank you. I'm looking forward to it, too."

"Talk soon," she says and hangs up.

If I worked for Gutted, the salary would be substantial, and I'd be good at it. Engineering always came naturally to me. It won't bring me joy, not like A Cup of Zodiac did, but beggars can't be picky.

My life with Gutted would probably be filled with long hours, coupled with lonely ones. Distancing myself from others would be for the best. For everyone.

If I'm going to make it to San Diego by Monday, I need to pack and get my car fixed. With that in mind, I force myself to get up and pack away my life. All into a single suitcase. I call my landlord and give my notice.

I leave the suitcase by the door and collapse back onto the couch. A deep exhaustion settles into my bones.

I'm about to doze when there's a bang on the front door, as if the police were trying to break it down.

I jerk up and tiptoe to the door.

"Open this door right now, or I'm breaking it down," yells Ruby.

I yank it open and snap, "You don't have to be such a Scorpio right now."

She ignores my quip and pushes her way into my place. She's dressed like she's ready for a bloodbath. Black from head to toe, a motorcycle jacket, and ass kicking boots.

She takes in the space and spins in a circle before her anger visibly leaks out of her. "You live *here?*"

She says it with so much disbelief. With everything else, I'd forgot how embarrassing my apartment is.

"What do you want?" I ask, shutting the door.

She places her hands on her hips, her indignation returning. "Why did you break up with him? Anders told me what happened."

"It's for the best."

"But you two are meant to be together."

"Real rich coming from you, someone who doesn't even believe in love."

"Exactly, this is coming from me, and I still think what you and Anders have is love. I've never been more certain of anything in my entire life."

Her words cause all the emotions I've been trying to hold back to surface.

I cover my face with my hands and sob. "But I... I'm not good for him."

"Bull fucking shit. You're scared and, by the looks of it, you're running." She gives my suitcase a pointed look.

"I've been following advice from a scam artist for months. It's led me down a wrong path."

"Did it really steer you wrong?" She throws her hands up in the air, exasperated. "If Beau wasn't Eric, would you really believe that? Really? Because I'm going to need you to use that amazing brain of yours and fucking think."

I pause. If Beau wasn't Eric, would I?

My brain rebels against the question. Everything is too jumbled to think clearly.

Ruby must sense this because she grabs me by my shoulders and looks me dead in the eye. "Did ZWOL give you fucking directions to Amore?"

And just like that, her words open the floodgates. All the horoscopes, and the level of detail ZWOL provided, flash through my mind. It recommended that I apply for a job at a coffee shop, and I did. But... it didn't tell me to apply to Amore. There must be thousands of coffee shops in Portland, and I chose Amore.

It recommended I get out in nature and even suggested even a Christmas tree farm, but it didn't mention which one to choose. I chose to go to the most accessible one. There were three options within a thirty-minute drive of my apartment.

When it mentioned love and hookups, it didn't give

name any names. Of course it didn't. It can't be that detailed.

Which means...

"I've been making decisions this entire time," I say. "It gave me the broad strokes, but I filled in the details."

"Fucking finally you get it. Beau slash Eric didn't make the app only for the Zoey Phillips in the world. The horoscope descriptions weren't a personal vendetta."

"But—"

"You were happy, even after the disaster that was your sister's wedding. How could you have made the wrong decisions if you were thriving?"

I open my mouth to argue with her logic, but quickly shut it. Was I thriving? I think back on the past months. I was in love, surrounded by friends, working on something I was passionate about.

I was... happy. I wasn't thinking about surviving, just enjoying and truly living.

I'm not sure why her words penetrate at this moment, because I'm starting to think Anders was trying to tell me the same thing. But sometimes we need to hear something at a certain time and in a certain way for it to resonate. And fuck, it's like she's kicked me in the teeth and made me pay attention. I feel like I'm thinking clearly for the first time since the TED Talk.

Before Addie died, I never used to question myself to this extent. But sometime after, it must've started getting worse. Until it was all I could think about and dwell on. I'm not sure if it was a defense mechanism or if the people in my life were conditioning me, or both, but I'm tired. Tired of second guessing everything.

Because if I cut out all my fear, it's simple. I love working at Amore and on A Cup of Zodiac. I love being friends with Ruby. But most of all, I love Anders and our life here. And I might've ruined it all.

I turn from her and sink onto the couch. "Everything's such a mess."

She settles next to me. "You can still fix it."

"But I'll eventually fuck up again and when that happens, everyone will leave me. Just like my family did."

"No, because if that happens, we'd help you. You have people in your life who truly love you and will stand by your side no matter what. Don't be stupid and throw it all away due to fear."

I blow out a long breath and lean my head back. She's right, I'm scared. Scared to be happy, scared to love, scared to rely on someone else. Because if I can protect myself, I won't get hurt.

But that's bullshit because I'm hurting now.

"Anders will be at the opening tomorrow," she says.

"He won't want me there, not after I left him to deal with everything by himself these past days."

"He hasn't been alone. We've all been pitching in, even his parents. But that's what I mean, we support each other. You aren't alone. Not anymore."

She's right, I'm not alone. But if I don't fix it, I might be.

Turns out regret is scarier than fear. Fear can keep me in the same place or situation, but regret has the ability to eat me alive. Just like it's done for the past forty odd hours.

It's about time I do something about it. I need to go to

Anders. To apologize and right the wrongs I've taken too long to realize.

And if he doesn't want me after it's all said and done, at least I will have tried.

Ruby pulls me into a hug and lets me cry.

Once my sobs die down, Ruby says, "A Cup of Zodiac looks amazing, by the way. Because of you, your decisions, your ideas, and your passion."

"It does?" I ask.

"Are you fishing for more compliments? Because I think I've reached my limit for the day."

"Bitch." I swat her arm with a laugh.

"You're going to be just fine." She grins and pats my thigh. "Just tell Anders how you really feel, scary bits and all. That's all you've got to do."

"You make it sound so easy."

"It can be. He loves you, and you love him. Everything else is just noise."

I nod. "You're right."

"One word of advice, though," she says. "Shower. Before you go to the shop tomorrow."

"Oh, fuck you," I groan.

She laughs and rubs her hands together. "My work here is done. Shower, eat, and come tomorrow prepared to grovel."

"Thank you," I say with so much meaning, I get teary-eyed again.

She lifts her shoulder. "That's what friends are for."

"No, that's what family's for."

* * *

I CAN'T WAIT until tomorrow. I need to see him now. After the quickest shower of my life, I run out the door and to his house.

Huffing and puffing, I ring the doorbell. But there's no answer. I step back and take in the windows, but there are no lights on.

I pull out my phone and try to call him, but it goes straight to voicemail.

Maybe he's at A Cup of Zodiac? Working on last-minute things?

I run, and a stitch plagues my side. Running wasn't a good idea, not when I haven't run since my last mandatory gym class back in high school. But I force myself to move faster, to continue.

I bang on the front door, but there are no sounds. No movement or light inside.

Fuck.

I run my fingers through my hair and pace. Where could he be?

I call him again, but it goes straight to voicemail again. This time I leave one. "Hey. It's me. Can we talk? Meet me at A Cup of Zodiac tomorrow at five a.m.? I... hope to see you then."

I hang up and trudge back to my place.

Tomorrow can't come soon enough.

CHAPTER 25

I rub my sweaty palms on my black pants. It's almost six. Anders didn't show at five, and for every minute since then, my heart has sunk. Lower and lower until it ended up buried so deep under the ground, I'm not sure if I'll ever be able to retrieve it.

It's ironic for my heart to die here on the steps of A Cup of Zodiac, the place that made me believe in love.

I Google therapists. I've been dealt blow after blow, and I'm not able to handle anything more by myself. I need help, professional help, to work through all my issues. To support me through... well, everything.

With a defeated sigh, I turn and begin the walk back to my apartment. Maybe I can return once it's open today. That way, he'll be forced to talk to me, and I can see him one last time before closing our chapter for good.

Footsteps pound the pavement behind me.

"Zoey," a voice bellows.

My shoulders hike to my ears.

It's Anders.

I whip around, and Anders runs toward me. His shoes are unlaced, his shirt is inside out, and his jacket isn't even zipped.

I curl my toes in my shoes to stay in place and not launch myself at him.

"I'm sorry I'm late," he says. "I just got your message."

"I don't think you've been late for anything in your entire life." My gaze roams over his face, taking in all the details. His beard is longer, more unruly than normal. There are dark circles under his bloodshot eyes, like he hasn't slept more than a handful of hours this week.

"I'm surprised you're here," he says. "I thought you didn't want anything to do with the shop. Or me."

"I lied."

He rocks back on his heels. "Why?"

"To protect you from myself. Seeing Eric fucked with my head so much and I went to a dark place. I convinced myself I'd ruin you, just like I ruined my life. I would never want to do that to you."

"You hurt me," he says.

"I'm so sorry."

"I'm sorry, too. For what I said. I didn't mean it." He closes his eyes and shudders. "But I guess it doesn't matter, though. Not when you're leaving."

"How—"

"Ruby saw the suitcase."

"Of course she did. And yes, I did set up an interview. For next week."

He blows out a breath. "Good for you."

"But I called and left a message this morning, cancelling it. Portland is my home. You're my home."

His gaze snaps to mine. "Do you mean it?"

"I do. I loved you before I was even brave enough to say it, and I'll love you for the rest of my life. But I'm scared." A noise escapes me, halfway between a cry and a gasp. "You have the power to destroy me, and at the first sign of trouble, I ran. I'm so sorry. You deserve better than that. Better than me."

"Oh Zoey." He closes the distance between us in the blink of an eye and cups my face in his hands. "You have the same power over me. That's why I left. I was scared, too. But even though I'm scared, being with you is worth it. You're worth it."

Of course, I begin to ugly sob at those words. I've got no chill.

He pulls my head to his chest and holds me.

"I fucked up on so many levels," I say.

"We both did, but I don't want to be scared you'll run every time life gets tough. I can't deal with that."

"I understand. I'm going to find a therapist and work on myself. If you don't want to be with me while I work through my issues, or if you don't want to wait for me to get my act together, I understand—"

I'm cut off by his lips pressing into mine. The kiss is sure, strong. It's a statement in response to my question. I deepen the kiss and relish the taste of him, the feel of him.

Kissing him is like finding my home.

Because he is.

He's my home.

Someone whistles. "Sorry to interrupt," Athena, the chef Theo introduced us to, says. "But we've got a shop to open in an hour."

I grin and say, "We'll be right there."

Anders grabs my hand and leads me to the shop. To our future.

* * *

WE BOTH FIX our appearance and tie on our aprons. A golden Leo for me, a green Taurus for Athena, and a purple Sagittarius for Anders.

We work together, making the final preparations. We've put months of hard work into this and it'll either pay off or fail spectacularly.

"Who's working at Amore today?" I ask.

"Theo, Ruby, and my mom. They're training two new people right now. And next week we'll train more people for here."

I grab his hand and squeeze it. This is huge for him, to trust other people to work at his shops. "I'm proud of you."

"Well, someone very smart made me see the light. Also, I'd like to spend more time with my girlfriend."

"Let's see if today goes well." I laugh and kiss him on the cheek.

"It will." He says it with so much confidence, even I begin to believe it.

When it's a few minutes before seven, we get into position and Anders nudges me toward the door. "You do the honors."

I send a small prayer up to the stars that this goes well and flip the sign over from closed to open. Athena snaps a few photos of Anders and me in front of the store and the logo etched into the window. It's of a coffee cup with the steam rising above made to look like zodiac symbols.

The line outside claps when Anders dips me and kisses me senseless in front of everyone.

Athena is responsible for food, while I prepare all the drinks. Anders will float between us both and man the register. We laugh and joke behind the counter and pull each customer into a conversation to make them feel at home. To make them want to be here and stay here.

And it works. We're so busy, I barely have time to breathe. I scarf down a quick lunch Athena made and get right back into it. I'm too caught up in every moment of the day to stop, even though Anders tries to get me to. He settles for pushing water and food on me to keep my energy up.

The concept is a hit, and it helps that many of our customers post on TikTok about their drink and food combination, the balcony, the decorations, everything. I make sure to comment on every single one and thank them for coming. We have our own hashtag on the wall to make finding the posts easier.

By the end of the day, after everyone leaves, Anders pulls a chair out for me. I collapse into it while he opens a bottle of champagne and pours us each a glass.

"We smashed our target today by lunchtime." Anders beams.

"No," I say in disbelief.

He shows me the paper. "Yes, all thanks to you."

"Thanks to both of us."

"I have something for you." Anders slides a folder over to me.

I open it and inside is a contract. It takes me a moment to read through it to understand fully what I'm looking at. "You're giving A Cup of Zodiac to me?"

"Full ownership. Not only have you done all the work, but I want you to feel safe. To know you always have something to fall back on, no matter what happens between us. It's something to call your own."

"It's too much." I try to push the contract back to him. "You don't need to give this to me to make me stay."

He stills my hand and flips through the pages until the end. It's signed and dated a week before Christmas.

I frown. "I don't understand."

"I knew this was yours from the minute you started helping me. You've worked too hard, and you're too good at this to ever feel afraid of being left with nothing in this world. I wanted to wait to give it to you after we opened, to ensure you were gaining a success."

I'm speechless. He's giving me a business and making me an owner. I'm now someone in control of my own future, and no one can take that away from me. He did this. For me. It's so selfless and unexpected. He continuously does things for me, and I want to show him I'm in this, in us, with every fiber of my being.

I place the contract back in the folder and close it. "I don't need a backup, because you're my future."

"You mean that?" he asks.

"I choose you. Forever."

He lifts me and I straddle his lap. "I like the sound of that."

So do I. It's freeing to finally make the leap, to trust

myself and my decisions. To allow myself to thrive and not hold back due to fear.

This. This is what I've been missing from my life for far too long. The freedom to live for me, not for my family or for a job title and degree.

Addie was right, Portland is magical. I've found myself and my passion while here, just like she did. I just have the added benefit of a Hot Lumberjack by my side, loving me.

All of me.

I'm not a number five anymore, or even a sixty.

I'm more of a nine: fun, happy, and adaptive. Think about it, nines can flip and turn into a six at a moment's notice... and what other number can do that?

EPILOGUE

FOUR MONTHS LATER

$\mathcal{M}$y arms shake as I continue to move my paddle in the water. The island we're aiming for isn't much farther. With renewed energy, I dig my paddle in the water and my kayak limps across the lake.

Why Addie thought it'd be a good idea for us to do something in nature during our Finish adventure boggles my mind. She'd be struggling as much as me, and I'd be laughing at her, at us. Just like Anders is now.

If nothing else, Addie would've made it a good story. At how we could barely make the trek out to a nearby island on smooth water since she was just as allergic to activity as me. Addie would've told her customers this story nonstop, but she'd be sure to add that it was all worth it. That the midnight sun in Finland is as dreamy as we imagined. Being on the water and seeing the sun reflected off it makes it all the more special.

I lift my face to the sky, the sun gently kissing me. A

light breeze tickles my arms and it's almost like Addie is here. With me. Taking in the beauty alongside me.

Stars, I hope so. She would've loved it here just based on the pulla alone. I'm going to need to add that cardamom spiced sweet bread to her recipe book. She would've liked that.

When we pull up to the island, our guide helps us out of the kayaks. He drags them further up the beach before leading us to some logs placed around a campfire. The guide promised us dinner, and I'm curious to see what he's going to cook on the fire.

Anders throws his arm around me, and I snuggle into him.

"It's beautiful," I say.

"It is. You holding up okay?"

"Yeah, I feel closer to Addie here. It's nice."

"Good."

The guide passes us some glasses of champagne while he pulls out pots and pans for dinner.

"Fancy," I say to Anders while I take a sip.

"We have a lot to celebrate."

"Yeah, these past months have been unreal," I say.

And they have. A Cup of Zodiac was named the most innovative coffee shop in Portland. Business is booming and we're planning to expand to different cities.

But best of all, Hayden saved my ass. When he found out about my Beau slash Eric drama, he approached Beau and threatened a massive lawsuit. Beau repaid us five times the amount we invested in his company. Even though my parents recovered their money and then some, I'm not ready to let them back in my life again.

No, I've cut them off as easily as they cut me off. Therapy helped me make that boundary for my mental health.

"I have one more surprise for you," he says.

"Careful, I'm going to get used to being spoiled by you." He's been surprising me nonstop on this trip with little things, like all the gluten-free food in Finland. And fresh flowers every morning. And a luxury boat trip to experience Finland by water. He disappeared this morning for hours and wouldn't tell me why.

"Good, you deserve it," he says. "You deserve the world, and I promise to give it to you. Every day of my life. I love how you hate coffee and yet own the best coffee shop in town. I love how brave you are when you experiment with new techniques, concepts, and flavor combinations. I love how you get superstitious about your horoscope. I love how your laugh can make someone's day, especially mine. I love how you push me out of my comfort zone and make me a better person. I love everything about you."

I blink through my tears. He rolls up his long-sleeved shirt and reveals a bandage on his arm.

I reach for the bandage, one that wasn't there this morning. "Are you okay?"

He nods, but his face is still serious. He peels off the bandage and reveals his watch tattoo, but it's no longer empty. The hour hand is on the eight and the minute hand is on the nine.

My fingers hover over the fresh tattoo. "You..." It's all I can manage.

Is this the exact time I entered the shop?

He once told me he wouldn't complete the tattoo until he found the woman he wants to marry.

I gasp and search his face.

He nods before reaching into his pocket. He pulls out a black velvet box and holds my shaking hands in his own while bending onto one knee.

"When I first saw you, I knew. It was like getting punched in the gut and I looked at the time. You didn't order, you weren't in a rush like everyone else. You said "ew" when I proposed a drink. I couldn't not notice you. When I had my break that morning, I wrote down the time you entered Amore in my notebook."

"Oh Anders—"

He places two fingers against my lips and smiles. "I promise to love you forever and to lift you up when you're down and worship you when you're on top of the world. Marry me?"

I grab his face and kiss him like he's my everything. And he is.

I pull back just an inch and whisper, "Yes. I love every part of you, and I promise to always support and care for you, no matter what."

He sits on the log and pulls me into his lap, so I'm straddling him.

"Careful, we have a guide nearby," I laugh.

He grins and opens the box. "You didn't even see the ring."

"I don't care about the ring, as long as I get you."

He takes my ring finger in his hand and slips it on. He kisses my hand and says, "I thought this ring would be fitting for a Leo."

I stare at the huge diamond on my finger. It must be over two carats, but it's no ordinary diamond. No, it's an emerald cut canary diamond. Small diamonds dot the band, and holy shit, it's gorgeous.

"It's perfect," I say.

Another breeze brushes against me. It's like Addie's saying she approves. I lay my head on his shoulder.

Grief is a journey. Sometimes silent, sometimes loud. But one necessary to endure, for on the other side is a depth of love and appreciation for the person. That never changes. Addie will always be with me, in my heart, in my memories, guiding me through life.

If it weren't for Anders, I'm not sure how long it would've taken for me to get to this level of peace.

But here I am because of him.

Because of his love for me.

And most importantly, because of the love I have for myself.

A NOTE TO MY READERS

Thank you for reading my book. I know it's extra effort to write a review, but I'd be forever grateful if you could leave one.

Your reviews and feedback help me reach more readers, especially as a debut self-published author. Thank you for your support!

Stay up to date on all the latest news by signing up to my newsletter.

ACKNOWLEDGMENTS

As an avid reader myself, my favorite part of every book I read is the acknowledgements section. I love to read about the spark of the idea that caused the story. This is why I'll strive to share a little background on each story I write.

First, I'm a horoscope whore so it was an obvious choice to make this part of the novel. But on a deeper level, I knew Zoey being celiac was critical to the story. It was born from my own diagnosis and dreams of experiencing a completely gluten-free bakery while I was living in a country that knew nothing about the disease. I couldn't even eat at a restaurant due to cross contamination and lack of menu options for someone like me. The desire to walk into an eatery completely free of worry was the initiation of this story.

The second thing I wanted to include in the story was my own experience of dealing with a sudden death. I, like Zoey, had previous experience with deaths that were predictable (e.g. due to an elderly person's long illness) but when my Uncle Lou died suddenly from a heart attack in his own driveway, the grief of losing him took on a new form. One I didn't expect. Losing someone suddenly leaves behind a whole host of shoulds, coulds, and regrets.

Zoey's journey with Addie helped me grieve my own loss. I love you, Uncle Lou.

Now, time for the awkward acknowledgements part where I list people's names and you, as the reader, have no idea who they are.

Thank you to my mom and sister. Without your endless encouragement, advice, brainstorming sessions, jokes, and late-night calls, this book wouldn't be what it is. I will forever be grateful for your endless support. I love you.

To my husband, you've always encouraged me to publish my stories and get my words out into the world. Thank you for supporting my writing in every way possible. I love you.

To my writing friends: Sandy, Gayle, Lisa, and Sara. Your feedback, encouragement, and support has kept me going this entire time. Thank you.

To Lizzie, without your endless enthusiasm, support, jokes, and amazing editing skills, I can honestly say this book wouldn't be what it is today. I'm so lucky to have you in my life. You make me a better writer, and I'm constantly in awe of your skills. And don't worry, next time, I'll redeem Virgos XD. Thank you times a million.

To Amy, thank you for your help with edits.

To Penny and Bronwen, without you, life would be a whole lot less fun. Thank you for being you and encouraging me every step of the way.

Lastly, and most importantly, thank you to you, my reader. Without you, all of this would be impossible. Thank you for taking a chance on me and reading this book. I can't wait for you to read Hayden and Bree's story next in book two.

ABOUT THE AUTHOR

Alexis Gorgun is a full-time author and perpetual expat who has mastered the art of packing, has more stamps on her passport than shoes in her closet, and has an undying love for the beach. She's currently based in the UK with her husband and two daughters. You can find her at www. alexisgorgun.com.